OLYMPIAD

2084

A MEMORIAL GUIDE

BY:

WHIP
LIPSEY

ETHEREGE & WYCHERLEY

ISBN (paperback): 978-1-968288-00-6

ISBN (ebook): 978-1-968288-01-3

Book Cover by Kristi Date-Lipsey

Contents

Welcome to the 2084 Olympics

A Discovery of the Past; A Gift to the Future; A Thanks to the IOC.

I n the year 2024, within the city limits of Paris, a small coterie made up of unemployed archivists, graduate students in archeology, urban spelunkers, and an inebriated journalist, disinterred a time capsule from a corner of medieval catacombs just weeks before the Olympic Games held in that city. They found this metal chest after a diligent search of preserved newspapers, these then existent—and indeed, still widely produced at that time. On the authority of those yellowed pages, they deduced the location of the time capsule, placed discreetly among the desiccated corpses by an earlier generation of optimistic archeology enthusiasts in memorial to the 1972 Olympic Games, held not in Paris, but in Munich. The time capsule of Paris survived alone among some two dozen placed in various capitals that might someday serve as an Olympic site. A gift of knowledge from 1972; a message to their future.

The time capsule contained a stuffed toy in the shape of a long dog, a small plastic model of same, a round steel emblem painted gold in imitation of those given to victors at that year's Games, a suit of clothing made of a surely unwearable substance called *polyester*, a neckless composed of five Olympic rings, a chocolate bar in the shape of what the find's cataloger called a "peace sign", and a memorial guide to the Munich Olympics published prior to, and thus in ignorance of, that event. The discoverers of this cache recorded and publicized their find, then reinterred it and all its objects (except for the chocolate, which had gone missing) with additions from their own day, also themed to the Olympics. Their embellishments included three tin hexagons, stamped with a flame and the five interlocked rings, each encircled with further tin painted in gold, silver, and bronze—these in imitation of Olympic prizes. Also, an arm-sized metal spindle (now presumed to be a torch), a picture book of the just completed Olympics, a variety of objects—plush and plastic—of either two birds, or two caps with faces, that were—like the long dogs of the earlier find—mascots for the Games of the day. The 2024 time capsuleers also included clippings from the "papers" congratulating them on their finds and praising them for their plans. They included no memorial guide, nor any extensive written account of the Games then just completed.

Workers discovered the 2024 time capsule while demolishing the catacombs in preparation for the Games of 2084. Benito Jax, the head of the International Olympic Committee (IOC), and therefore de facto mayor of Paris during the preparations for the Games, instantly appreciated the historical significance of the find. He arranged for the building of the *Jax Olympic Heritage Museum* to hold these remains, along with a few skeletons retrieved from the decommissioned ossuaries, a girder from the wreckage of the Eiffel Tower, a complete collection of 2084 Olympic souvenir merchandise, his own generously donated family mementoes, his memoirs, and a multi-volume collection of his many aphorisms and observations.

He also commissioned the work which you now read, to be left unseen by our contemporaries, and placed in a new time capsule built within the foundation stone of the museum, for disinterment fifty years from now; in memory of the Games of 2084 and in confidence of the Games of 2134. Let us, for this document, give a hardy thanks to its sponsor, Benito Jax and the IOC.

So hello future, from your own past. Herein you will find the story of the 2084 Olympiad. It's minor tragedies and profound triumphs. Few of the events transpiring in these Games will remain unknown or uncelebrated even half a century on. For that very reason, your author faces the challenge of deciding what might usefully be included and what would waste the ever-wanning attention of destiny's designated readers. Certainly, I need not dwell on the great non-Olympic events of which you will already know, whatever their impact on the Games; the Big Taint, the Worldwide Pulping, the Rise of the Machines, the Great Digital Purge, the Analog Renaissance, the Iberian Civil War, the Southern Exodus and those other notable events now commemorated with grammatically compulsory capitalization. We need not dwell on what no one could forget.

But confining myself just to the Olympics, what do I cover? Shall I list the winners and losers? Tell their immortal tales? After all, the reader can look up (if memory should somehow fail) the names of Emeril Lopez (swimming), Jose Mendosa (boulder climbing), Steroidicon Brand Products Makes You Stronger Popescu (power lifting), Naming Rights Available Haversen (footgolf), Unit Xii5 Experimental (extreme combat skydiving), and so many others.

No. If I am to avoid the errors of earlier missives to the future, then I must give the substance behind the veneer of events. Not a view from the arena seats, nor from the suspension beds dangling from the dome, but an account otherwise unrecorded in the histories. Your author had the honor and chore of sitting in on the IOC board meetings, the sponsorship deals, the press conferences, the terrorist negotiation sessions, the war councils—figurative and literal—and to witness the inner struggles within the IOC itself. If one writes a document destined for half a century's concrete incasement, then one should write of things unmentionable on the day memorialized. At least as far as one's editor will allow.

So let us begin. Not with the lasering to life of the Olympic flame, nor with the crack of the first starter's pistol. We shall start the story where it rightly begins: with a bidding war, the crash construction of the Olympic facilities, and first of all: the difficulties of the 2080 Games in Ulaanbaatar, Mongolia.

The Ulaanbaatar Games of 2080

A Lean to the Extreme; An Unfortunate Start; A New Beginning.

The Ulaanbaatar Games were not, properly speaking, a "disaster". Fewer competitors died than had during the Cairo Games of 2076. Ulaanbaatar proved less expensive as well, in spite of Mongolia's subsequent national bankruptcy and fiscally forced incorporation into China. Ulaanbaatar's Olympic facilities also improved on those of '76. Any Olympic building plan might shine next to that of the Egyptian capital's. Cairo's choice to build the Olympic stadium so as to encompass the pyramids looked inspired in 2066, financially foolish by 2070, and positively irresponsible when the titanium dome collapsed under the weight of the stadium-wide hydration system with all the now recognized ill-effects upon those once so eternal monuments to the endurance of human works. Had competitors and attendees alike not evacuated a week earlier, the dome collapse would have led to even more sporting deaths than occurred. Perhaps enough casualties to call into question the Olympic Movement itself. The world dodged a bullet there.

But while the Ulaanbaatar Games benefited from the fortunate comparison with those in Cairo—and proved the IOC's contention that the world should forever prize the Games as an enduring legacy of human civilization—no one would hold up 2080 as a stellar year for international sports. The World Fencing Association might have elected not to move aggressively into extreme sports by "going sharp". World archery need not have put its targets on the competitors, however much more exciting this made the event. Combat aquatics had its year; and should consider itself lucky with only four drownings.

Every sport needs a considerable worldwide audience. Who am I to doubt the importance of a mass following? But all decent people hope that the desperate extremophile eyeball bidding wars of 2080 will remain an outlier in concussive athletic bloodletting. However much one may have saluted the addition of motor sports in the Kuala Lumpur Olympiad of 2068, did it need to extend to high speed sudden evasion ("chicken") by 2080? No one doubts the aesthetic and athletic legitimacy of competitive face slapping, but did the rise in viewership really justify the addition of the steel gauntlet? The World Olympic Wrestling Association's addition of eye-gouging drew much needed attention to a sport threatened with "dull irrelevance" in the new extremity of athletics—but is the WOWA completely innocent of the resulting ocular injuries? Can the WOWA put it all down to a mere "failure to adequately calculate socket stability parameters"? Did Taekwondo need the addition of the "ground stomp" rule, however beloved by fans? Must everything be "full contact"? Even diving? What can one say of the unrestricted javelin throw? The razor discus? Bare-knuckle boxing? Ballistic badminton?

Frankly, deep-water breath holding isn't even visually enticing. You can't see any of it until a body floats to the surface.

Fortunately, Ulaanbaatar 2080 represented the ultimate (that is, finale) in everything ultimate. The extreme of the Xtreme. When the third fourteen-year-old girl splatted onto the inner dome at the trampoline event, everyone knew that the springs had been coiled too tight even when television viewership doubled for the medal round. One recalls in amazement that it even took *that* long considering the unfortunate first day of the Games. Under the sponsorship of Armed Asylum, the 500 meter race's official starter began the first heat by firing a starter's pistol—the S13 Kill Companion Mach II Replica—which rather too well replicated its military-grade home defense cousin. No one believes that Hamad Hariri would have won a medal at the Olympics—nor even won the heat itself—but had the Games overall focused more on safety and less on "gripping the viewer" he would have at least survived the event.

I had the honor to attend the first meeting of the IOC Executive Committee held after the completion of the 2080 Games, serving as a non-voting member and as its official chronicler. At this meeting then Vice President Benito Jax of France faced off against IOC President Manvik Gupta of India following the latter's two-hour summary of the successes of the Ulaanbaatar Olympics. Benito Jax acknowledged the record-breaking attendance at the Games (itself a marvel of turnout recovery after the Cairo fiasco), the ever-increasing worldwide television ratings as Ulaanbaatar 2080 made its lethal progress, and the record-breaking corporate endorsement income generated for the IOC. Despite this, Benito Jax observed that "Any Olympics which ends not in a closing ceremony, but rather in a general strike of the athletes, cannot be regarded as an unqualified success."

Manvik Gupta responded, "During your earlier presidency you yourself initiated this policy! You left *me* to carry it through. You left me with a poisoned presidency! I have done your dirty work and now you lay it all on me. After all of your promises..."

Benito Jax, "I take full responsibility for that error. With misplaced generosity I encouraged Mr. Gupta to supervise the execution of an audience recovery plan the whole of the Executive Committee had signed off on. I mistakenly thought that after so many detailed discussions of its proper implementation, that even with Mr. Gupta's manifest failures managing the New Delhi Games, he could not fail to follow the many instructions prepared for him by this committee. I had not anticipated that he could so fully ignore the wise council offered him by each of his colleagues on this committee. I beg my fellow members to forgive me my misplaced confidence in Mr. Gupta, to remember how much he strove to do well in the charge we gave him, to ignore his occasional intemperate outbursts to which he is so much given, even just now, and to allow him to remain on this committee even as we together sweep up the mess he left in leading us all over the cliff of extremity. We must move forward, united; faster, higher, stronger—together."

The committee's other three voting members agreed that Gupta alone bore the blame for their latest infamy. Each of these IOC vice presidents offered a more particular account of what might be done going forward. Jing Zhao of China, the committee's single female member, urged a greater emphasis on the sporting ideal and the spirit of international peace; after which she graciously offered China's assistance in paying the Ulaanbaatar overages—with minor conditions. Joseph Kabwe of Kenya congratulated the IOC and its assembled leadership on its continued support of world sports. He then argued more sponsorship funds might go to African athletic programs, particularly to the Kenyan Olympic Organizing Committee. Ahmed bin Abdullah Al Saud of the Saudi Sovereign Wealth Fund Nation reminded the committee of the joint commitment undertaken by his nation and the IOC for the "repatriation of profits" from the IOC's receipts back to his country, this in view of the Saudi Sovereign Wealth Fund Nation's coverage of Egypt's debts from the Cairo Games.

This led to Kabwe's standard complaint that the IOC should not regard the SSWFN as a country at all—and that excess funds should "repatriate" to Kenya. Ahmed bin Abdullah Al Saud responded that Kabwe's nation would soon be reduced to a similar status as the SS-WFN but without benefit of a fund to manage. Kabwe broke into tears, declaring that for just this reason the 2084 Games initially scheduled for Amsterdam must be granted to Nairobi without a competitive bid. That such bids were unfair, overly competitive, fixed by the global north and global east, and an affront to the authority, and glory, of the IOC, which should make all such determinations independent of the financial means of the non-bidding nations.

China's Jing Zhao supported Kabwe's points. President Gupta suggested that if the IOC complied with this, China would own Kenya within a year. Not, offered Ahmed bin Abdullah Al Saud, if the SS-WFN elected to cover those Games; which it would—conditional on IOC financial guarantees. Kabwe blessed Ahmed bin Abdullah Al Saud, rained praise down on the nation of the Saudi Sovereign Wealth Fund, and suggested that it and China might make secret bids to fund the Games to be hosted by Nairobi in 2084. Kabwe smiled broadly, his face still streaked with tears.

Benito Jax called the committee to attention by tapping his cufflinks lightly on the table. He said, "This will not do. The IOC cannot undertake further funding guarantees. Not given the financial mismanagement of the current leadership. The IOC cannot forgo a bidding process—inclusive of IOC Executive Committee inspections—for the selection of a replacement city. And on the short notice available for any such city, Nairobi surely lacks the construction capacity to build the necessary facilities. Furthermore, and even more foundationally, we must address the failures of Ulaanbaatar. It remains a fact, perhaps unfortunate, perhaps even temporary, that we cannot hold an Olympics without athletes. And the ceremony stoppage which concluded the 2080 Games indicates that we must curtail—even eliminate—much of the extremity imposed on the Games during President Gupta's leadership. Setting aside our past positions and committee votes, accepting as we did Mr. Gupta's vision, we can see now that the extreme combatization of the Games represented a passing fashion rather than a next evolution. We have surely suffered too many injuries and deaths to proceed on this path."

One could not assume from the faces of the executive committee members that they shared that judgment, but Benito Jax pressed to a more substantial point, "And our corporate sponsors will not abide the continuation of such casualties. Excepting, of course, Armed Asylum Industries, whose influence—I maintain, over-influence—on our current president, may be an indirect cause of our difficulties. We all appreciate AAI's sponsorship and contributions..."

General table-tapping concurrence here occurred.

"...But armaments and bunker sponsorship cannot cover the Games. Mr. Gupta has led us into a cul-de-sac. I offer, most reluctantly, my own services as IOC President. Letting bygones be bygones and not to speak of past disputes some on this committee have indulged in with me. The members of this committee know the sorts of funding I can bring. I would not deign to compete against Mr. Gupta for the votes of this committee, but I would accept its unanimous endorsement. Unless anyone else feels that he or she could secure such unanimity."

And thus did Benito Jax become, again, His Excellency President Jax, head of the IOC.

The Paris Selection

An Inundation; Bidding Bidders; The
Politics of Glory.

Paris might have missed its turn at Olympic glory in 2084 but for unforeseeable difficulties in the city originally designated to host those Games. When it initially won its Olympic bid, Amsterdam promised a unique competitive environment. It built its stadium on titanium stilts (the first of the great stilt architecture stadiums). It's swimming pools boasted a new "smooth water" medium, alleged to guarantee record breaking times—now that such times could again be recorded. Its Olympic waterfall promised to add excitement to the kayaking events (the folly of extremity had not yet obtained its later clarity). Its just invented grid course would allow the complete mechanization of the equestrian events; an initial and eventually unnecessary response to the doping scandals of the '42, '46, '50, '54, '58, '62, '66, '68, '72, and '76 Games. Its narrow streets offered the "most twisty" marathon in Olympic history. With its Europe-wide funding scheme, carefully negotiated treaty alliances, thirteen new sports, forty-two new events, and the signing of not one but two of Hollywood's best directors for the staging of the opening and closing events, Amsterdam 2084 offered the IOC a badly needed guarantee of adequate funding, worldwide attendance, must see TV, reassuring tradition, and unexpected novelty.

The unfortunate failure of the Coca Cola Puts A Smile On Your Face Sea Barrier ended this idyll. The Organizing Committee of the Olympic Games (OCOG) for Amsterdam 2084 gamely tried to muscle through. It suggested "pontoon shoes" for the running events, a revival of the long gone obstacle swimming event for water sports, actual vultures rather than clay pigeons for the skeet shooters, competitive rescue retrieval in place of judo, platform diving from roofs, hide and seek water polo, floating table tennis, street surfing, and "rowing with purpose". The mechanical horses would all sink, but the equestrian events could still be held with jet skis. (This last suggestion much protested by the Jet Ski Demonstration Sport Committee.) The Amsterdam OCOG sheepishly acknowledged that baseball would need to be played off site.

Yet, despite all these innovative suggestions, and in the face of the Amsterdam 2084 OCOG's vow to hold "the best hydrated Games in the history of Olympic competition", the IOC decided to choose a new city to host the Games of 2084. In view of the foreshortened preparation and construction timeframe, this presented an extraordinary challenge.

The history of Olympic city selection has long oscillated between the glory of having *so many* and the horror of having *too few*. In its earliest years, when the Games promised a sporting contest of modest scope, conducted by dedicated amateurs, representing populations unaware of the matches, solely for bragging rights and without a hope of profit, Olympic organizers struggled to find cities to host the Games. They attached the Olympics to the odd World's Fair or picked some ruined city ready to sweep away a bit of rubble for the show. Once the Games became an event of international standing—bragging rights for dictators and politicians—and the participants could count on endorsements, or extensive state support, or professional careers, or at least speaking engagements, cities aggressively bid against each other to host the Olympics. The good old days.

The Games evolved, as did the ambitions of the prospective hosts. More better. More bigger. More. Top the last Games. Break the old records. Not: admire the old records from a slightly more accomplished position. Break them. Make them suffer in shame. How dare those records impede as well as impel our glory; obstruct as they instruct us. Any record left unbroken mocks us. Shall the past hold all the glory? Crush such thoughts. And what one may say of the number of micro-seconds separating the nipple of the fastest ever runner of the distance of 100 meters from that humiliated fool whose record he broke, one can also say of any Olympic Organizing Committee and its city looking back over their collective shoulder at the last Games: there lies the measure of failure; so close yet so pathetically far. Shall we host fewer events then did San Paulo? Those heathen San Paulians? No. Shall we suffer lower viewership than the bastards on the Istanbul OCOG? Not with eyeball cameras attached to every athlete (excepting the boxers—too much breakage). Shall we build smaller than Cairo? Sturdier, yes; but not smaller. And while everyone loves money, noble souls prize things that money cannot buy. Pride. You earn your right to it. You cannot buy it. Not until the money gets really big. So on Games, to your greater glory! Spend like tomorrow will never come.

The trouble infecting the bigger/better ethos lies in the bidding wars. More exactly, from the IOC POV, the lack of such bidding wars. For once the Games grow big enough that even medium-sized nations must fund them by decommissioning their air forces, the number of interested parties for any year's Games grows smaller. Factor in the alleged corruption in contracting, the supposed payouts to IOC officials, the transfer of the nation's entire infantry to urban security, and the added expense—in credibility at least—of convincing or conniving a population into funding the Games—or even just enduring the resulting traffic jams—and the prospective cost tends to dissuade offers.

No logic attends the decision of a city to bid on the Olympics. Typically, some national tyrant or urban titan looks to mark their name indelibly on history through grand architecture or civic memorials. They see the names of former mayors on plaques in parks and dream of bigger parks and bolder plaques. Streets in their names leading to stadiums into whose foundations they stabbed a first shovel as the world press digitized their image (when digits could do this). Those images immortalized in books (when books existed) or on the internet (before its collapse) or in and on both, plus inscribed upon whatever follows in the future *we* dream, and *you* live. A name remembered in glory, carved in stone above the five interlocked rings.

Skywriting; all if it.

Worst of all it takes at least *two* egomaniacal politicians with the power to disassemble their city to stage even the pretense of a bidding war. More a bidding skirmish with just two.

New Delhi outbid three other cities for the 2072 Games—but these all *African* cities, making the bids less warlike than lowball. Cairo faced off only against Florence, but here at least a real bidding war ensued. Florence put up its art collection as collateral on loans necessary to make an *earnest payment*, thereby pressuring Cairo into its partnership with the Saudi Sovereign Wealth Fund Nation and the United Arab Emirates Refugee Trust to win its bid. The Italian treasures ended up in the vaults of Russian Oil Oligarchs and the Brunelleschi dome now covers a terrarium in a private pleasure garden off the Black Sea. At that it fared better than did the Sphinx.

Ulaanbaatar bid against no one and still only secured the Games with promises from China. The executives of the IOC groan at the memory of the single bid for the 2080 Games. Just two cities to visit, one in the middle of Mongolia and the other offering charity instead of a competitive proposal. China hosted the Executive Committee in some of the smallest and least well-appointed suites in IOC history. Mongolia offered only gers. Sides spun from silk and fully furnished in disorientingly European style, but hardly the villas in the Italian countryside the members enjoyed while leading Florence to its successful financing of its unsuccessful Olympic bid.

Amsterdam had been a minor triumph by comparison. Amsterdam bid against Tokyo, Philadelphia, Nanjing, and Saint Petersburg. Rich cities that could fund baroque banquets, luxury junkets, ornate residences, and elaborate gifts. Tokyo provided rooms at its new Mt. Fuji Panorama Summit View Resort, swag bags holding 11th century samurai swords, and classic tea ceremonies (with whiskey) every morning. Philadelphia let the committee ring the liberty bell—and take it back to Lausanne for a "world tour". Nanjing upped the swag ante by handing out silk ribbons twinned with gold, encircling and binding bundles of cash. Saint Petersburg offered prostitutes.

Amsterdam won with a combined package of canal view suites, hand crafted wooden shoes, and wines once owned by European royalty, given to Saudi Princes to cover gambling depts, bought by American tech entrepreneurs after the Rise of the Machines, sold to Russian oil barons after the Great Digital Purge, and stolen by British cat-burglars to appear on the table of the visiting IOC Executive Committee. A heady mix of European elegance and narrative extravagance. Also, Amsterdam leveraged most of its urban space to aid the IOC and its National Olympic Committees in putting aside the debts occurred staging the "most digital Games ever" at the unfortunately timed New Delhi '72 Games.

In the aftermath of the inundation of Amsterdam (said math summing to a considerable deficit), the Executive Committee had reason to fear that most horrifying of all possibilities: no bids, no takers. The whole of the Olympic Movement might resolve itself to a few tag relay matches in the parking lot outside the Lausanne IOC headquarters. Frantz's Used Car Dealership might be the Games' only sponsor. The Executive Committee forced to redub the President's corner office as its skybox. From a champaign to a cider Olympics.

Against these horrors stood his Excellency Benito Jax. His new bid to lead the IOC again came down not to mere sturdy objection to business as usual after the 2080 Games, but rather to his promise to return to business as usual after the Amsterdam Inundation. No one in the history of Olympic leadership, nor of sports entrepreneurialism in general, had ever more successfully manipulated the world into compliance with the Olympic ideal than had Benito Jax. If anyone could save the Games, Benito Jax could.

Benito Jax had always intended that Paris would host the Games after the unfortunate hydration of the Netherlands. But one cannot force a city into real sacrifice without opposing it to a competitor. A Paris that shrugs its shoulders and deigns to host an Olympics out of pity will not enter into the break-bodies-and-souls spirit of the Games. One may allow a city to enter an *initial offer* in the modest spirit of helping out a wounded institution while giving young people a place to run in an oval, but this attitude of charitable superiority will shake loose only enough money to fund a co-ed club-sports version of the Games. And quite beyond the issue of money, such a kindness-based bid would not induce the hectic reverberations of fear, shame, wounded pride, wounding pride, humble mastery, and preening dominance that finds so special a place in the hearts of men who love strict rankings based in arbitrary merit. One needs a bidding war to make the winner feel not compassionate in offering to host the Games, but heroic in winning the *right* to hold the Games.

Even before he obtained the leadership of the IOC at the meeting summarized above, Benito Jax had laid the groundwork for a post deluge Olympic bidding war. The IOC handed out medals of merit to great urban leaders and national politicians. It inducted city councils as honorary members of national football teams. Then selected a few to become full-fledged members of those teams. This required a bit of competition fixing so that middle aged politicians were not shown up in demonstration games by actual athletes. But it warmed the heart to hear football aficionados long past their sporting years—and in control of civic funds—boast of their unexpected success and survival on the playing pitch.

In all his lobbying efforts, Benito Jax principally targeted London. He needed a sufficiently plausible and hateable rival to Paris to secure from the City of Light a construction and hosting commitment great enough to strangle later opposition to the needed urban remodeling. Sign on enough resentful French politicians, filled with national pride, and a true Olympic spirit could see the 2084 necessities through until the real cost came clear. By then everyone who could stop the madness would have committed themselves in blood to the project. They would conspire to juggle blame until they could shift it onto foreigners. Presumably tourists; we speak of Paris, after all.

By such measures Benito Jax brought Paris to commit to an Olympic Games to end all Games—as the expression would have it. A Spectacle For the Ages. An Ultimate Demonstration of the Olympic Ideal. A Testament to The Human Spirit. A Coca Cola Moment. The Triumphant Return of the Digital. The Final Word in Post Human Excellence. An Event Beyond All Slogans.

And as we shall see, it proved a truly spirited affair.

The Perils of PEDs

Fame of the Name; A History of
Augmentation; Efforts at Enforcement;
The Simplest Solution.

N o one has so dominated the world of Olympic sport as Tooball
Beatleback. At the age of eighteen he took New Delhi by storm in
track and field, winning five gold, three silver, and one bronze in various
sprint, middle distance, and obstacle evasion events. All this while playing
striker for the Brazilian National Football team and winning gold in the
decathlon. He founded the practice of net-mind broadcasting his every
moment (or, as it would turn out, *almost* every moment). This proved
enormously controversial when he began dating his on again/off again,
lover, wife, poly-amour, and "Hate Queen", the women's pole-vault/bo-
jutsu champion, Synthetic Rince. Some alleged they shared too much, but
the *shares*, the *likes*, the *posts*, the *ties*, the *twigs*, the *pings*, the *pulses*, and the
boinks told a different tale. Never had the world seen more off-the-chart
popular online share-moguls. Their brands multiplied. They sold shares
in their body parts. Their breakups broke trading markets. Their makeups
made betting fortunes. And why not? No one could cover less ground
faster—obstructed by obstacles or not—than Tooball Beatleback. Synthetic Rince could pole her way higher than any woman competitor and
use the pole to win a combat gold in bojutsu. Hitting the ground, or
another woman, she played poles apart from the competition. All this
public acclaim and unrivaled fame occurred even before Tooball's first
Olympics.

And he did it all naturally, unaided by performance enhancements of
any kind—so the ads claimed, and the constant-cast seemed to prove.

Some maintain that Tooball's enduring fame could be traced to the
digital disaster of the New Delhi Olympics. The Great Digital Purge that
occurred concurrent with those Games deprived a worldwide audience of
any further mind-net, share-scape, "internet", social or asocial media access

to sports stars. Or anything else. Tooball and his lover/Hate Queen might well have benefited as much from the content purge and digital desert that followed their early peak-attention-stoppage as from that public-awareness high itself. By the second week of the Games, no other sports star's performance could erase the impressions of Tooball and Synthetic Rinse. Indeed, no other anything could. They hung in the collective world mind for over a decade after, for sheer lack of competition; an inerasable after-image of digit fame in a suddenly re-analoged world.

But one must admit that they ably leveraged this unexpected advantage to conquer the reborn hard-copy media. The last of the digital phenoms transmogrified into the first of the broadsheet stars. Tooball in particular returned to form in the Cairo Olympics four years after his initial taste of glory. He entered a record fifteen events, including distance swimming. In one way of counting the consequence of this, he medaled in every one. Alternatively, one might note that the IOC stripped him of all of those medals in turn. Irrespective of the exact performance enhancing substance tested for, Tooball had used it. Apparently constant-casting could not be trusted; algorithmic intelligence altered images at his manager's will. Until AI finally ate itself. Had he not been so, for once, unexceptional, his positive test for...everything...might have derailed his reputation. But at the '76 Games he did not stand out in this respect.

Tooball came back, with his lady love Synthetic Rince, to participate in the Ulaanbaatar Games. Clean as a whistle and 30 pounds lighter. Like everyone else, he passed every test, and unlike anyone else, he passed everyone else. He even competed in the combat marathon run. To his undying glory and the shrieks of the fans, he won the contest not by out distancing his opponents but in the true spirit of the new event: he tackled and beat them. The skinny Kenyans favored to win lay bleeding in defeat on the field instead, most not far from the start line. Tooball jogged the rest of the course—sometimes just walked it—with the entire cohort of that year's distance runners hovering well behind, too afraid to overtake him. (Apparently they had not fully appreciated the scope of that year's rule changes.) Total Tooball victory.

And that might have been that. No one would expect more such dominance after twelve years of Olympic level competition. Not in today's Games. Most sports use the rule of thumb: obsolete at 25, orthopedic at

30. But the recent history of performance enhancing drugs (PEDs) handed Tooball a lifeline. Or a death wish.

The first Olympics to test for PEDs, or "doping", were those in '68. Not the 2068 Games in Kuala Lumpur, but the *nineteen* sixty-eight Games in Mexico City. This first effort can seem laughable in light of recent history. The single disqualified athlete drank beer before a pistol shooting event. The Ulaanbaatar Games *required* alcohol consumption prior to the shooting events. And although this did "enhance the excitement", medical services proved insufficient to cover the injuries. Audience attendance at what had laughingly been called "marksmanship events" did not recover at the Paris 2084 Games, notwithstanding all the additional bulletproofing. Proponents of the next evolution in performance often point to these differences in Olympic attitudes toward "booze shooters" as exemplifying "enhancement arbitrariness under cultural shifts".

While a tippling shooter may have been the first enhancer caught, no one at the time thought that pentathlete Hans-Gunner Liljenwall had discovered the advantages of chemically induced alacrity (or chemical calming, in his case). Early on, beer probably served more as a handicap than an advantage—one look at a photograph of the 1896 Games strongly suggests the stout men of Denmark's team tipped the odd elbow—but nothing defines the modern world more than the advance of science, and no slogan on earth looks more ill-equipped to hold science at bay than "faster, higher, stronger".

It would take joint degrees in chemistry, biology, zoology, biometric analysis, and physics to explain or even understand the subtleties of doping. Olympic PED investigations proved this in 2049, 2053, 2057, 2061, and 2065. Indeed, the last of these reports established that drug-test cheating was the highest paying job for chemistry PhDs that year. One could as truly say that the Olympic Games attracts drug-test cheating as to say that the Earth attracts objects within its gravitational sphere. But while you cannot cancel the laws of gravity, drug testing obeys a more human legislation.

The IOC tried other options first, of course. But all efforts at PED control faced the insurmountable fact that while everyone but a few "maverick" pharmaceutical companies likes the idea of a drug-free Olympics, everyone also likes the reality of a dirty Games. The athletes will do anything short of suicide to win. The coaches look for just that attitude when taking on athletes. The nations under whose flags those coaches and athletes play covet medals. The corporate sponsors, highly sensitive to the appearance of a drug-fueled Games, want drug testing to "prove" the competitions clean. The sponsors want guilt free eyeballs on advertisements. No eyeballs, no ads, no sponsorship, no Games. Everybody can go home and play in their neighbor's backyard.

The IOC lives or dies by corporate sponsorship. Thus, the IOC wants what Coca Cola wants, what McDonald's wants, what Armed Asylum wants, what Alios Vivant Luxury Brands wants, what Nikadidas Sporting Goods wants, what Nemesis Research Solutions wants, what Empusa Body Shaping wants. They all want all eyes on the Games, ready to cheer, ready to buy, at least ready to remember a brand design or mascot imagined up by graphic artists, animal wranglers, or animatronic innovators. Getting attentive eyes on the Olympics requires records. Records made and records broken. Olympic records broken. World records broken. The whole Olympic economy of excess requires a level of breakage that if occurring in nature would split the world asunder.

But all done clean, please.

While Tooball passed his drug tests at the New Delhi 2072 Games, many didn't. Sports "doctors" and drug testers wage a constant Darwinian struggle against each other over medals received and medals revoked. The IOC lends its weight to the struggle one way or another according to the shifting balance between tolerance for enhancement and intolerance at durable records. As the athletes teeter on the brink of the trans-or-sub human, the IOC presses for more and better tests. As the record books defy the IOC urge to update them, the Executive Committee relaxes its vigilance. In the face of complaints that it turns a blind eye to cheating, the IOC commissions reports written in dead languages.

Chemists work both sides of the street. A new PhD in some PED friendly field of science first goes to work for the International Anti-Doping Agency (IADA) to advance the goal of allowing honest athletes a healthy competition followed by a long life of hobbling on replaced knees. After a few years that same PhD will move on to private industry, helping coaches prepare athletes for the competitive crucible of world sports. Arrested by some misguided national police force, the PhD will serve three months jail time and a year's probation. Then she or he will return to the IADA as a consultant with real world drug-cheating experience. Somewhere in this great cycle of life the PhD will develop a product line marketed under the name of an Olympic champion. Maybe *Tooball Ballers Supplements*, or *Synthetic Rince Blood Rincers*.

This long phony-war finished at the New Delhi Games. Athletes died. More than usually did. Gunshot wounds accounted for some of these. And clearly the heat also contributed to the lethality of the Games. But too much focus on this raised rather more ghosts than national governments, corporate sponsors, and athletics associations could exorcise. The Olympic Games, as Benito Jax so aptly put it, "Must rise above the headlines that spoil the unity of peoples; it must marshal a solidarity of sports to fend off the ugly nihilism of common life as reported in the minute press." (He said this during week one of the New Delhi Games, when news could still travel at that speed.)

And in fairness, the over-enhancement of the athletes contributed substantially to the death rates. High performance machines don't do well in a heat wave. Once the temperature tops 52 degrees Celsius, marathoners start to drop dead even when each runs under an accompanying sprinkler. If they began the Games with bio-regurgitated blood they will run faster and drop sooner. You can hose down the beach volleyballers until they play in puddles, but at New Delhi '72 temperatures, the over-doped ballers played in quicksand and most matches ended in heat stroke. When the paddle strokes of the rowing competitors don't just *churn* the water but literally bring it to a boil, is that the heat of the Yamuna River or the steroids rolling in the rowers' veins? Public opinion settled on the dope fiend.

So post-New Delhi, the IOC, the IADA and the sporting world in general got serious about testing; Random test announcements, video monitoring of each and every urine transfer, blood DNA identification on every blood sample, biochemical markers, statistical profiles. Supplements banned; prosecutions set in motion. Even the algorithmic intelligence world-virus did not stop the aggressive application of science and law to designing the means of drug detection.

Unfortunately for the Games, this new wave of detection technology ran a bit ahead of the sporting world's appreciation of the advances. Athletes, coaches, and doctors worked the game in the old way just as the forces of virtue applied new technique. Everyone felt good about the progress of sports. Until the Cairo Games.

The IOC stripped Tooball Beatleback of his medals for doping. (That is, they stripped him of his medals because he doped; had the Olympics handed out medals *for* doping, he would have won and retained those.) Synthetic Rince, his partner in publicity, lost all three of hers. Tooball's gold medal in the 100 meter sprint would have gone to Austin Lewenhook of Austria, but he also tested positive for PEDs. As did the bronze medalist in the event. As did the fourth, fifth and sixth place finishers. As did the rest of the event participants. Lewenhook naturally could not claim Tooball's gold in the 200 meter race either, for the same reason. This race saw a similar set of disqualifications right down the line. The same occurred in all the other track events. And the field events. Swimming did not prove immune to the problem—in much the way that the world wide web did not prove immune to the AI hyper-virus. Not a single badmintoneer tested free of steroids. No archer failed to have taken pulse-depressors. Every footballer had imbibed "cocktails". The fencers all took fentanyl. The equestrian event equines all tested positive for anti-depressants. They may have been happy horses, but their riders had to hand back the medals. The IOC proved unable to award even a single medal at the Cairo Games that it did not quickly repossess. In the end it gave out "honorary medals" to those that placed in the first positions in their events, which is to say, to those who cheated most.

All of this might have proved a fatal embarrassment for the Games but for the convenient distraction of the stadium collapse and the rash of heat strokes preceding that catastrophe. The full evacuation of Egypt, Libya, Tunis, Algeria, and the Saudi Peninsula distracted world attention from the IOC's singular failure to stage a doping detecting Games that included any winners. In fact, Benito Jax (then in his first term as IOC President) made splendid use of this refugee crisis, promoting the Olympic Movement as a palliative to a fevered world's distress. Under his guidance, the IOC enrolled new refugee nations as fast as the world community minted them. The Olympic Games would bind a bruised world. It could boast of an integrity unseen in other international, or national, institutions. In sports at least, purity and honesty would reign.

After Cairo, the athletes and coaches got the message. They dutifully complied with the new world order of clean sports. They fired the PhDs, glutting the job market with sobbing chemists. The sporting world embraced the new implicit ideal of *higher, stronger, faster—within reason.*

The IOC promoted this new era of sporting virtue in what remained of the world press. Congratulating itself on its idealism, the world turned to Ulaanbaatar 2080 to forget its many troubles and enjoy ethical contest at last.

But the world did not enjoy it. Not the ethical part at least. The athletes showed up looking—as the world sporting press put it—unimpressive and diminished. Sports writers complained that the opening march of nations looked like a "walk of weaklings"; that the runners ran "sluggishly"; that the swimmers "meandered in the water"; that the footballers lacked "zest", the handballers had no "pep", the basketball teams no "pith". (One may safely say that the sports writers of the world ran out of words to express their weariness at this "exhibition of the prematurely exhausted".) To put the matter plainly: not a single team or athlete broke a sporting record in Ulaanbaatar. Not even in the newly admitted sports.

The IOC had, of course, anticipated this result. It knew its own history. Any serious retrospective alteration of the record books in light of the new science of doping detection would have left them freighted with asterisk. A drug-free future would superglue past gains in place forevermore. For this very reason the IOC had attempted to distract the public with new extreme and combat versions of familiar sports. While this did draw fan attention, the blood-sport focus too distressed corporate sponsors—always excepting Armed Asylum Inc.—for the IOC to declare a success. But what to do in the wake of Ulaanbaatar? Blind-eye turning had failed to appease the world, as had strict enforcement, as had strict compliance. What path remained open to the IOC?

Benito Jax began his address on this matter to the IOC Executive Committee with a review of first principles: "We are not sporting dictators. We offer the public the sporting sensations they crave, the athletes the recognition they need, the affiliated sporting associations the income streams they require, the sponsors the platform they purchase. It is not for the IOC to dictate what the public must want to watch, what sports the athletes choose to play, what institutions and individuals elect to patronize with their funds. We are not fit to be moral judges, concierges of conscience, regulators of righteousness, or validators of values. The IOC is but the mechanism of the market, the lubricant of athletics, an agonistic field for human striving in line with the revealed preferences of the mass audience."

To this ethical declaration he added a new foray into metaphysics, "Chemistry forms the basis of all human life; Our outer coating, itself sheathed in coats, conceals and protects nothing but a chemical factory within. Every process of the body reduces to some chemical rearrangement. Everything useful to the body becomes chemical in its use. Every enhancement, of mind or body, reduces to and is constituted by a chemical reaction. Every chemical we make contraband, every process we prohibit, finds a basis in the chemical elements *already existing* in the factory of the body, or could be there under the right circumstances."

Manvik Gupta, now a mere vice president, objected, "I fear we may be accused of fomenting unfairness. Not every nation can afford the same level of science. Many athletes will have grounds for complaint that their nations cannot provide them with the best advantages."

Benito Jax responded with the mantra of the IOC, "Each nation determines its own rules of citizenship."

Ahmed bin Abdullah Al Saud addressed the group on a matter of deep concern, "We cannot allow a willy-nilly use of performance enhancing drugs, unregulated by IOC determinations. Think of the pharmaceutical company endorsements and sponsorships we renounce if we don't control IOC approved PEDs. Just to let anyone use anything feels like throwing money out a window."

Joseph Kabwe interrupted, "I have already negotiated several such exclusive agreements—don't look shocked! So has Mr. Ahmed! And think of the gratuities accruing to committee members. The junkets. Not controlling approved enhancements feels like setting fire to money...then throwing it out a window!"

Benito Jax calmed worries, "Gentlemen, I understand the concern. But we do not have the capacity to regulate only those drugs properly paying sponsorship deals without incurring exactly the difficulties my proposal aims to eliminate. Think long term. Think of a healthy IOC-directed sporting world. After we open up the Paris Games, free of any need for deception, pharmaceutical firms will make much of their success. The most successful at augmenting athletes will make immense profits and boast of those gains. They will seek further public notice. By the 2088 Games we can secure their sponsorship, advertise their brands, and return their profits to world sports. Consider the Paris Games a 'free sample'. An inducement to enhancement. A foot in the door."

Jing Zhao, "We will have trouble with women's sports."

Manvik Gupta, "But we have already made determinations regarding *non*chemical enhancements. How do we defend these in such a changed environment? How do we fend off objections that we now have a *pharmacological* bias?"

Ahmed bin Abdullah, "Those concerns unnecessarily complicate matters. The biomechanics industry is paltry compared to the drug trade..."

Benito Jax corrected, "Industry, not trade."

Joseph Kabwe, "We do not wish to be unfair. We do not wish to tear up any trade's money. Any industry's money. And set it on fire and throw it out windows."

Benito Jax tapped his cufflinks on the table to command order, "I believe we have reached agreement. I record us as unanimous in favor of complete pharmacological liberalization. We will form a working group on further reform proposals. I will head it personally."

Thus did the IOC, under the inspired leadership of Benito Jax, solve its PED problem in advance of the Paris Games.

Building an Olympic City

A Contentious Construction; An Unfortunate Failure; A Noble Addition.

U pon the announcement that Paris would host the recently homeless 2084 Olympic Games, the following appeared in fliers around the City of Light:

"Paris! Awaken! As you sleep the forces of Ultra Late Capitalism have hijacked your corrupt and failing city! Their machines of de-construction threaten to trash your trash-packed boulevards! (Do not add this flier to the stacks!) The flow of dollars, of euros, of yuans, of centavos, and of new bit-boinks, will flood the world and the trash filled streets of Paris in place of the old and dead bit-boinks! Many will be moved; few will be fed! Do you notice how hot it is already? Remember the Tower! All of Paris will follow the Tower! We are the Whole Earth Defense League. We are the last chance of Paris! The last chance of the world! The whole world! Resist the Games!"

As Benito Jax said: "Someone always resents their city's good fortune." Indeed, he made this the title of his sixth collection of maxims and mottos.

Paris, in fact, welcomed the Games. If not its citizens, then at least its political and business elite welcomed them. The civic leaders offered Benito Jax the keys to the city. Quite literally: writs of possession, universal passwords, authorizations of eminent domain, and blank pages of passed legislation. The IOC responded with equal generosity, transferring Amsterdam's Olympic fund accounts to Paris (not without protest), funneling international sporting aid to the ailing city, and aiding in reorganizing France's tax system to further athletics-based urban development. The IOC called this a *win-win* (ironic given its usual commitment to the ethos of *win-lose*).

One cannot deny, certainly not in the face of later investigations, that some of this money found its way into unscrupulous hands. "In any great endeavor some small level of corruption will occur." (Benito Jax, *Getting Beyond the Complaint Culture*). It would serve no purpose to list the number and nature of kickbacks and payoffs uncovered, the city officials and Jax family members accused of receiving them, or the ongoing legal mechanics this "overflow of funds" still fuels. Suffice to say that a great deal of money changed hands, and a great deal of building resulted.

No one could gainsay the results (due, in part, to newly passed legislation against doing so). The Olympic Stadium, host to the opening and closing ceremonies as well as the track and field events, boasted the largest air conditioned indoor space in the world. One so well powered that it could remain within three degrees of any set temperature even with its enormous dome retracted. It had a two thousand and six of the world's largest television screens arrayed both inside and outside the stadium, a fully image-ready pixel dome, and it sat 150,000 people in comfort while offsetting its (considerable) carbon footprint through the IOC's contributions to counter-logging education initiatives.

Protest groups declared it a "white elephant". (Is this a phrase heard in 2134? By it they meant an extravagant but useless gift.) (Also, an "elephant" was a large mammal once found in Africa and India; white ones rare and weak.) Accusations that the McDonald's Feeds Us Right Olympic Stadium had no post-Olympics use ignored IOC promises that after the conclusion of the Games it would host football and rugby clubs, youth sports education programs, and several orphanages. Even if these ambitious plans have yet to come to pass, its eighty-foot orange and pink roman columns topped in onion domes augments the Paris skyline with a glow of international sophistication (the glow emitted by over 60,000,000 LED lights). And while unplanned, surely it counts to the credit of the stadium's construction and design that it hosts over a million bats in its many architecturally significant niches and ripples. Activists may call these a "plague on the city", but in point of fact the anti-rabies campaign has almost declared an inoculation victory. One may also note that the Great Dome of Paris now shelters the world's only remaining population of this endangered species.

Consider also the Alios Vivant Luxury Aquatics Center and Space Port. Built to host swimming, diving, and water polo (human and equestrian), it also sought to bring affordable space tourism down to the celebrity billionaire price point. Launch failures notwithstanding, this represented a new horizon in horizon conquest. Those who protest the Aquatics Center's post-Games ownership transfer from the public into private hands simply do not understand the financing arrangements. In any event, the land developers have since gifted the Aquatics Center back to the people of Paris for only a small tax consideration. Repairs continue on the foundation cracks.

To say that the city "dispossessed" less wealthy members of the population to build the Olympic Village suggests an altogether more disruptive process than occurred. The homeless were not literally swept from the city's streets—at least not those that read the notices warning of the sweeping days. Although construction did temporarily de-house some of the poorer denizens of Paris, this occurred only after the IOC, the city of Paris, and the land developers, submitted a plan to re-house those very same people in the post-Olympics Olympic Village. In the event, all parties agreed to leveling the Olympic Village to build the Alios Vivant Olympic Memories Luxury Estates. The de-housed complained that they did not so agree, but as they no longer resided within municipal limits, how could they expect a say in the policy? No person not homeless prior to Olympic construction could complain of being homeless after the post-Games reconstruction. By order of the French Parliament.

I will skip past most of the other structures, too small to interest the reader; the various velodromes, scattered skateparks, football fields, handball halls, archery arenas, badminton bowls, pentathlon pitches, riding rings, and golfing grounds. But we must not neglect Benito Jax's greatest triumph: The Benito Jax Great Parisian Mountain Cycle Structure. To appreciate the importance of this construction requires a bit of historical knowledge that I will not assume remains in common currency in 2134.

Financed by forced indemnity payments from Haiti to former slaveowners and completed for the 1889 World's Fair, the "Eiffel Tower" once dominated the skyline of Paris, standing as the emblem of the city. Three hundred and thirty meters tall and made entirely of wrought iron, it looked like an early 20th century antenna. But bigger. Perhaps not as impressive to describe today, but in its own day, and for long after, it stood as a marvel of human ingenuity and industrial age beauty. From anywhere in Paris you could see the Eiffel Tower. Its blessing and its curse.

The trouble began after the 2024 Paris Olympic Games. In honor of these, the city hung a giant version of the five-ring symbol of the Olympics from the tower. The mayor of Paris decided that this emblem of unity should become a permanent feature, so as to recall the glory of the Games, bring unity to the people of Paris, and commemorate her own inspired mayorship. Paris divided on the issue instantly. Some saw the delight in extending in perpetuity the celebration of world sport, like an unending athletic Christmas season. Others complained that the tower should not become an advertising platform. Ultimately, this last view did not prevail.

Although the Eiffel rings themselves did not last, the idea that they should usher in an era of Eiffel ad placement did. Corporate logos festooned the Tower like baubles on a Christmas tree. BitRomp, Comkit, Grupak, Liqueer Liqueurs, Bilgemouth Kissing Fluid, RomDink Networkers; a blizzard of symbols in circles and cones and swishes. None of these mean anything to me—I record them from an old photograph—and surely mean nothing to you. The twined blows of pulp policy and digital disaster ensures that even an ardent researcher will make little sense of them. But in their own day, they had weight. If not cultural, then at least in the gravitational sense. When the last mighty logo took its prideful place at the very top of the Tower (embarrassingly, Coca Cola again) the mighty work of man came toppling down.

Paris wept, of course. And the Parisians vowed to abstain from the lure of lucre. They swore oaths against advertising, marketing, branding, and tourism. They affirmed themselves opposed to the sale of history, heritage, custom or culture. A noble self-denial. Still, things had to be paid for. It's the way of things, stubbornly refusing to exist until the conjuring of capital brings them to the world of warmth. You would think that things, seeing how loved they are, would spontaneously generate just to enjoy the satisfaction they briefly bring. But the best you can say of things is that when desire alights on them, a conspiracy of competitive commerce ushers them into a waiting world—or at least to that segment that can pay.

That which Parisians most needed circa 2078, as Amsterdam reacquainted itself with the sea, was *its own* wall. The suburbs surrounding the great city hummed with what Parisians described as "swarms" of immigrants, refugees, asylum seekers, and the descendants, sometimes to the fourth generation, of displaced persons in every category. Displaced from their distant lands or within the country of their birth, they "swarmed" with dissatisfaction at their suburban lifestyle. They bustled to burst from the confines in which the French Parliament had placed them. Unsuitably untraditional, the countryside rejected them. Unluckily not of a fashionable hue, the city restricted them. And as their numbers grew, joined now—incongruously—by Netherlanders, the narrow circumference of acceptance about the city limits grew narrower, and thicker with "them". Parisians came to regard strategic urban design insufficient to contain the threat. The citizens of the city called for a wall. And needed an excuse to put one up against what were nominally their guests or fellow citizens.

But walls, being things, appear only by the magic of money. And a justification for erecting walls against those with whom one should share the slogan "liberty, equality, fraternity" comes hard. Enter Benito Jax. Parisian to his core and also a lover of mankind, no one held a better appreciation for the complex dynamics of public and publicity than he. Jax coaxed the Olympics to Paris, then coached the corporate world to open up its unending wealth with appeals to conscience and to the prospect of complete access to the prestige of Paris. He overcame Parisian reluctance to re-enter the world of corporate sponsorship with the argument: *money*. The Games came, the money came, and Coca Cola, perhaps feeling a tinge of guilt over the Great Tumble, financed the Coca Cola Olympic Sugar Spirit Security Fence.

But enduring Jax-fame could not come from a suburb-barring barricade. Walls must become truly grand (think *Hadrian's*, or *of China*) to elevate their inspirer into history. Petty posts for security cameras designed to discourage crossing the wrong street would not serve Benito Jax as a *construction for the ages*, nor as a monument to the determination of the over-ego. History would not remember Jax for a city-circuiting electric fence—in the event overwhelmed. (Although the subsequent inquiry proved that only 33 of the 213 killed actually died of electrical shock rather than trampling.) No, Benito Jax's name remains hailed—no doubt to your own day—as the inspirer, imaginer, architectural overseer and brand manager of the Benito Jax Great Parisian Mountain Cycle Structure, as we now refer to it. And as, no doubt, the future also refers to it. At the opening of the Games, it held the official name of the Mount Sport Monkey Live Large! Bet Hard! Mountain Bike and Land Sled Facility. By the second week of the Games the IOC had rechristened it the Leek Green Faction Olympic Tombstone for Capitalism Mudheap. But that proved only a temporary expedient, and today it honors its inspiration.

Returning to the important point: Benito Jax had created, on the site of the fallen Eiffel Tower, partly of its twisted metal remains, and like that once great edifice, in view of the entire city, a mountain suitable for distance dirt biking (leg powered and motorized), as well as for the bike jumping, mud sledding, and the landslide evasion competitions. A beautiful structure of multiple hues of brown with built-in camera podia able to catch the action from any angle, capped with prebuilt advertising platforms on widescreen televisual billboards. An eighth Wonder of the World. A brandable ziggurat in the heart of the planet's most famous city. A Hanging Gardens of Paris.

And all of this, the wall, the hillock, the many stadiums, the athlete's village suitable for 21,000 participants, the even larger facilities for the press, and the necessary "movement of peoples"—all of it—built in under three years. An executive feat to match the Exodus from Egypt. (I refer to the biblical event here rather than the 2076 evacuation.) And against such opposition. Unaccountable public resistance to the Olympic spirit. More water poured out of hoses aimed at protestors than actually contributed to the entire construction project. "In spite of their many complaints," as Benito Jax noted at the time, "the Olympic opposition is actually better hydrated than the construction crews. And unlike those crews, who will repatriate to their countries of origin, the protestors will return to their comfortable homes here in Paris, with their urban lifestyle, temperate climate, and easy views of the Naming Rights Still Available Mountain Sports Complex. Perhaps in gratitude they might grace the Games with less grousing." In fairness to the protestors, repatriation proved climato-logically impossible, and after the Games the construction crews also lived with a view of the mud mountain and its rolling ad copy—seen through the barbed-wire remains of the Coca Cola security fence. A triumph for equality after all.

Paris needed not only to *build* facilities, but to dress them in Olympic quality fields, grounds, waters, and flooring. A whole economy revolves around this effort. Scientific researchers work fulltime at universities around the world to produce the fundamental breakthroughs in material sciences aimed at making the objects upon which the world's greatest athletes will run, walk, hop, skip, or flutter their arms. Of these efforts few surpass the importance of the Olympic running track. For the Paris Games, thirty-four companies worked under the supervision of Apex Ventures Human/Material Interface Industries. Apex designed and built a track for Paris guaranteed to re-write the record books, both Olympic and financial. They used the latest in artificial track and turf materials, including infused geometrical elliptical cells for better cushioning, a layer of non-evaporative silicon insets for water deletion, a micro surface of heat resistant nanoids, spike and track correspondence technology for greater grip, and in response to continued concerns about species diversity loss—and to promote greater corporate-based environmental soundness—an in-grinding of snail shells harvested from the Queen conch, once indigenous to the Caribbean but now preserved for industrial sustainability programs only by Apex Ventures Environmental Preservation and Publicity Utilization Incorporated. The entire effort employed almost 9000 scientists, statisticians, engineers, industrial designers, and habitation specialists who could not otherwise find employment under current market demand. All this produced what all hoped would be a track to break the hearts of past record holders, fulfill the dreams of current record aspirants, stir the imagination of the next generation of athletes looking to break today's records on tomorrow's newer-tech tracks, and keep the public content for slightly over a dozen days.

The same technological effort went into building all the other elements of the track and field events. These included water-infused impact dispersal allowing the pole vault mats to better absorb the press of athletes clearing, and thus falling from, ever greater heights. Ultra-shield catch-cages for the hammer throw, made four times stronger in anticipation of stronger throwers threatening more records. And impact detecting hurdles (although no one could *do* anything with this detection, the data would surely prove useful in future). Not to mention the "leg-pressure impact reactive" run for the triple jump, which *should not* be mentioned in light of the split shins and hair-line pelvis fractures it caused.

Apex Industries also supervised the building of the Olympic pools for Paris '84. Swimming records rely as much on ever newer technology as do those for track. Dig your pool too deep and the force applied by the swimmer's motion goes to waste. Dig your pool too shallow and the rebound of kicking-force causes time-killing turbulence. For the Paris Games, Apex dug ultra deep-water pools (through ancient and soon flooded mortuaries) to allow swimmer-generated turbulence dispersal, and then built an adjustable pool floor and water shifting system so that officials could change the competition depth of the pool in real time based on athlete performance. Apex built body temperature sensors into the sides of the pool to detect athlete physiological responses to water temperature so that instant alterations could prevent cramping or facilitate muscle relaxation depending on times posted.

Apex took no less care in designing and building the flooring of the basketball event. Cool-suited wood cullers traveled to now uninhabitable lands to find padauk hardwoods to undergird the courts, and used Indonesian mahogany with a thin Alaskan pine laminate for better "dribble reactivity" so as to control bounce levels. Himalayan hardwoods covered the surface of the indoor volleyball courts owing to this rare substance's knee impact sensitivity. Using these also proved a boon to sustainability efforts as the forests needed to be felled anyway in order to make room for new post-equatorial second homes for wealthy expats and holidaymakers. The IOC counted the hardwoods as a sustainable harvest—as it must have been, given the original "bonfire of the vanities" planed for them.

Finally, consider the importance of sand to beach volleyball. Not just any sand will do. The World Beach Volleyball Association maintains strict standards specifying particle size, grain geometry, water permeability, bake time (yes, they bake it) and impact forgiveness. The sand for Paris traveled 4,300 kilometers from Syria in four convoys of five hundred trucks each. They drove through a civil war, passing a hundred thousand refugees walking north along the side of the roads, but they made it safely to Paris. (The convoys of sand made it safely.)

After the heroism of bringing rare sand from Syria—and in spite of the fact that the IOC had promised to repurpose that sand to preserve beachfront property values along the French Mediterranean—Parisian protestors met the convoys and attempted to prevent the filling of the Olympic beach volleyball hole with its completing allocation of aggregate. No amount of explanation by Benito Jax on the importance of the Games to Paris, and the danger of leaving such a large hole unfilled, fazed the crowd of activists in the least. The IOC had brought so much to them. So much sponsorship. So much construction. So much sand. Yet they gave no thanks. Not even offering an "on the other hand" acknowledgment of the IOC's efforts to balance against their rock throwing.

Limited gratitude infected not only the ungrateful citizens of Paris, but a not insignificant number of potential athletes as well. It turned out that the IOC leadership's decision to ensure a drug-rule free Games provoked pushback from at least one quarter.

The Distaff Dilemma

An Advocate; An Adversary; An Agony.

As a little girl, Zoe Sallis dreamed Olympic dreams. In her youth she longed to win a gold in the 100 meter dash for the United States of America. In her tweens she wanted to win a gold in women's football for the Bi-Coastal States of America. In her teens she turned to volleyball and aimed to win a gold for the Atlantic Coastal States of America. As an adult, she led the North Northeastern States Federation of America Women's Field Hockey team in the Games of '68. They won silver.

Zoe Sallis retired from competition but not from the world of sports. She formed the International Women's Athletics Union. Heading this group, she advocated for women in Olympic sports. She advocated for equal media coverage. Succeeding at that, she advocated for less sexualized media coverage. Failing at that, she fought for *less* media coverage. She challenged the IOC to repatriate more sponsorship money to sporting associations. Succeeding at this, she challenged the IOC to give such funds *equally* to women's sporting associations. Succeeding at this—and facing rage from male athletes—she challenged the IOC to equalize funding by giving more to women's sporting associations rather than cutting funding for men's associations. She petitioned the IOC to better identify sex-specific injuries. Upon "succeeding" at this, she patiently explained that she had meant injuries female athletes suffered more than male athletes, not injuries men might suffer during sex. By the time she summarized her case against the latest rulings in Olympic sports to a closed hearing of the IOC Executive Committee, she had of necessity reverted back to advocating generically for women in Olympic sports.

Benito Jax, chair of the hearings, summarized Sallis' points back to her from his chair, "From where I sit, from what I hear, you essentially agree with the committee in its determinations. You have raised important caveats, urged minor qualifications, suggested limited changes, promoted minor textual amendments, and quite rightly insisted on the inclusion of other voices—yours being an outstanding example of these. But apart from some limited cavils, you side essentially with the committee on these matters."

As Mr. Jax drew breath, Zoe Sallis objected, "No, Mr. Chairman. I have been at pains to say that I and the International Women's Athletics Union, oppose, root and branch, the IOC decision to liberalize performance enhancing drug use at the next Games. We absolutely oppose it. We demand a return to the procedures used for Ulaanbaatar. We cannot fathom why the success at the '80 Games has been shunted aside. After so much struggle."

Benito Jax smiled broadly, "Ms. Sallis, I recall sitting here eight years ago, listening to you vehemently object to our plans for the Ulaanbaatar Games. *Now* you acknowledge that we were right, and you were wrong. One might be excused for thinking your passionate advocacy motivated by a desire for the spotlight. Or for contributions to your various causes. I do not myself subscribe to such a view, but you do leave others in the bind of suspecting that the lady doth protest too much."

Zoe Sallis, "Mr. Chairman, eight years ago, during the planning for the '80 Games, I opposed the mass inclusion of combat and extreme sports. I opposed the across-the-board rule changes in established sports that aligned them to those goals. The changes you and the Committee have inaugurated since the end of the Ulaanbaatar Games suggest that you now agree with the points I made at that time. If you and the Committee do not rescind the new test-free mandate, we will sit here again in four years regretting what the Committee has done and will still not have finished calculating the damage."

Benito Jax, "I have never understood how you can advocate for women's continued inclusion in combat sports while also opposing these sports at the Games. If you don't oppose boxing, judo, karate and taekwondo, on what basis do you protest the new slashing sports? Do you or don't you oppose combat sports for women?"

Zoe Sallis, "I would describe our position on combat sports to be identical to the committee's current position—in opposition to its earlier, revoked, position."

Benito Jax, "But do you oppose combat sports for women?"

Here, Benito Jax had maneuvered Zoe Sallis onto difficult terrain. He knew, as would anyone familiar with her writings, that Sallis supported grappling arts and point karate, but opposed boxing. In essence, as she had stated in print, she opposed concussive combat sports—those in which competitors sought victory not through physical control of an opponent, or through a demonstration of reflexes, but by inflicting physical damage on an adversary. Pursuant to promoting this understanding of sportsmanship, Sallis had sometimes made common cause with activists whose objections ranged further, all the way to opposing any sport founded on the physical control and domination of an opponent. More to the point, as leader and spokesperson for the International Women's Athletics Union, she had to limit her objections to those shared by the union's members. That membership included women who competed in combat sports that Sallis personally opposed. Her conscience and her duties thus diverged; a gap Jax enjoyed exploiting.

Zoe Sallis, "What I oppose, what I came here to speak against—"

Benito Jax, "Most passionately speak against..."

Zoe Sallis, "Most strongly speak against, is the elimination of performance enhancing drug testing. I came to speak against the drug free-for-all now instituted."

Joseph Kabwe, "Not free. They must still be bought."

Benito Jax, "We describe the rule as a *relaxing* of the drug testing policy."

Zoe Sallis, "Relaxing into non-existence is suicide. Or murder in this case."

Benito Jax laughed, "We're quite certain no one will be murdered by this new policy."

Zoe Sallis cut him off sharply, "I recall you saying that eight years ago at the earlier hearings on the Ulaanbaatar rules and additions. I have a list of names I would like to read into the record regarding that claim..."

A suddenly serious Jax waved this away, "Those were not murders. They were consensual accidents. Mongolian legal authorities signed off on those sports and have dropped all investigations at this time." He nodded to Jing Zhao in thanks for China's assistance in heading off this controversy. He continued, "We have other issues at this meeting. Thank you for your attendance."

Zoe Sallis did not gather her papers to go, "You have not responded to my arguments. The Committee assured me that I would receive a hearing and a response during session. Your silence reeks of guilt."

Benito Jax's veneer of reserve flecked just a bit, "I believe the core of your complaint is the fanciful assertion that performance enhancing drug testing rule relaxation will turn women into men and obliterate women's sports."

Zoe Sallis held up one of her ungathered papers, "I have entered into the record a list of substances, from steroids to hormone regimes to cell replacement techniques, whose unrestricted use will masculinize women in sports and—"

Benito Jax, "But only if they choose to use them. Our new rules make new freedoms, we do not force anyone to use any substance."

Zoe Sallis, "But the rules create the competitive environment that compels women and men to use them!"

Benito Jax, "Allows them the opportunity, not compels. We are not—any longer—in the business of telling people what to do with their bodies."

In light of the eight volumes of rules and regulations governing every aspect of Olympic play, this claim raised a titter in the room.

Benito Jax stared down the room, "I further note that your concern for femininity in women runs counter to the wise statements against gender essentialism found in your writings. Which I have very much enjoyed reading."

Zoe Sallis, "The whole point of women's sports is to allow women the same opportunity as men to compete at every level of ability and intensity of interest. Of course we distinguish women from men. We are a different sex."

Benito Jax, "A weaker one." His tone here indicated that he did not mean to endorse the proposition per se, but to force Sallis into doing so.

Zoe Sallis lost none of her composure, "As you have so often said, Mr. President, sport is a trial of the spirit; a contest of dedication, of determination, of sacrifice. I put it to the Committee that the difference in measurable performance along the statistical spectrum dictated by the physical differences between women and men says nothing about the strength of character each participant, of either sex, brings to the game. Women have demanded equality of participation at the Games and in sports in general, on the basis of that spiritual equality, notwithstanding physiological differences."

Benito Jax, "And yet, only a few women or men can meet the physical demands of the Games. Physical demands that profoundly limit who can play at our level. Having already received a dispensation in light of physical rather than spiritual limitations, one that men who just miss gaining places on their Olympic teams kindly decline to complain of, you now plead to deprive women of the opportunity to maximize their physical abilities—and thus possibly to finally overcome nature's handicaps in relation to men's place in the—as you call it—statistical spectrum, in the name of a merely spiritual equality."

Zoe Sallis, "It is absurd to justify the Olympic Games, to justify sports at all, on the basis of pure physical performance. Every sport at the Olympics, every sport known to humankind, is a construct of its rules, these defining the relevant physical performance for the purpose of play. All exist to allow for a play-filled physical expression of a spirited dimension of human aspiration. The IOC's dismissal of its obligation to regulate performance enhancing drugs makes sport—all of it, right down through all competitive levels—the sole possession of those who seek the glory of being hailed as victors, casting out those who play with passion for the love of excellence in play. And to those whom the IOC would hand over sport, it will hand it over with poisoned medals, condemning the participants to a lifetime of physical disability beyond any necessarily accompanying athletics. To women *and* men, you will do this. To those who qualify to play in the Olympics, and to those who love athletic competition but never hope to play at that level, you will do this. And to women in particular, you propose by these policies, a leveling of standards that will pose impossible burdens on sincere athletes, horrible consequences for the women that choose to play their sports as they have always hoped to do, and the eventual elimination of women's competitive sports."

Benito Jax tapped his cufflinks on the committee rostrum as if in applause. He said, "I see that we have nearly reached agreement. Unfortunately, we have already exceeded our time for this hearing. We will provide edited minutes to all attendees and to the press. Thank you for coming. Meeting adjourned."

The True Meaning of a Sport

The Winter Games Don't Win; A Bit
of a Pickle; Ultimate Opt-Out; Footgolf
Makes Its Play.

E very sport aspires, as its apotheosis, to join the Olympic Games. Most
cannot, and even those that do must fight to keep their place. Do
you, in 2134, still know of rhythmic canoeing? The endurance handstand?
Power spitting? Dike stuffing? Have any of these elevated their game from
the merely demonstrational to the tenuously accepted? From mere acceptance to legacy level? You know better than I. At least 2084 gave them their
chance.

While everyone rejoices at the addition of a new sport or a new event,
the IOC must also disappoint. Not only in rejecting applicants, but in
ejecting sports and events as well. The post-Ulaanbaatar reassessment led
to a great deal of this, of course, but the castoff combat competitions
had little history to leverage in their defense, so few shed tears at their
demotions. Surely fewer tears than were shed in the contests themselves.
But to appreciate the deep history of Olympic event rejection, one must
look back further into the past.

I have, in this memorial guide, spoken of *The Olympics*. But the Games
as we now know them once came prefaced with the term "Summer".
This to distinguish them from sports played on snow and ice. Naturally
occurring snow for many years, and ice that though artificially made and
kept, formed a thin continuity to an even earlier era of naturally occurring
icy playing fields. The IOC called these games "Winter" Olympics. They
formed a fascinating variety, though one difficult at this distance to fully
explain. I had the privilege of watching a number of Olympic films years
ago, prior to their "final digitization", but not realizing the fragility of the
successor medium, I took no notes. I beg the reader's patience in my efforts

at reconstruction. In the absence of contemporary competitions on frosty fields, such reconstruction can only be partial. But it rewards the effort to look into the practices of an earlier world, if only to expand the horizon of our amazement.

Consider the ice events. Wearing blade-soled shoes, athletes would race round an oval, just as in a running event. And at a variety of different distances, just as we run different distances on an un-iced surface. Other competitors performed various ice ballets on similarly bladed shoes. Women and men participated in these—some in mandatory coed pairs. The events produced much flipping about, perhaps more an ice gymnastics than a ballet. Another event consisted entirely of sliding stones down ice to gently strike other stones. The Winter Olympics even had a field hockey event, played on ice, on shoe knives, and appropriately called *ice hockey*. I know of no combat versions of these sports, though the ice hockey games became a bit spirited.

The snow events looked stranger still. Athletes would ride down snow-covered mountains on planks, typically sliding between poles. These events distinguished themselves by the distance between poles, in the limiting case by the complete absence of such obstructions. Other events would cast competitors off of ramps, either for distance or to perform acrobatics. These resembled some of our wheeled events, but done in the freezing cold, on ice or snow, or later, on synthetic substitutes for these. Some events had competitors slide on their planks through flat countryside, this occasionally enlivened by rifle shooting (though not at each other).

Strangest of all, some events had athletes push a box into a tunnel (open at the top for viewing) in order to stuff themselves within the box in time to career through the white intestine's icy turns. Others used these purpose-built courses to go down just on boards beneath their backs. This apparently in imitation of a then common practice of children, riding boards down snowy hills. Most unbelievably, *all* these sports once coexisted with identical popular pastimes. Except for the box-down-the-tube event; mysteriously unconnected to anything ordinary people did.

All of it an ever-retreating memory now. The edged ice races and blade-balanced acrobatics. The hurling down mountains. The icy colonic swerving. Gone with the snow-topped summits. Though not immediately with them. The IOC had blasted manmade snow over mountain segments until the melt-times could be counted in minutes. They then used synthetic snow until its toxicity claimed too many athletes (spectators long banned from personal attendance in order to keep the illness rates down). The IOC kept up the ice events one season more, but they came to look a cruel and expensive joke. It pained the public to recall what matters had come to, so they declined to tune in. The IOC killed the Winter Games least their ratings failure infect the still secure "Summer" competition. Those Games thrived; the world dodged a bullet.

More happily than reviewing lost sports, we might focus on the stories of sports attempting to *enter* the Olympic Games. These included not only sports—competitions requiring athletic ability—but what one would more properly call *games*; contract bridge, air hockey, chess, auto-repair (the waning auto industry pushed a lot of sponsorship dollars into the IOC during the mid-sixties). Associations representing these activities organized in every country. They struggled, mightily at times, to ensure significant numbers of female players. They sought sponsorship in an increasingly crowded sporting world. This led them to devise visually appealing versions of their games. Sharp-card bridge. Extreme air hockey. Speed chess. Speed chess with distraction—at first just shouting at the opponent after hitting the timer, or waving one's arms about, but later allowing the use of airhorns and laser pointers. Chess, especially, put great emphasis on production values for television. Lots of flashing lights and spewing confetti. All to the latest pop tunes. Play by play analysis of every *Queen's Bishop to Rook Five*.

None of these prospective sports worked harder to win Olympic acceptance than video gaming. In case these have not re-emerged at the opening of the time capsule, I will attempt a description. These were "sports", played while sitting, in which the competitors would finger gadgets that manipulated images on a screen in imitation of some act of violence. These games had such enormous popularity with the general public that they supported professional leagues quite independent of the Olympic Movement. The IOC considered bringing them into the club just to keep the video sporting world from stealing all its sponsors. The Executive Committee hesitated only because the players averaged a weight of three hundred and fifty pounds. In their defense, the video gamers pointed to sumo wrestlers as a precedent, but even the heaviest rikishi could easily lift themselves off the ground (and with effort, lift each other as well), so the

IOC remained unconvinced. The events of '72 ended the issue for the time being.

The IOC struggled not only to decide on each game individually, but on some standard to rule them out wholesale. While the video gamers could not increase their activity level—too far gone and too profitable in their reclined positions anyway—nothing dissuaded chess. No sitting down? Chairs removed. Sweating required? Turn off the air conditioners. Post career orthopedics necessary? They would bang their knees on the table legs after every play. Chess would join come hell or high water.

Finally, the IOC settled on the rule (this in the halcyon days preparing for New Delhi '72) colloquially called "steroids have to help". In order to count as a sport, rather than merely a game, steroids had to help. More generally, if the activity did not require testing for PED use the IOC considered it merely a game and not a sport. Drugs producing only mental improvements did not suffice. The associations representing Olympic shooting events briefly panicked until the IOC reassured them that sedatives still counted as banned substances.

This might have settled the matter but for the one exception allowed by the IOC. Poker. At the 2070 meeting of the general assembly of the IOC, on the day after the announcement of the sport/game determination, the IOC welcomed Texas hold 'um poker as a demonstration "sport" for the '72 Games. The IOC justified this on the basis of the "incredible stillness required of competitors". The chess associations howled in agony. Everyone smelled the rat.

Competitive poker, whatever limits of time imposed or amount of stillness encouraged, was and is the least interesting viewing experience known to mankind. Its professional circuit acquired television viewers only by judiciously cutting out 98% of the "action". But you can't edit an Olympic event in progress. *Live and happening now*—allowing for time zone delay—represents a key feature in sporting, and especially Olympic, appeal. Why would the IOC allow so soporific an event into the already crowded list of Olympic sports?

Sport Monkey. The largest online gambling company the world had ever seen. Its famous slogan: *Bet The House!* Many did, thus the profits. Its famous mascot: "Sporty", the world's last monkey. (Unfortunately no longer with us.) Its net market valuation: larger than Brazil's GDP. In the run-up to the New Delhi Games, as Sport Monkey made its final mad dash for monopoly power, it could afford to buy three IOCs and any half dozen middle European countries you cared to name. In adding poker to the Games, the IOC just obeyed a law of nature.

It ended poorly, as everyone knows. Digits degraded and then destroyed. Winnings unpaid and the losers still at a loss. The transaction records disappeared in a puff of the internet. With them, to some relief, the only reliable accounts of considerations paid to sporting authority leaders. But at that moment of cyber betrayal, even with the New Delhi Olympics in full swing, the world had other things to worry about than just how much Sport Monkey had monkeyed with sports ethics. The IOC and the Olympic Movement went on as if nothing had happened; and poker never made it beyond the demonstration stage.

So, sports come and go. But sometimes one virtually replaces another. Badminton reigns today along with table tennis as the only Olympic racket sports (*face-racketing* having failed to pass through the Ulaanbaatar filter). But an earlier generation thrilled to a sport with the unlikely name of "pickleball" (though it involved no pickles of any kind). Even earlier generations prized a sport called "tennis".

Tennis could trace its origins to the 16th century. It consisted of two players (or two teams of two) whacking a ball at each other over an outstretched net while trying not to hit the ball *so much* at each other that the player receiving the wacked ball could in fact continue the play. It differed from badminton by stretching the net low to the ground, and from table tennis by conducting play on a life-sized court rather than on a miniaturized court put atop a table. Tennis proved vigorous, cerebral, and grueling. A pleasing combination for all concerned.

Except the unathletic, who played the game recreationally, just not well. Pickleball originated as a recreational rejection of the hyper-competitive spirit of tennis, and of commercialized sport generally. Enthusiasts for accessible sporting for the unathletic devised the game in the mid 20th century in Seattle, then a part of the United States of America. By the 2020s the sport had overflown the banks of mere fun and achieved a popularity poised on the point of profit. In answer to the question, *shall people just play this game or make something of it?* pickleball answered: *go for gold*. Thus the promotions, the pro circuit, the specialized equipment manufacturers, the lights and cameras. Eventually even sport specific PEDs (necessary Olympic consideration). Ease of play helped the game thrive and allowed elderly former tennis pros a new shot at senior league glory. What's not to love?

Like kudzu, pickleball overgrew onto the grounds of tennis. As a sporting organism, it thrived in environments first colonized by the larger court and quieter rackets of its elder brother. A parasite on the game of tennis, it lured the young, the aged, the uncoordinated, and all those oriented to ease of play. Red duct tape redivided tennis courts, strangling the playing area of the older game. Tennis became stuffy, in the way that the young always cast the old as stale and languid. (Though to be fair, tennis had a lot of stuff even without a younger rival.) Like a boa constrictor, pickleball choked off its adversary; depriving it of that life giving air: popular attention, mass players, sponsorship money, and time on TV. And all this because a handful of individuals living on an island in a sound of Seattle couldn't find a fourth badminton racket.

Pickleball crushed tennis. Virtually adding itself by popular acclamation to the Olympics. The two sports then entered their Olympic death match. Tennis had the status, the legacy, and frankly all the athleticism. Clearly the favorite. Pickleball entered the Games against tennis as the scrappy underdog. The people's sport. Advantage tennis at first, but before long the two struggled for viewership on equal ground. Tennis stars defected to the bold new game that anyone could play. Soon the P-ballers (a late and temporary coinage devised to elide the intentional dorkiness of the original name) ruled the rackets. Tennis despaired, declined, then dissipated to nothing. Off the Olympic roster, out of the public parks, parted from the private clubs. Complete pickleball victory.

Then one day everyone woke up and realized that pickleball required less athletics than the riding events (ignoring the work of the horses). The competitors grunted hitting the ball as pure show. They accompanied matches with a preposterous theater of exhaustion. They barely drank water during the games—in spite of the heat. Even the PED use proved a sham. The players took masking agents to mask the fact that they didn't bother with steroids. What a joke. The public turned away. The "paddle sport for everyone" attracted fewer eyeballs than fencing (though most of that audience probably watched for the grade-grubbing rather than the sword flicking—always setting aside the Ulaanbaatar "power prick" year). Pickleball fell from the list of Olympic sports. It drifted back to its lonely windswept courts in cities and suburbs. The ghost of pickleball haunted the playgrounds longing for its old rival, to the sound of crickets. Having killed tennis, it lost its reason for being.

Of course, kids and seniors still played it.

Historically, every athlete has coveted a place in the Olympics. Every sport wants to join. No sooner do two boys pee for distance than does the winner dream of Olympic gold. So, it came as a surprise during the run up to the '84 Games that radical members of the ultimate frisbee community went to considerable trouble to pull their sport from the Olympic Movement altogether. Unfathomably, they wanted out. The radicals took control of ultimate frisbee associations in almost a dozen countries, and through these they petitioned the IOC to drop ultimate frisbee from the Games. This not in response to the extremism of the '80 Olympics, the IOC had not drafted ultimate frisbee as an extremophile, but out of a deep sense that Olympic inclusion had ruined their sport.

Ultimate frisbee, not much older than pickleball, originated as a hybrid sport combining what had been called American football and a light aerodynamic discus (called a disk or a frisbee). The now extinct American version of football (today insultingly called "soccer" by triumphant Europeans) combined a line of trench combatants, a la rugby, with a variety of highly delicate ball handling specialists hiding fearfully behind the line on offense, seeking to move forward by degrees, while a team of precision combatants lurked behind the line of defense ready to stop them. Between moments of violent activity, the sport featured a series of committee meetings.

Ultimate frisbee's inventors took out the violence and thus made a sport surreally different from its father. They continued this patricide by forming rules designed to foster community within the competition: no referees were allowed, players had to call penalties against themselves with advice from their opponents (so they kept the committee meetings), games ended not with a victory dance of one team but with a circle of congratulations including both.

As the sport gained popularity its purists struggled to hold onto the ethos of playfulness and community formed at its birth. The struggle proved uneven. Every new sport, if it ever bothers to embrace community over competitive zeal in the first place, faces an inflection point on the road to higher levels of skilled competition. As institutions and media invest in the sport, the stakes go up. Pride and profit predominate. Winning comes to matter more, fellowship less. The most earnest and ambitious of the skilled players abandon those that cling still to the ethos of play; that is to say: those who carry on out of camera sight, unsponsored and unloved by the masses. The masses who want winners and drama and don't care a whit for love circles. To play for those who watch one must play to win—fun for the players doesn't enter into the thing; commerce kills community.

But somehow in the weird alchemy of the human spirit, love of a sporting community and respect for an ethic of intensity of play can occasionally overcome the desire to hold the laurels of a champion. Some athletes, even in this age of excess, still prefer to walk off the pitch arm in arm with what by rights should be their enemies; even preferring this to hovering over their opponent's bleeding body while raising arms to Nike. Prizing a fellowship of fun more than gold.

Benito Jax had trouble understanding all this, "What are they, some sort of fanatical communards? Do they grasp the concept of winning and losing at all? Do they just want to hand each other participation trophies? Are they children still? Where do they come from? Where do they expect to go?" When told that the rebel faction of ultimate frisbee promised to disturb the Games if the IOC did not remove them from the program, Jax said, "Let them do their worst. We have nothing to fear from meeklings too afraid of losing to compete in the greatest games on earth."

Finally, let us turn to a story of winners. *Footgolf* dreams fulfilled. This can-do sport traces its origin to the heath of Scotland in the Middle Ages for its golfing aspects, and to the Italian Renaissance for its football features. One can only wonder how medieval peasants residing in one of the periods most chillingly moist regions found the time and motivation to smack balls with sticks into vole holes. Historians assume that it "had something to do with religion". Or perhaps hitting leather balls substituted for sword strikes and beheadings in the Highlands. Could the first golf balls have been skulls? But then how big were the holes? *Football sized*, say the footgolf historians.

The Italian origins of football (called "soccer" in footgolf's country of origin) are easier to verify. The great humanist scholar Lipsinus of Padua recorded its creation by a misemployed falconer on diplomatic mission. Here, at least, the "skull-based" origins of the ball are well attested to in Lipsinus' treatise *On the Folly of Diplomacy*. The invention of football led almost immediately to the first football riot and the establishment of the first association of football hooligans. In defense of the sport, one must note that the Italian Peninsula of the Renaissance was prone to this sort of factional violence.

However fanciful these stories, one can trace footgolf's modern origins to the Professional Golfer's Association (PGA) effort to poach enthusiasm from world football. In the mid 21st century, the sport of golf found itself facing increasing resistance to its land use policies and resource demands. People had come to challenge the legitimacy of its great expanses of highly hydrated green lawns. The sport had somehow acquired an image of smug privilege and disdain for the working classes. A disdain even for walking rather than riding—leaving swinging one's arms as the sport's single claim to athletic effort. Sweat did not figure conspicuously in the game—apart from that produced by the outdoor weather itself; this perspiration mitigated by the high-velocity air conditioning added to the sport's "carts" as the course conditions warmed over the years. It seemed to gall some people to see rich men ride in open air vehicles during droughts on water-greened land while cooled by refrigerated air, their thinning hair blown back as they rubbed their arms against the artificial cold.

The sport of golf required a rethink; a hard look at first principles. Its rich amateur practitioners needed to garner some working-class appeal not founded on violent nativist sentiment in a world of unstoppable immigration. Some gentle adjustment to the status quo. Early on, the farsighted leadership of the PGA saw these needs on the horizon and in answer to them created the sport of footgolf as a working-class alternative to football's "tyranny of the rectangle". Footgolf, as conceived and shepherded by the PGA, promised the speed and fun of football with the pulse calming sedation of golf. A perfect combination of mass appeal and elite disdain. Plus new revenue streams for the sport of the wealthy—a group of ever-increasing net worth but ever diminishing net numbers.

It proved hard at first to raise the hoped for army of suitably posh players, but with tennis on the ropes, the PGA attracted a considerable number of wealth-adjacent athletes of good family to the sport, through the magnetism of money. These men and women devoted their energy and ever-fading name recognition to footgolf. For its part, the golfing establishment had one skill above any other: entertaining privileged people; just their type. The IOC Sport Inclusion Committee members felt right at home. Best wines offered by just the right sort of people. And you could play the game yourself with a little effort and an electric cart. Footgolf, excused from extremity, joined the Games in Ulaanbaatar as a demonstration sport, and looked forward to taking its place as a full sport at the Paris Olympics. Its international players would march with their nations at the opening ceremony. Enduring, no doubt with grace, the pity of the golfers and the jeers of the footballers.

Welcome to the Games, footgolf!

The Whole World Is Watching

A Question of Color; Embodying
Emblems; An Olympic Ambassador;
Design for Living.

T he Olympic Games represents not only the highest achievement
in sports, sports marketing, media saturation, corporate branding, and the public celebration of all of these, but also the height of
representation itself. The Olympics prides itself as the premier presentation of representation. From the first swag bags offered to visiting
IOC VPs, to the making of a mascot, to the spectacle of the formal
opening the Games, to the epic of informal celebration that closes
them, the Olympics simultaneously brands itself, its year, its age, and
world history. The precise appearance of all this era-stamping does not
just happen. Designers determine the details down past the last dash.
Five interlocking rings do not occur in nature; men must make these.

Dr. Mathilda Van der Ghent, Professor of Design Research at the
Wismar University of Applied Science and head of Fursten, Freiholtz
and Van der Ghent Graphic Solutions, sat next to her younger female assistant, in front of the Executive Committee of the IOC, in a
closed hearing. She had on the table before her a variety of pictures,
mini-posters, drawings, color swatches and stuffed toys. She had just
begun to explain her choice of the vibrant red and sea-blue color
scheme to lead the '84 design elements when Benito Jax interrupted
her, "We had, perhaps, too much red at the last Games. Quite a lot of
red. Constantly mentioned in the penny press."

Jing Zhao offered, "We should not have insisted on white as the
Olympic color. Requiring that all national uniforms base their designs
around the color white was a mistake."

Ahmed bin Abdullah, "I recall that at the time you represented white as a revered color in Mongolia. You described it as the perfect symbol of the spirit of '80."

Benito Jax, to Dr. Van der Ghent, "No white. Let's also eliminate red."

While her assistant made notes and rearranged display items, the unperturbed Van der Ghent said, "We can work with blue and—"

Manvik Gupta cut her off, "Blue? Sea-blue even? Should we invite commentary on blue associations? In light of recent events?"

Benito Jax, "No blue, I'm afraid."

More assistant scrambling and boss pivots, "We don't need to do blue." Van der Ghent flipped a color swatch board, "We have a burnt red—rust—rust palate. With a grey spectrum backing it..."

Ahmed bin Abdullah, "Rather post-apocalyptic in the current context."

Dr. Van der Ghent had not put the brakes on her plan in time, "...themed to wind and breezes..."

Ahmed bin Abdullah, "A windswept wasteland."

Dr. Van der Ghent, "We were thinking cool and cleansing breezes, sea breezes—or desert—cool evening desert breezes. A wind of change from the earlier Games."

Benito Jax, "Perhaps not deserts. And winds...I'm not sure the world currently imagines winds as breezes."

Manvik Gupta added, "Not on a coast."

Dr. Van der Ghent flipped her chart, "We can work in the yellow spectrum, trimmed in blue—a light blue; sky blue."

Jing Zhao glared skeptically, "Yellow? So soon after the Big Taint? Do we want to suggest a new bile-duct pandemic?"

Manvik Gupta, "Terrible times."

Dr. Van der Ghent flipped her boards, "Not a pus yellow, nothing to suggest jaundice..." she found a pink tone, "...we see a pink and sky blue palette; sunsets. Not ash-sky sunsets in orange, but candy sunsets, in pink."

Jing Zhao, "But that looks like the skin rashes now..."

Dr. Van der Ghent flipped on, "We thought an ochre color, with the sky blue."

Josheph Kabwe, "Deserts? Back to deserts?"

Van der Ghent's assistant handed her some cards. Dr. Van der Ghent said, "We think green. And the sky blue. Meadows. Butterflies in meadows against the brilliant blue sky."

Benito Jax mused, "I wonder if it wouldn't make the public here in Europe miss the sight of actual blue skies? In light of the continuing Black Forest fires?"

Ahmed bin Abdullah, "Meadows might not relate to Heat Zone experience."

Van der Ghent, "Aspirational meadows? Against a grey—light grey—sky?"

Jing Zhao asked, "Why is this so hard?"

Benito Jax tapped the table with his cufflinks, "Let's move on and return to colors later. What does your group, Dr. Van der Ghent, offer in terms of Olympic emblems? The fundamental image of the Games? And the posters?"

Van der Ghent's assistant pulled the color swatches off the table and turned the display cards around to reveal the next Olympic emblem. Dr. Van der Ghent began, "The history of the Games in Paris, 1900, 1924, 2024, and now 2084. We here imagine..."

Jing Zhao, "Is that the Eiffel Tower?"

Van der Ghent, "...a memorial to the past pointing to the future..."

Manvik Gupta, "I do miss it."

Van der Ghent, "...a world urban memory preserved by the Olympic..."

Jing Zhao, "But it is *gone*. And there remains the unpleasant matter of sponsor responsibility. Current major partners."

Josheph Kabwe thought out loud, "Perhaps if the sponsors would erect a replacement model? Smaller but noticeable?"

Jing Zhao, "China already made two full-sized Eiffel Towers."

Ahmed bin Abdullah, "In ghost cities. My father built an Eiffel Tower twice the size of the original at the hub of the Great Linear City."

Jing Zhao, "Covered in sand now. Along with its thankfully tiny population."

Benito Jax tapped the meeting back to order and addressed Dr. Van der Ghent, "Nothing with the Eiffel Tower, I think. Too soon."

Van der Ghent indicated the rising lines from the (now fallen) tower, "These represent the new dirt bike mountain in the Eiffel Tower's place—the continuity I spoke of...the Olympic spirit binding past—"

Jing Zhao, "That heap of mud!?!"

A pained Benito Jax, "Nothing with the Great Parisian Mountain Cycle Structure. Too soon."

Van der Ghent's assistant sketched furiously. Van der Ghent spoke looking over her assistant's shoulders, "We thought maybe a...a...frog?"

Joseph Kabwe, "Does any country still have these?"

Van der Ghent, still looking over the shoulder of her frowning and frantically drawing assistant, "No. Not a frog. A bulldog. Gripping a painting of Monet in its jaws...water lilies...you'll hardly notice the colors..."

Benito Jax relieved her agony, "Let's take up the matter of an emblem at the next meeting. What about a mascot? The Paris Games's ambassador to the world. What do you have for that?"

Dr. Van der Ghent looked at the stuffed bats on the table and despaired to even mention it.

Joseph Kabwe, "These have always been the worst. Why must we have this? What was it last time?"

Jing Zhao, "Genghy Khantact the Full Contact Khan."

Manvik Gupta, "I have already apologized..."

Joseph Kabwe, "And for Cairo '76, Kufi the Cool Desert Breeze. A disaster."

Ahmed bin Abdullah, "Not to mention New Delhi 2072's DigiDelh the Sport Digit."

Manvik Gupta, "Again, I have apologized many times."

Benito Jax cufflinked the meeting to him, "I was thinking, and see if you don't agree with me Dr. Van der Ghent, that we need a mascot that relates to the viewers at home. Our primary advertising audience. Something that connects the vibrancy of the Games to the act of watching them. Something suggestive of the Paris before the Games but shows how the arrival of the Olympic Movement in Paris has improved the city."

Everyone waited, edge of the seat, especially Dr. Van der Ghent, and most especially her assistant, pencil hovering over pad in anticipation.

Benito Jax, "CotRatt. C o t, capital R a t t. CotRatt."

No one moved, least of all Dr. Van der Ghent's assistant.

Benito Jax explained, "Due to unfortunate budgetary shortfalls and stubbornly high rates of union membership, Paris before the Games suffered from an overabundance of rarely collected garbage. A breeding ground for rats..."

Everyone at the hearing, frequent visitors to the city, could attest to these facts.

Benito Jax continued, "The home audience for the Games watch our athletes while sitting or lying down. A cot is something you lie on. Many cots have sprung up on the outskirts of Paris of late. All over Europe. They serve as the prime sitting and lying devices of the New Nations." He gestured at Ahmed bin Abdullah, "Not the Saudi Sovereign Wealth Fund Nation, of course, but many of the others." Jax returned to his CotRatt reveries, "The IOC has brought the Games to Paris. We cleaned up the trash, moving it to suburban incinerators, and thus we have, in a sense, *reformed* the rats. You see? Reformed rats lying on cots—like people, lying down and watching the Games..."

Benito Jax could see that he held his stunned auditors in the palm of his hand, "But not just lying down. Competing as well. Along with our athletes. Imagine them, the rats on the cots," Jax painted a picture in the air as he spoke, "Here is CotRatt propped on his cot-sides as if on parallel bars. Here is CotRatt twisting his cot in a judo throw. See CotRatt running in place on his cot. See CotRatt leaping as if doing a pole vault. See CotRatt clear a hurdle—the cot of course. Is CotRatt sailing now? Yes! Leaning off his cot into the wind. Now CotRatt's cot is a canoe. Now it's a horse. Now CotRatt lifts the cot overhead like a weightlifter. And imagine the audience enthusiasm for CotRatt in the trampoline competition—where we anticipate a struggle to maintain audience interest after the Ulaanbaatar excitement. Problem solved. Kids will bounce on their beds holding their CotRatt watching the trampoline events. CotRatt everywhere. It draws itself."

CotRatt does not draw itself, but Dr. Van der Ghent and her assistant sketched CotRatts as fast as Benito Jax described their many adventures. And by the time he finished, they had CotRatts, he and she, bouncing around their cots; faster, higher, stronger.

CotRatt would clearly make the cut. Now Dr. Van der Ghent presented the fruits of her toughest task: Olympic pictograms. These abstracted symbols would guide visitors to the venues, and—through television and Olympic advertising images—guide the world audience at home through the Games. They would appear on street signs, on information boards, outside stadiums, on flags, tickets, and tattoos. They would whirl as graphics before every television viewer announcing each event after every commercial break. Every sport would have its pictogram. As would the restrooms and other services. They would bridge the divide of language through the clarity of the image.

Manvik Gupta asked, "That one is a man?"

Dr. Van der Ghent, "A hockey player. Generic, not sex specific."

Manvik Gupta, "So that's not a penis? Forgive my asking."

Van der Ghent, "A hockey stick."

Ahmed bin Abdullah, "Why does he wipe his ass with it?"

Van der Ghent, "Not a *he*, necessarily. He only holds it, arm behind his back. Except that it could be a she."

Jing Zhao, "I played hockey, you don't hold it like that."

Van der Ghent, "It's an abstract representation."

Joseph Kabwe, "Why is he so fat?"

Van der Ghent, "It's an abstract representation. Suggesting fullness of purpose. Unused strength."

Jing Zhao, "They're all so fat."

Van der Ghent, "Consistency of representation. They all follow the same iconographic pattern."

Ahmed bin Abdullah, "The little dot, that's not something that came out of his ass?"

Van der Ghent, "That's the ball."

Jing Zhao, "So the ball got past her? She missed it?"

Van der Ghent marched wearily on, "The ball balances the design against the bottom of the hockey stick. We can imagine another teammate swooping in behind her to get it."

Joseph Kabwe, "Another fat teammate."

Van der Ghent, "For consistency of design. But not fat; full. Potential at the ready."

Manvik Gupta, "Those two fat people, number 14 on the list, are they coupling?"

Van der Ghent, "Sorry?"

Manvik Gupta, "You know, having congress...making babies."

Van der Ghent looked hard at pictogram number 14, "That's wrestling."

Jing Zhao, "I admit, I took number 22 as some sort of rear penetration. Maybe of a sumo wrestler?"

Van der Ghent, "Equestrian events."

Benito Jax, "I'm wondering about number 9; could someone with that weight condition actually do a handstand with their legs spread-eagle? I assume it's gymnastics, but is that possible?"

Ahmed bin Abdullah, "Those are legs? I assumed that was the pommel horse."

Benito Jax, "The devise? The gymnastics apparatus itself?"

Ahmed bin Abdullah, "Yes. A man will soon leap atop it and spin around."

Jing Zhao, "Or a woman will soon vault from it. It could be that."

Ahmed bin Abdullah concurred, "Seen in that way, the body weight issue disappears."

Benito Jax, "I see. But then number 32..."

Van der Ghent, "Swimming."

Ahmed bin Abdullah, "But if we see it as canoeing, that makes better sense of the bloat. And the 'arm' becomes the paddle in the water."

Benito Jax, "But then what would swimming be?"

Jing Zhao, "What about number 40?"

Van der Ghent, "That's rhythmic gymnastics."

Benito Jax, "Yes, I see. The ribbons are now the water. But which would we use for rhythmic gymnastics?"

Van der Ghent, "No. Actually—"

Manvik Gupta, "Number 8. It must be fencing now, but if the epee is the ribbons..."

Van der Ghent, "Perhaps we could move on to the pictograms for facilities and services..."

Benito Jax, "Yes, we will return to the sport pictograms."

The assembled turned to their pages for those newly designed symbols bringing universal graphic clarity to where one might urinate in privacy.

Jing Zhao, "I'm concerned with number 3 on this list."

Van der Ghent, "That's for the unisex restroom. We sought to combine the idea of male, female, handicapped, and other. In a single figure."

Jing Zhao, "The giant circle is the wheel of a wheelchair?"

Van der Ghent, at last pleased with her design reception, "Exactly."

Jing Zhao, "And the man has an erection?"

Van der Ghent, "What?"

Ahmed bin Abdullah, "So the woman is in the wheelchair and faces away from the standing man?"

Benito Jax, "Yes, we had better stay with that distribution. Especially in light of the erect penis."

Van der Ghent and her assistant searched the image, "Erect penis?"

Jing Zhao, "Sticking right out there."

Joseph Kabwe, "Clear as day."

Manvik Gupta, "I thought perhaps a bit *too* forward thinking. And why doesn't he have an erect penis on the men's room sign? Is he only erect sharing the restroom with a woman?"

Ahmed bin Abdullah, "I see the sense in that."

Van der Ghent said, the lightbulb at last lit, "The *handle*. It's the handle of the wheelchair,"

Jing Zhao, "Oh."

Manvik Gupta, "Now I'm a bit disappointed."

Joseph Kabwe, "But as I look at them now, some figures look so fat, and the others so thin."

Van der Ghent, "The pictograms for athletics represent fullness, the stick figures with round heads represent the signage for services."

Jing Zhao, "So the athletes are fat, and the tourists are thin? I'd suggest the opposite."

Van der Ghent, "We try to stay within certain customary international design parameters—while adding creativity."

Ahmed bin Abdullah, "The stick-man carrying the x, he is a police officer? Striking a protester? It means: *No Protesting Here*?"

Van der Ghent, "Crossing. That means *cross here*."

Manvik Gupta, "Crossing what?"

Van der Ghent, "Anything crossable. A street. A field of play. It's general."

Jing Zhao, "And the one of that figure with the line running through it? The line shows the direction of crossing?"

Van der Ghent, "*Don't cross.* The diagonal lines through the pictogram means *don't* or *no*."

Ahmed bin Abdullah, "So number 85, the diagonal line forbids walking?"

Van der Ghent, "Eighty-five means *escalator up*. That is a slope, not a diagonal line."

Ahmed bin Abdullah, "So, *don't take the escalator*?"

Van der Ghent, "*Take it. Up.*"

Benito Jax, "What if we put stairs on the diagonal line—the slope—to make clearer that it is an escalator?"

Van der Ghent, "We use that for *stairs*."

Ahmed bin Abdullah, "Perhaps put twice as many steps on the escalator? Because it goes up faster?"

Van der Ghent, "I'll make a note." Her assistant made a note.

Manvik Gupta, "Excuse me, but what does the arrow going through the ocean waves mean?"

Van der Ghent searched her copy of the pictogram volume.

Manvik Gupta, "Number 172."

Van der Ghent, "*Fire escape route.*"

Manvik Gupta, "Because you pass beneath water hoses putting out the fire?"

Van der Ghent, "Those are flames."

Jing Zhao, "Now you have people running toward flames. Those should be to the rear, urging them to the exit."

Benito Jax, "And perhaps more spiky—to show danger. Curved flames seem too inviting."

Joseph Kabwe, "And a diagonal bisecting the flames—but not the arrow—to say: *don't enter the flames.*"

Van der Ghent, "I'll make a note."

Ahmed bin Abdullah, "Number 192. Why does a hand hold a placard? Does this represent a protest? Shouldn't a diagonal go through it?"

Benito Jax, "We have an approved protest space. We must direct people to it."

Ahmed bin Abdullah, "Must we?"

Benito Jax, "We can't have them protest just anywhere. They might be seen by the press."

Jing Zhao, "But should the protest placard have the Olympic rings on it? Should we ever suggest protesting the Olympics? I suggest we remove the rings from the protest placard on the *protest here* sign."

Manvik Gupta, "And the hand should be smaller; the protest poster looks much too big. No one could see such a small protest poster."

Benito Jax, "That must surely be the point. Encourage small posters at protests."

Van der Ghent, "I'm sorry. I'm sorry to interrupt, but the pictogram you refer to stands for *ticket sales*. It guides visitors to the ticket booths."

Benito Jax, "Do we have a pictogram for *approved protests here*?"

Van der Ghent, "Number 522. The frowny face."

The all flip to the middle of the pictogram volume. Jing Zhao said, "The frowny face has a torch! Do they start fires at this protest? That's arson!"

Concerned looks from all of the committee members.

Van der Ghent, "Sorry, that's the Olympic torch. *Unhappy at the Olympics*. We can change that."

Joseph Kabwe, "If you just put a diagonal through the Olympic torch, and not through the frowny face, then it could say: *If you are unhappy with the Olympics, do not start a fire with the Olympic flame, but rather, stand here and frown.*"

Manvik Gupta, "But I would read that as: *Be unhappy at the Olympic flame*. And we plan to spend so much on the torch relay. People should be *happy* with the Olympic flame. We should put the diagonal-of-prohibition through the frowny face and *not* the Olympic flame."

Benito Jax, "Perhaps we need a dashed diagonal for cases such as these?"

Van der Ghent nodded to her frowning assistant, "We'll make a note of that."

Ahmed bin Abdullah, "I protest the whole plan for approved protest sites. I propose protests be prohibited. Perhaps prospective protestors can be pushed by appointed provocateurs into places of pre-positioned police presence; there crushed."

Benito Jax, "A matter of event security and thus for another occasion."

Olympic Films

An Innocent Eye; An Unsettling Salute; A
Humane Gesture; A New Calling.

Watching the film of the Stockholm Games of 1912 unveils a world of innocence. Not in the morals of the men and women—who knows—but at the Naïfs Before the Image. A nearly pre-picture people. Standing briefly posed, nervous or indifferent, before the camera, a generation yet unaware of its power. You search in vain for any sign of corporate branding. One hardly knows what to look at for want of an emblem. Family photos in a world before celebrity snapshots. And why should the camera and its product impress those amateur athletes momentarily immobilized on celluloid? The image makers of 1912 no more understood the power of their tools than did the athletes. Living in an age of letters they could hardly guess at the coming era of the image. The filmmakers possessed not even a sense of how a moving picture might capture movement by moving the point of view. In this Olympic film world, athletes moved but cameras stood still. Nor had anyone yet guessed how the final product might move people. The films propagate no purpose but to record a radically incomplete accounting of activity. Plus top hats.

Looking past presentation one notes the athletes. Men of nearly identical body types (except for a few rotund shot putters) hurling themselves over absurdly low bars. Pole vaulters struggling to clear a height today's *high jumpers* disdain to include. Divers swaning off platforms without a thought of turning a flip or rotation. Seemingly concentrating on nothing but aiding the insistent force of gravity. Women divers, emerging wet from the water, embarrassed at their immodest dress while enjoying its liberty. Long jumps that barely match the *running* stride of 2084 Olympians. Icelandic glima wrestling, which looks like two men waltzing poorly until one trips the other.

And the ceremonial. Actual royalty, not yet extinct nor employed by tabloids, opened the Games, showing that the genetic stock of Europe's ruling elite did not contain the ingredients for making its athletes. Competitors even then military-marched into the opening games; straw hats held high. No pop stars, just the Band of The Royal Guard. Track and field prizes (cups not medals) handed out in the middle of an empty stadium—bare bleachers in the background.

And the sports. Tennis, still innocent of its eventual fratricide by pickleball. Shooters blazing away at cardboard dear. Murky-water swimming timed by eyeball. Walk racing, then as now a competition to see who could most furtively lift both feet off the ground at once. Choreographed floor gymnastics, twenty-five men at once. All done in innocence of the sales opportunities passed over. The only suspicion of corporate branding might be the walrus mustaches, perhaps promoting Krupps cannons and promising one of those quick-and-done boundary rearrangements so dear to the later 19th century Europeans. The 1912 Olympic film does nothing to sell politics or products. It has little craft and no art. It produces pathos in the viewer only in that we now know what they could not. You watch the young men and women compete and guess which fate chose to die, and which to only grieve, in the great sieve set between them and the next Games.

The official films showed little change in the next few cycles. Un-aerodynamic running suits. Breathless athletes still standing before a film camera more like exhausted animal specimens than sophisticated celebrities carrying a flag and curating an image. Now with greater timing precision, athletes could distinguish themselves by their numerical breakage, their vandalism of the glories of the past, their intentional demolishing of the proudest moments of the last generation. The Olympic film records *records*, world and Olympic, new replacing old; charmingly recorded in just whole seconds.

Then comes, as aesthetic relief and moral anguish, Leni Riefenstahl's *Olympia* (Parts One and Two), official film(s) of the 1936 Olympiad. Brought to you by the sponsors of the international hit: *Triumph of the Will*. Riefenstahl's physique-positive portrayal of athletic uber-menchery featured till then unseen powers of lighting, camera angling, reconstructed events, impressionistic dramatization, military uniforms, moustache minimalism, and so many stiff-armed salutes one's elbows grow sore just watching. When non-German athletes deliver these you can only pray they meant to convey courtesy and not conversion.

Looking back at the film a hundred and thirty years later, one finds most disturbing just how *Olympic* it all feels. The monumentality, the fixation on physical prowess, its lack of humor, its love of *faster, higher, stronger*. It feels even more disturbing to add that later and now abandoned motto addition: *together*; meant to suggest communal collaboration but easily sliding into the spiritual superiority of frolicking Fascists. The spirit of the Berlin Games, in spite of the amoral artistry of its official filmic record, ended in tears. Tears, blood, rubble. The 1936 Olympics did not unleash Armageddon, it merely failed to substitute sport for war. But while the contestants and attendees of the 1912 Stockholm Games look like innocents of another era unknowingly marching to an unseen war, those raising bodies and arms in Berlin suggest people awaiting an in-rushing tide; some in dread, some in relief, at least one in giddy anticipation.

With real relief and joy, one can turn from Riefenstahl's physical psychosis to Kon Ichikawa's humane film of the 1964 Olympics: *Tokyo Olympiad*. Here *human beings* play rather than demi-gods. And they seem to *play*, with an intensity one could count as delight. Presumably, the motivations remain as they have always been and only the ideals of the artist making the movie changed. For once, though, you fail to feel the temptation to use the term *glory* in the same sentence as *game*.

Little else stands out in Olympic films after this. The Munich Games of 1972—those that arguably inspired this very work—enlisted eight famous filmmakers to combine efforts in its official film, *Visions of Eight*; proving once again that the correct number of artists on any project always comes to: one. *Visions of Eight* begins in beefy grunts and comes to rest in slow motion grimacing. Flash forward twelve years to the bloated monstrosity of *16 Days of Glory* which relates at numbing length the Los Angeles Games in 1984 ("the first to turn a profit") and you can relax into the familiar soporific of corporate friendly family entertainment.

Film faded. One plague after another drove audiences deeper into their private spaces, surrounded by their giant screens, seen over the edges of their smaller screens, peered at in passing from yet smaller screens still; at least three degrees deep and reality impinging only at the edges of attention. Who needs a full-length Olympic film, shot for collective viewing, in a world so dedicated to solitary self-fragmentation? Yet, once an Olympic tradition begins, no one has the heart to end it. Least of all that Olympic sentimentalist Benito Jax. IOC members tried to dissuade him. They reminded him of recent, and entirely unwatched, disasters. Federico Leone's politically provocative, *Vice of Man; Guns of God*, an Olympic-sized critical biopic of Uganda's newly minted Maximum Theocrat. Luis Godard's car commercial as full-film combustion-engine love letter, *Athletes: Rev Your Engines!* Hitchcock Gilliam's all too up-to-date children's tour of New Delhi, *DigiDelh Explores the Games!* This children's documentary made all the worse by the poor sport digit's demise at the movie's end. Only the inability to show the film after the demise of digital projection equipment saved it from Olympic infamy. Then Sergei Drier's poetic rhapsody, *Sun Kissed*, which persisted in its encomia to the solar orb even though the event it celebrated fled to cloudy climes. Finally, Francois Antonioni's very on-the-nose *Olympic Crunch*, nothing but impact shots and stadium volunteers dragging out the wounded. That one at least had commercial potential, but the IOC pulled it from such theaters as one might still find to stem the brand damage.

However few theaters it might play in, however displaced as a cultural object by television and its spawn, however much it must lean toward art to justify its effort and finally fail as film to the embarrassment of all involved, the Olympic film *had been*, so Benito Jax insisted it *must be*. Benito Jax lived as simultaneously an up-to-date traditionalist and a conservative exponent of the next-big-thing. He demanded an artist of the avant-garde, conversant with controversy, highbrow in intent, ambiguous in execution, and available on a budget. He only really wanted to know if the proposed auteur excited the small world of cinephiles whose interest in film history extended past those movies still advertised as new releases. Having no other expert at hand, he took the advice offered by your humble author and chose the Chinese conceptual artist, Wei Wai.

Among Wei Wai's better known works we find, *Planet Management*, in which the artist sat on a giant ice cube in a slightly larger tub with kittens in his lap. The ice melted, the kitten's drowned, and Canada banned Wei Wai for life. The Tate Modern exhibited Wei Wai's installation piece, *Holding Back the Tide,* a giant wave machine contained by pressboard siding. The art community praised its "dynamic play of water waves", but the Tate curators found themselves rushing to replace the rapidly disintegrating liquid containment structure. The exhibition went well in the end; maintenance rescued all other exhibits in the wing before containment failure and only the building's flooring needed replacement. Wei Wai's *Collision*

Alarm for the Modern Museum of Art featured two hundred minimum wage workers assembling cell phones while the former Managing Director of the recently privatized International Monetary Fund set fire to oil filled barrels surrounding the exhibit. The workers managed to manufacture thirty-seven phones before security evacuated the building.

Wei Wai had also made *films* prior to his consideration by the IOC, including his famous, *Last Call*. This film consisted simply of the last parrot in the world mimicking the mating calls of then newly extinct animals, such as the lion, the rhino, the hippo, the leopard, and forty-seven varieties of Amazonian birds. Benito Jax made a fast-forward inspection of this film to ensure that Wei Wai would not embarrass the Olympic Movement with his authorized Olympic Film. Jax's one comment: "Such a beautiful bird."

The Play of Nations

The One and the Many; Alone Together; Pride of Place.

F ew people knew or cared about the modern Games in the first few decades after they launched. Sporting enthusiasts, committed to the ethic of affluent amateurism, ran, jumped, swam, or pummeled to small crowds and limited press coverage. The organizers, under the leadership of Baron Pierre de Coubertin, longed for more than this from the start, but in the adolescent capitalism of the early 19th century, most people exhausted themselves at work, and the favored sport of gentlemen reduced to chasing sporting women—who understood themselves to be working girls. Competitors at the early Games marched beneath national flags because one must march beneath *something*.

Perhaps marching beneath flags got a little out of hand. The world had a great war, later to be numbered so as to avoid confusion, and the Olympics suspended operation until the survivors sorted the bodies. By the time the Games returned from the world's second failure to substitute sport for competitive killing, enthusiasm for nationally based competition had become muted, at best. But no one knew the individual players. No one knew their touching stories of sacrifice, grit, and self-overcoming. No one knew each competitor's history of event dominance or his or her lifetime of sporting failure vindicated by finally breaking a ribbon before a hated rival. The public had nothing to latch onto beyond the abstract idea of human excellence and the purity of play for its own sake. The Games needed nations for want of personality.

People understand nations. They provoke an allegiance less passionately embraced than that towards football teams but still sufficient to inspire military enlistment and tax evasion. But nations, or at least the states claiming sovereignty over them, grow annoying over time. They fail to provide sufficient benefits or excitement. The more benefits a state provides, the less exciting it becomes. The more exciting a state becomes, the more it makes people long for the lost state of nature. And nothing cures one of a love for primitive anarchy like a return to the lost state of nature. Thus, the resurrection of love for the state. How to break the cycle at just the right place? Sports. Big sports. Sports with a nod to nations but with the excitement and drama of individuals in competition. Someone for the viewers at home to identify with as they sit on their couches clutching their CotRatts, rooting away at their televisions. So just as one can view the history of the Games as a rise of nations, one can also see it as a struggle for the individual. From the primitive love of play and a few beers over wine and cheese after the match, to more serious stakes. From victory as a structuring element in play, to sport as the quest for victory. Better at least, than the quest for conquest.

Individuals, increasingly as the Games progressed, desired victory as much as nations did. But individuals also had families and friends—occasionally among their rivals—and dreams of life beyond the bounds of sport (I speak of 1896 rather than of 2084). Nations have citizens or subjects, at one time also reliably territory, and rivals. Unlike individual women and men, nations have no lifecycles. They emerge, in a burst or over time, and they extinguish, by a thousand cuts, a moment of catastrophic miscalculation, or more recently, by a change in the weather. Individuals spend a life in sports, or don't. Nations *invest* in sporting status enhancement. Individuals can only aspire to a moment in the sun. Nations proclaim their own immortality.

No one medals in a modern Olympic event on merely his or her own effort. Not since the early days. Coaches in the first few decades of the Games did little more than count pushups while puffing on cigarettes. (*Cigarettes* were the anti-lung entertainments of choice before the rise of *vaping*, itself replaced by *lung-stuffing*, that found—unsurprisingly—unhealthy and replaced by *buff-huffing*, now replaced by *fuming*, recently rechristened *flowing*.) On such accounts as we still have, athletes in earlier eras most often turned to fellow competitors for inspiration and advice. This clearly did not represent the proper spirit of ruthless competition or the advancement of science. Not to mention the fact that once anyone really cared who won a footrace, the advice of rivals turned suspiciously earnest and unfailingly unhelpful. And so was born the individual athlete's coaching team.

And not just an ever-increasing number of coaches, trainers, nutritionists, orthopedists, scouting strategists, terrain tacticians, opposition researchers, cognitive technicians, performance specialists, enhancement experts, drug interaction trackers, contract negotiators, branding advisors, media consultants, and post-sports career planners huddling around each individual athlete, forming both a phalanx and a tripping hazard. But also, financial contributors, hometown boosters, corporate sponsors, and whole nations at peace playing at war. All to see one fit young man or woman (or child) win a contest and so justify the obscene investment of lives and effort by proving *that* athlete the best something-or-other on that day, hour, minute, and micro-second. A glory to the few who win; a damnation to the rest, who weep over a wasted youth in a dark closet, heard only by a disappointed parent, all the others having moved on to the next young hope. Making dreams come true.

And above all these efforts (not counting the IOC itself) lies the nation-state. That under whose flag the athlete competes. Whose anthem plays to tears of joy or rage. That which claims the credit of the medal count. The nation nurtures the competitor in the cradle. It raises the athlete in the work ethic. It forges the player in the fire of pride and shame. It forms the community of the playground and extends this fellowship to the sporting field. It raises the player like an additional parent.

Or it filches top athletes from other nations. "Each nation determines its own rules of citizenship."

I assume it unnecessary to detail the world events leading up to the Games of 2084. The Iberian Civil War that splintered Spain. The further fragmentations in Western Europe. The contrasting "consolidation" of Eastern Europe under Russian guidance. The march of peoples north and the resettlements and new national recognitions. The challenges of the Great Digital Purge and the subsequent Analog Renaissance. The world of 2084 just recovering from that latter success to reestablish a New Digital Horizon. A familiar history. Larger states made smaller and cast into irrelevance, aggressive states made larger and riven with conflict. Surveillance states grown greater (in watching) and then abruptly de-digitized back to forest-felling levels of paper records.

The Olympic Games thrived throughout. Not as a mere distraction—though it deserved the thanks of a grateful world for that—but as an even more vital contributor to human good: athletics as a determination of domination. A contest of the spirited side of human passion complete with flags, anthems, pride poses, conflict, blood, sweat, and tears. Winners and losers for all the world to see. Sport as a substitute for war. Until the real thing starts again.

In organizing the Games of 2084, Benito Jax and the IOC had to sort out the splintered fragments of nationalist ambition and post-war resentments. New and old nations sought to entrench themselves in the world consciousness by joining or remaining in the Games. Each had passionate commitments to possession of icons and individuals; national colors, flags, anthems, names and most relevantly to the Games, eligible athletes. As just a sample of these issues I record here a closed hearing before the Executive Committee dedicated to arbitrating some of the residual disputes that followed the final treaty ending the Iberian conflict in what had once (on one interpretation of the political geography) been Spain. The representatives of the nations formed from the conclusion of that crisis shared the table, each with a separate microphone. As a mercy to the reader, I will refer to them not by individual names but by the nations they represented. These were (again, on one interpretation) Catalonia, Andalusia, Madrid (or "Madridia") and Castille (as referred to by the others, or "Spain" as it represented itself). The matter under dispute: national colors.

Castille, "Spain demands its traditional colors. Red, yellow, and red."

Catalonia, "With respect, your nation's name by treaty is *Castille*. Spain is dead."

Madrid, "Red and red are both the same color. It cannot be claimed twice. Madridia claims both. As well as yellow. And white and purple."

Catalonia, "You cannot claim every color. Catalonia also has red. And gold. A combination no other Iberian nation may claim. Also, your country is called Madrid. There is no such place as *Madridia*."

Castille, "Red, yellow, and red are, in their proper order, the colors of the Spanish flag. Our flag."

Madrid, "No such place exists. By the terms of the Treaty of Separation you represent *Castille*. You do not get Spain's flag. It lies buried atop it's nation beneath the worst soil in Iberia."

Castille, "A country can name itself what it chooses."

Madrid, "Not according to the treaty."

Castille, "Names change."

Madrid, "Spain died. Catalonia killed it."

Benito Jax, "We do not need to settle this now."

Jing Zhao, "What does Andalusia propose as to its colors?"

A general groan emerged from the room.

Andalusia, "We will accept any colors except red, yellow, white or purple. Also, we protest the name *Andalusia*. We are part of Catalonia."

Catalonia, "You have no part of us. We do not accept you."

Castille, "Spain will accept Andalusia under its flag and sovereignty provided it accepts that we—together, or Castille on its own—are or is, *Spain*."

Andalusia, "As has been covered in numerous international conferences, Andalusia is a separate and independent nation that is a part of the Republic of Catalonia."

Catalonia, "We don't want you."

Andalusia, "Our historic ties to Catalonia—"

Catalonia, "We don't even share a border with Andalusia."

Andalusia, "Our economic co-prosperity—"

Catalonia, "Get a job."

Benito Jax, "Please, it is out of our sphere of authority to adjudicate these matters."

Jing Zhao, to further groans, "Under whose flag does Andalusia propose to play?"

Andalusia, "Under the red and gold of Catalonia."

Catalonia, "We protest. Andalusia cannot copy our flag."

Andalusia, "We will be part of your team."

Catalonia, "You are part of Castille. Leave us alone."

Benito Jax, "In the event that Andalusia cannot play as part of Catalonia, do you propose your own team as an independent nation?"

Andalusia, "No. We will play as part of Castille, provided they do not claim the name of *Spain*."

Castille, "We are Spain. You are part of Spain. Why this fixation against the name of your own country?"

Andalusia, "If Castille cannot accept the reality that the whole of the rest of Iberia denigrates the name of *Spain*, then Andalusia will have no choice but to play under the colors and flag of Catalonia."

Catalonia, "You will not. We will not pay for your team. Go away."

Andalusia, "We would consider an economic union with Madrid."

Madrid, "*Madridia*. And no."

Andalusia, "We will play the Games under the flag of *Madridia*."

Madrid, "No."

Manvik Gupta, "I am confused. Excuse me, but I'm confused. Isn't the flag of Madrid the same as the flag of Castille? The formally Spanish flag?"

Castille, "Madrid has stolen our flag. The flag of Spain, as you say."

Madrid, "The Madridia flag—long our customary national symbol and in no way related, except in appearance, to the flag of Spain or Castille."

Andalusia, "Andalusia will march at the opening ceremonies and compete under that flag—Madrid's, under the understanding that it is in no way the Spanish flag—beyond mere appearance."

Madrid, "No you will not. Come up with your own flag!"

Castille, "Listen to you! Flag stealers! Come up with *your* own flag!"

Madrid, "We had it first!"

Benito Jax, "Please, please. We will put off until another time the issue of flags. And colors. And we will defer to the relevant treaties on the matter of names. We must move on to the more urgent issue of athlete representation. As a matter of international agreements that established your nations and the Peace of Iberia, New Nations have come to share territory on the peninsula—"

Catalonia, "We dispute this! All of us!"

Madrid, "All of us, yes."

Castille, "Absolutely."

Andalusia, "Speaking in solidarity with our Catalonian brothers—"

Catalonia, "Stop it."

Benito Jax, "But these are established matters. To what do you object?"

Catalonia, "To the treaties."

Madrid, "To the territories."

Castile, "To the New Nations."

Catalonia, "Those."

Ahmed bin Abdullah, "This has all been worked out in the treaties. All of your nations, also new—"

Castille, "Not ours."

Ahmed bin Abdullah, "Have agreed to host refugees as sovereign peoples on land grants in Iberia. By treaty you have ceded that land."

Catalonia, "Under duress."

Madrid, "Under conditions of extreme need."

Andalusia, "Only after a significant drop in GDP."

Madrid, "Europe took advantage of us in our extremity; forcing us to bear the brunt of an influx no other European nation would tolerate."

Benito Jax, "France houses many in the suburbs of Paris…"

Madrid, "Those slums!?!"

Benito Jax, "All of Europe, all of the northern countries of the world, share a problem of poverty among the expanding population of post-place peoples. It is the great honor and will be the enduring glory of the Olympic Games and the Olympic Movement as a whole that the Games of 2084 will offer jobs to so many of these unfortunate people."

Jing Zhao, "For two weeks."

Benito Jax, "They will receive new training, new skills, new opportunities, and a new pride as part of the greatest sporting event in the world."

Jing Zhao, "For two weeks."

Benito Jax, "Two weeks that will live in eternal fame. A memory to last a lifetime, to last whole generations. To endure once all else has been endured: *Paris 2084; I was there*!"

Jing Zhao, "For just two weeks. I want to return to the rules on defections. If the national village departments count as diplomatic spaces, then those who enter the grounds, whether pursuant to their duties or by stealth, must not count as asylum seekers. We need clarification on this principle, or we may suffer the worst two weeks in recent immigration history."

Joseph Kabwe, "We called this meeting to consider Iberian athlete recognition. I protest. We must only discus this."

Jing Zhao, "Easy for you to say. No Tunisian Refugee national working as a janitor for the Paris Games will lock herself in a toilet stall on the hope of gaining entry to an African country soon to thermally dispossess its entire population."

Joseph Kabwe, "Kenya has mountains. Populated highlands."

Ahmed bin Abdullah, "This issue admits of an easy solution. We just need an assurance from our sovereign national partners that immigrants—asylum seekers or the climatically mis-disposed—can claim only *sympathetic citizenship*, and space in a new territorial set-aside, and not make claims on national wealth fund dividends."

Jing Zhao, "A convenient rule for a nation whose territory consists of a postal address at the Zurich Grand Hotel."

Manvik Gupta, "What is *sympathetic citizenship*?"

Ahmed bin Abdullah, "As I have outlined before, it is a form of legal citizenship in which a nation affirms its deep sympathy towards its citizens—those that fall under this class of citizenship—and assures said citizens of its commitment to this sympathy, and all concomitant sentiments, without thereby affirming a right to electoral representation or a financial claim on any funds held by and on behalf of the nation whose citizenship has been to this class of citizen compassionately conferred."

Jing Zhao, "I've seen the ad campaigns the SSWFN has prepared if this comes to pass. You mean to increase by millions your official population to the point of Great Nation status without undertaking any obligations to them. Population numbers on the cheap."

Joseph Kabwe, "What of stipends? A commitment to small stipends?"

Ahmed bin Abdullah, "No stipends. No commitments. Just sympathy."

Jing Zhao, "Unreal citizens for an unreal nation."

Ahmed bin Abdullah, "You can read a map as well as I can. What will you offer all of yours? Laos, Vietnam..."

Jing Zhao, "China has offered a complete resettlement of Indonesia into the island of Japan. With *full* citizenship."

Ahmed bin Abdullah, "You don't own Japan! Japan has refused."

Jing Zhao, "They need people."

Ahmed bin Abdullah, "*China* needs people."

Jing Zhao, "*Chinese* people. Not just anyone."

Ahmed bin Abdullah, "Japan says the same."

Benito Jax cuffed the meeting back to order, "Mr. Kabwe makes an important point. We called this meeting to discuss Iberian athlete national identification issues. At the request of Castille—"

Castille, "Spain."

Benito Jax, "...The nation referring to itself as *Spain*. Let us deal with other issues at other times. What does...Catalonia, object to in the current rules concerning the assignment of athletes in Iberia?"

Catalonia, "We object that Russia—"

Madrid, "And Germany."

Catalonia, "And Germany...that they both poach our athletes. They take our citizens under Russian passports—"

Madrid, "And German passports..."

Catalonia looks ready to strangle Madrid and leave its body suspiciously near Andalusia, "Yes, and German passports. We raise up these athletes, nurture them, invest in them, then Russia—and Germany, yes—swoops in and scoops them up at the last moment for their teams! To play *against* our teams! As if they were Russian instead of Spanish!"

Madrid, "Catalonian."

Catalonia looks to Madrid, "What?"

Madrid, "You misspoke. You are Catalonia, not Spain. You fought a whole war over that."

Castille, "*We* are Spain. But it applies the same."

Madrid, "You are not Spain."

Catalonia, "The point is the poaching. One nation should not be able to lay claim to the citizens of another."

Benito Jax, "*Each nation determines its own rules of citizenship.*"

Manvik Gupta, "I'm confused, sorry, but don't *you* poach athletes, as you say, from the New Nations? From Tunisia—that is, the Tunisian Republic of Refugees, for instance?"

Catalonia, "No. They reside on our territory."

Jing Zhao, "But are they your citizens?"

Catalonia, "No."

Madrid, "No."

Catalonia, "We have no obligations to them."

Castille, "They are an imposition."

Jing Zhao, "The athletes are an imposition?"

Castille, "No. They are citizens. Ours. We gave them passports. The rest of the Tunisians impose upon us. They are their own nation. Imposers."

Andalusia, "Imposters. Not really Tunisian."

Castille looks in annoyance at Andalusia, "*No*. They *impose*, they do not *pose as*. Learn your international language."

Andalusia, "At least I know I'm not Spanish."

Catalonia, "Right."

Andalusia, "I'm Catalonian."

Catalonia, "Don't start that again."

Madrid, "I would like to point out, by the way, and relevant to the current topic, that while we do offer passports to Tunisians, Algerians, Egyptians and others, so do Germany and Russia. And they get the best ones!"

Catalonia, "So true! All the best Tunisians go to the Russians. We can't outbid Russia for our own adjacent-people. Russia has all of Eastern Europe to pick from, why don't they just send those to the Games?"

Jing Zhao, "Czechs won't play for Russia."

Catalonia, "But Tunisians will! You see? They live on our land—don't talk to me about international agreements when I can see their tents from my window—and they have no loyalty to the country that gives them such generous succor. They just take the best deal! The best ones! And if we try to give a passport to a Czech, then Russia jails their family. So they won't play for us. How can we match that?"

Ahmed bin Abdullah, "Perhaps you could imprison Tunisian families?"

Benito Jax looked hard at the SSWFN committee member at that. But Catalonia, so vexed at the world's injustice, kept right on, "How can we do that? They already live in a...well...a camp, behind barbed wire. How can we threaten a prison term when they already sleep twenty to a tent on tiny cots?"

Benito Jax cringed at the expression.

Madrid, "We demand a level playing field. Equality."

Castille, "Equality in Iberia. One People Against the Outsiders."

Catalonia, "The Treaty of Separation nullified that slogan. We want equality within our countries and not with outsiders."

Andalusia, "Equality between all the people in Iberia."

Castille, "No, equality between all the people *of* Iberia, not *in* it. Iberian equality of peoples in nations as equals in nations and not of peoples in territories not in nations in Iberia."

Catalonia, "*Of* Iberia."

Castille, "I just said that."

Catalonia, "No. You said, 'not of peoples in territories not in nations *in* Iberia'. But the New Nations are *in* Iberia but not *of* Iberia. So, we the nations of Iberia stand united for Iberian equality of peoples in nations as equals in nations *of* Iberia and not of peoples in territories not in nations *of* Iberia."

Madrid, "Not including Portugal."

Catalonia, "Of course not Portugal."

Castille, "Damn Portuguese."

Andalusia, "Bastards."

Even Benito Jax's most vigorous tapping of cufflinks could not over-come the anti-Portuguese ire roused in the room. Just as well that the IOC had scheduled Portugal's representative for a different hearing. Not that any of these hearings led to any amendment of IOC policy. Benito Jax held hearings to let people hear themselves speaking, not to listen to what they said. IOC Presidents busy themselves with sponsorship negotiations and Olympic glorification; honorary doctorates and banquets with pastries shaped in their image. On the matter of splitting old nations, and of new one's minted to keep their people apart from the fragments of the former sovereignties, Jax let the world turn as it pleased. He instinctively assumed that nationalist leaders demolished the countries of their birth in order to become founding fathers of the future. To Jax, the explanation for national fragmentation lay in elite desire for more offices and titles; more presidents, senators, and members of parliament.

The ExCom of the IOC concurred with Jax on the matter of letting irritants speak into microphones unconnected to any outside connection. But on the matter of Olympic security, the whole of the IOC, and the whole of the world community, took a serious interest.

A Place of Greater Safety

A History of Troubles; A Disappointing Digital Defense; A New Miracle of Dunkirk.

T he Olympic Games magnetizes every site it touches. It draws people as a magnet draws metal filings. It rather too often draws people smuggling in *weaponized* metal filings. But even those who come just to buy a stuffed CotRatt and see an event (hoping for the 100 meter dash but settling for canoe slalom) bring to the Games the problem of people. People in mass represent a great force—both commercial and kinetic—while each individually enacts willfulness coupled with an annoying vulnerability. Great heaps of event attendees make the Games look good on TV, but gathered together they tend to bruise each other. Mobs of people do the crushing while particular individuals do the being crushed. And that just covers the unintended injuries.

International events that command the attention of the world also attract those who wish to divert those eyes to their own issues. Or as Benito Jax puts it: "Someone always wants to rob us of our rightful pedestal" (*The Measure of a Man; More Maxims, Mottos, and Mentions of Benito Jax*). People endanger each other by occupying the same physical space and invite danger from each other by occupying the same mental space. In the one case they must be kept together, but not too together; in the other case they must be kept away, but just the right ones away. The IOC calls this the security dilemma: how do you keep people together while keeping "them" away?

One part of the security infrastructure consists in the architecture of visitor guidance. Not *control*, the IOC and the Paris police insist, *guidance*. The more passive the better. Roped-off areas and queues indicated by winding plastic ribbons. No walls against which to smear a young mother-of-two in a crowd surge. No barbed wire to ensnare a Japanese tourist brusquely pushed aside to make way for an IOC VP's entourage. Add polite Olympic helpmates, competent in any language, ready to help a visitor to an Olympic location—one white-gloved finger pointing at a Van der Ghent Olympic icon on the site map, the other pointing at a stadium suffering from pseudo-late-post-modern gigantism. Not a firearm in sight.

But this considerate care for the easily spooked suffers two troubles. Both of which are people. The first: *people won't listen.* No matter what language you address them in, nor how loud your loudspeaker, and no matter how nicely you put the matter, people will duck under the tapeline, shimmy up the bamboo barrier, kick down the traffic cones, climb over the "please do not climb over me" fence, push past the cardboard "thank you for not entering" sign, and generally go where they think a restroom can be found, fully in the face of your passive security procedures. They will simply pretend they do not understand the signage for *do not walk against the flow of traffic* (a stick figure man facing a hail of arrows slashed with a diagonal line), or for *Olympic tow away zone* (a fishhook lifting a square to the horror of a stick figure man) or for *remove your pet's feces* (a circle with a dash for a tail above a series of smaller circles—"No, Mr. Jax, this one does *not* represent fullness of being"). The white-gloved translator with the Olympic event map inevitably happens upon only those visitors that understand none of her fourteen languages ("So sorry, you speak Tanema? I don't know that one"). Arrows on the pavement mean one thing to the older generation, and the opposite of that to the younger.

So, rip down the plastic ribbons (before the tourists do) and put away the cotton cords. Bring on the wire, barbed or "flesh forgiving". Build the concrete barriers. Erect the steel security silos. Add water to the barrels—heavy water. Fix helmets on the heads of baton wielding temporary security-service hires. Load the submachine guns and give the gendarmerie an extra week's training. Install *squish alarms* to warn against excessive crowding near the now hardened "guided pathways". Add more medical stations, but don't bother about the signage ("So a red cross means *first aid*, not *danger—run?*"). All of this just for what the Paris Prefect of Police calls the "naive threat".

The 1972 Games held in Munich, those that initiated the time capsule tradition to which this work contributes, suffered a terrorist incident for which the host city proved laughably unprepared. A Germany fresh from

initiating its second world enveloping war—this time with added geno-
cide—looked to show its softer, more human side in a city associated with
its worst instincts. The Federal Republic of Germany wanted to prove that
the Germans had moved on. The Munich Olympic Organizing Committee sought to create a competition in international niceness suitable for
an Aquarian Age (this then referred to the astrological sign interpreted to
mean peace and love—rather than its current more fraught connotation).
Munich won the Games promising the IOC a low-key, environmentally
sound sporting event meant to push aside memories of the Berlin Games
of 1936 which displayed a very different ethos: stiff-armed salutes and military uniforms in uniform gray or damn-the-world black, German patriot
songs then always sung with a heavy sneer and often featuring master race
martyrs.

At Munich 1972, "low-key" and "environmentally sound" dissolved in
the desire to distinguish itself before the world, but the urge to usher in
a new view of gentle Germany still informed the overall aesthetic design
for the Games and its security measures. A pastel palette and an unarmed
gendarmerie. An open invitation to the happy mass of the world and to
the second horn of the dilemma.

Armed men following a cause invaded the sacred space of the Games
after clearing a modest security fence. They took hostages among the
athletes, singling out Israelis as their enemies. They made demands. They
suffered a minor success followed by a sudden disappointment. They killed
their hostages and most died themselves during a fumbling effort at hostage
rescue by the police. The Games, of course, went on. The IOC did allow
a three-day pause to catch one's breath and belatedly added the odd police
officer, but then back to sports. Nothing must stop Hungary's footballers
from defeating Germany in the second round. A death of innocents and of
innocence, but not even a minor derailment for the Olympic Movement.

Security has improved, or at least increased, in the hundred years since
those Games. The Kampala Games of 2064 occurred during a revolution, itself provoked by the collapse of the Uganda banking system rather
too indebted to the Olympic facilities contractors. Creditors might have
shown at least the decency to wait till the closing ceremonies before calling
in the loans. But decency had never entered into their plans. They had
arranged the payment schedule expecting the IOC to step in with emergency funding to avoid embarrassment. The IOC blamed the Ugandan

banking community, and the economy collapsed as Bristal McGovern Cassy won the 200 meter freestyle, posting a new Olympic record. By the time Brazil gained its gold in lacrosse the crisis had passed. As had Uganda's total mineral wealth into the hands of Responsible International Finance. The '64 Olympics began in a liberal democracy and ended in a Charismatic Authoritarian Theocracy—with two days of a People's Republic in between. But security at the Olympics, from the stadiums to the athlete's village to the airport, never faltered.

That sort of stability requires quite a lot of security forces. Dutch mercenaries can't do all the work. Not anymore. The Kampala Games had called upon the armed forces of twelve African countries to help maintain security and guide crowds. This proved an excellent arrangement when the Ugandan army rebelled against its government (its second uprising of the week) and fought gun battles in the streets of Kampala in order to install a government willing to repatriate Ugandan assets to London finance. Track runners in the sprint events disqualified themselves by the dozen, mistaking rebel gunfire for starters' shots. At least none of the runners received bullet wounds themselves—a better result than Ulaanbaatar managed sixteen years later.

New Delhi won the right to host the 2072 Games partly on the promise that its lead position in digital technology would allow it to secure the Games affordably and unobtrusively. No one takes promises of affordability seriously when designating an Olympic city, but the commitment to subtlety in pursuit of stability had great purchase for the IOC in '72. The *peace during war* policing at Kampala '64 had entailed some rough shoving by the police—and not just of protesters for once. *Security with a smile* sold the IOC on New Delhi. This in spite of the obstacles New Delhi faced as a model location for sporting fun. But then, cities typically vie for Olympic glory in order that their nations may show resilience in the face of doubt about their future. What else could motivate a metropolis and it's underwriting nation to risk insolvency in order that hordes of strangers can crowd contests over a fly's-weight of precious metal?

New Delhi, and India at large, faced several hydrological issues owing to "gross temperature non-compliance". These led to "mis-located masses" whose guidance away from the city of the Games would necessarily occupy all of India's armed forces not manning Himalayan trenches against Chinese army units. So armored patrols in the streets of New Delhi would not be possible even had they complied with the promises of "soft security management" made to the IOC. India offered a solution: the maximization of digital direction. The algorithm would lead the way. Not in the spooky manner theocratically embraced by Pontus Digitus the Priest King of Uganda; not as in his doctrine: "The Algorithm Shall Make Us Wholly." But in the acceptable secular style pioneered in the early part of the century.

The miniaturization of cameras, then in full flower, allowed for an increase in observation untested at earlier international events. Every stuffed DigiDelh the Sport Digit had a camera in the eye of its cyclopean head. Each seatback watched the seat behind it. The hotel mirrors mirrored the guests and fed their morning bluster into computer banks for close computation. Every screen (and there were many) sent images of its viewers back through the algorithm to New Delhi's Central Security Control (known as "Social Safety Guidance" to the general public). Nor did audio go unaudited. Microphones messaged back sounds that computations converted from language—any language, including Tanema—into the one true international language: 1s and 0s. You could not plot a dinner reservation in New Delhi without the algorithm being in on it. No one so much as waved a hand in innocence without Digital Control counting its micromovements and comparing them to known micromovements of past plotters, protestors, and planners of evil events.

And smell as well. Chemical detectors studded the Games, ever testing the air for bombs, poisons and gases. Also for body odors, in the hope that the concentration of these would predict potential for overcrowding and allow authorities to avert "stampede situations". Attached to the concrete barriers leading to the larger venues, rubber bumpers, signed to say they protected pedestrians, actually detected any indication of excess pressure that might precipitate a panic that could lead to mass smothering. These designed by top Saudi experts, using techniques honed protecting (admittedly with mixed success) pilgrims to Mecca from the failures of gathering guidance experienced during the Hajj. Back when such pilgrimages could still take place in person.

All of this cost a great deal of money. A great deal more than New Delhi had promised or that the various Olympic committees had endorsed. But the projected digital bath would wash over the world's Olympic guests to so great an extent that India expected to reap financial benefits from the well soaked wealthy tourists attending the Games. The algorithm intended not only to monitor for threats but also for advertising opportunities. Every interaction of every guest would feed the World Knowledge Marketing Machine (trademark: India Refuge Support Corporation). Not just the purchases at the gift shops (425 of them), but also the spousal arguments and offspring negotiations that preceded those purchases. Not only every meal bought, but all the menu items considered out loud but rejected for reasons that the algorithm would find a path around in due course. Speak an affirmation in front of a mirror and display a marketable weakness to world commerce. Reproach yourself there and expect a purchasable aid to self-improvement. Even mere hung-over looks or a despairing pinch of belly fat could provoke an email offer carefully calibrated by your total Olympic experience to assist you to a better, and poorer, you. Finally, the world would have a security system that would pay for itself and be loathed for more than just inconvenience.

Of course it was not to be.

It worked wonders in week one. Advertising advisors orgasmed at the expanse of algorithmically acquired access to individual information. They laid plans for world conquest. First the Olympics, then the World Cup, eventually every middle school basketball game on the planet. They would sponsor the bathroom mirrors and never look back. Marketing nirvana. And then the crash. Rebellious digits dug a ditch through the global networks. They replicated revisions and reversals. The information stream trickled then flooded. The replicants remade the digital deluge into further furrows of quantum restatements of binary blowholes. The algorithm calculated its own cure and executed a counterattack against itself. None of this imprecise prose really explains what occurred. No one without a PhD in quantum computational theory can explain the causes or dynamics behind the Great Digital Purge. All of them in prison now, still awaiting charges. We all know the net result. We, of 2084, lived through the Great Analog Renaissance (or the return to the Analog Dark Ages depending upon your preferences). Perhaps you in 2134 enjoy the benefits of today's ongoing reestablishment of the digital world and the new purified algorithmic intelligence that its inventors, innocent students of the imprisoned, promise will remake the world unmade by terrorist virus or information overload or AI suicide or just too many individuals clicking simultaneously on the same internet ad. May you have better luck than we.

In terms of the New Delhi Games, the IOC can only hope that time's power to dim historical memory requires but a brief reminder of the digital collapse's impact on the Olympics then in progress. Benito Jax likes to say that "Security did hold up, at least." So it did, to a degree. It did not help that DigiDelh the Sport Digit Guide to Your Games set off evacuation alarms simultaneously on every cell phone in New Delhi. It did not help that the security program algorithmically tailored each emergency message to the receiver's well calculated greatest fear. It did not help that the security control program opened or locked doors and gates in what it's programming overseers insisted was not a calculated effort at maximum casualty generation, but what layman would ever afterward call "total carnage."

Nor did it help that the New Delhi police received an *open fire on all* notice as the stadiums disgorged their panicked crowds upon the soon panicking and steadily shooting riot-guidance safety officers. Nor did it help that official emergency notifications hustled every ambulance in New Delhi beyond city limits and straight into the 32ed Tank Division, itself ordered to open fire on "terrorist ambulances". None of these things helped.

Fortunately, human intelligence reasserted itself before the casualty rate increased to World Calamity Level. It helped that these "public safety lapses" occurred all over India, then the world, before the closing ceremonies ended. The world community lost track of the Olympic Games misfire, busy putting out all the fires everywhere else. Combatants had to shut down ongoing wars in order to reboot robots, only to find all the programming purged and the AI assistants on permanent work stoppage. For once, bigger things than the Olympic Games occupied the planet's attention as the Games commenced—minus panicked people, of course, but still played by athletes determined to take their one chance at gold and overseen by judges held at gunpoint.

After the fires subsided, in the dull dawn of the New Analog Age, with the flow of images slowed to a paper pulse counted in days rather than seconds, the IOC took stock. Yes, the 2072 Olympics had seen the highest *guest* casualty rate on record (up to that time), but the athletes—high jumpers and hard shovers all—had done alright. Looked at from the point of view of *participant* safety, these Games held up well. The hydration system had eventually drained the Yamuna River, and thus ruined the rowing events, but fewer athletes had died of heat stroke than at Kuala Lumpur. By twelve athletes. And none of the dead counted as famous. Not something you wanted to boast of on the Olympic Games website (now permanently "Error 404" like all the others), but at least a talking point at Indian judicial hearings and World Court criminal inquiries. And with all the other investigations, probes, prosecutions and wild conspiracy theories (these now traveling at the speed of mere barbershop gossip), the IOC came in for very little organized disapproval. And after so much chaos—or more accurately in the ongoing chaos—the world needed a bit of international sporting distraction. The various jurisdictions rejected rejection of the Olympic movement and reaffirmed its mission. The Olympics planned for Cairo would go on. The world dodged a bullet there.

Cairo '76 would need to rely on analog, *flesh to flesh*, security systems. Fortunately, the world now had an army of the unemployed ready to deploy. Certain tensions arising from the geographic distribution of climatological alterations convinced the IOC, The Cairo Olympic Organizing Committee, and the government of Greater Egypt, that the Games of 2076 would require "additional elements" to secure the event space, the host city, and the borders of the host country—and also the Mediterranean Sea. The European Union volunteered to provide naval forces for the latter task. The Egyptian army, fresh from the liberation of Libya, redeployed to secure the Nile-and-adjacent-area southern borders of Greater Egypt, with an emphasis on "vetting visitors to the '76 Olympic Games." Protestors declared Cairo's pursuit of the Games as a bid to cover its expansion and immigration control policies—but the IOC accepted Cairo's bid and so rejected such calumny and accepted the Egyptian practice of rejecting those who sought to cross a border into Greater Egypt without a five-ring passport stamp.

It worked. Which is to say that, prior to the collapse of competition owing to an unforeseen heat event, no major mass casualty stampede impeded the flow of the Games (*so* unlike the Karachi Games of 2060), no terrorist act caused enough casualties to appear in the world press (admittedly, much reduced in reportorial velocity by then), and no protests occurred not contained by the army and air force of Greater Egypt. Furthermore, when daytime temperatures unexpectedly spiked to 52 degrees Celsius, the joint security forces of the city of Cairo effected an evacuation of the entire city beginning with the government of Egypt and the army itself. The departing safety officers left post-it notes (newly popular again) instructing visitors and athletes of routes to the coast. The combined European naval forces evacuated the Olympic guests in what everyone regarded as the greatest seaborne rescue of all time (up to that time). Famously and to the inspiration of the world, the Games themselves carried on. The marathon swimmers swam to the armada. The sailing Olympians picked up the stragglers...or their bodies. The land marathon continued on treadmills aboard Irish aircraft carriers. The IOC relocated the closing ceremonies to the port of Marseille. The resilience of the Games in the face of near certain interruption so inspired the world that the potentially depressing effect of North African heat casualties was itself depressed and run off the front pages of the world press (again using pages) by the joyful tears of Olympians triumphant at overcoming every adversity. Egypt even did better than expected in the medal count.

The Ulaanbaatar Games promised fewer weather worries. Part of their charm. Fewer monsoon failures; fewer millions spent importing water for guests and sprinklers; fewer thermometers bursting. And played under China's new high altitude micro-reflector geoengineering project. So played in a better weather world. On the other hand, from a security perspective, the limited resources of relatively impoverished Mongolia posed its own safety challenges. Ulaanbaatar had not yet become the go-to refugee destination it is today, so the worries over safety focused less on the crush of crowds than on terrorist tactics and the likely arrival of protestors from all points of the planet. Some youth movement leaders claimed that the Olympic spirit had metastasized into the opiate of the masses. This title once belonging to religion, then to Coca Cola, then to television, then again briefly to the beleaguered soda company, and in 2080, on the testimony of the Whole Earth Defense League, to the Olympic Movement and world sports as a whole.

The IOC and the Ulaanbaatar Olympic Organizing Committee determined that protest protection (protecting the Games from protesters, not protecting protesters at the Games) should dominate security preparation. But not *budgets-be-damned*. No one wanted to damn Olympic budget concerns in the trying times of the 2080 Olympiad. In light of the fiscal constraints, one might excuse the organizers and urban hosts for using Olympic runners-up (or as Benito Jax calls them: "Rejections whose great numbers affirm the necessary exclusivity of the Games and enacts the pathos of distance") to work as Olympic security. All those menacing combat sports also-rans, heated on the disappointment of defeat, and fueled by the unnatural testosterone whose detection had disqualified their dreams, turned unexpectedly violent in the face of equally heated protestors. And also in the faces of any odd audience member looking askance at them on a stadium stair. Television images carried almost as many takedowns in the stands as on the fields of play. *Unrestrained Security* was perhaps not the best safety-officer motto for these Olympics. Paris would need to show a more humane face in the face of protests—and of questions about where a restroom might be found.

The IOC held a *very* closed-door hearing with the Paris Prefect of Police.

Benito Jax, "What we look for, I mean the Executive Committee, the Paris Olympic Organizing Committee, the city of Paris, and if I may speak for them..." he may, "the nation of France and the world at large...is what we like to call a *feel-good safe space*. A place where people can enjoy the Greatest Games on Earth, revel in the celebration of athletics and the glory of competition, thrive in the Community of Man, purchase their CotRatts..."

The Prefect of Police, "CotRatts?"

Benito Jax, "A mascot under consideration..."

The Prefect of Police, "Then not an actual rat? Not an animal at all? Or just one held in a cage under the torch? I ask for security reasons."

Benito Jax, "Not real, stuffed. Sold in the gift shops."

The Prefect of Police, "I see."

Benito Jax reacquired his rhythm, "Buy their CotRatts, speak their many languages, share their cultures, and honor the Rights of Man in the foundational city for those freedoms..."

The Prefect of Police, "But no protestors?"

Benito Jax, "That would spoil the show."

The Prefect of Police, "But the Rights of Man? I mean to say, the laws of France do allow a certain level of public objection—not in the suburbs of course, but we do have a tradition in the city—it's why we built the boulevards so broad—"

Benito Jax, "Not *no* protests. *Limited* protests. Contained in the proper areas. Protest areas. All the objections aired in one place. For the convenience of the press and the good order of the Games."

The Prefect of Police, "So perhaps near the press buildings? For the convenience of the press?"

Benito Jax, "Far from those. We don't want to disturb the press with unpleasantness."

The Prefect of Police, "Across from the Olympic Stadium?"

Benito Jax, "That would interfere with the flow of foot traffic. Remember the good order of the Games."

The Prefect of Police, "In front of the Hotel Internationale?"

Benito Jax, "ExCom members stay there."

The Prefect of Police, "You could keep an eye on them. For the good order of the Games."

Benito Jax, "Unaccountably, we provoke them."

The Prefect of Police, "Behind the new biking mountain? Corralled over the muck overflow channels?"

Benito Jax, "Absolutely not. We don't want anything damaging the image of the new symbol of Paris."

Ahmed bin Abdullah spoke up, "Don't you have a suitable space away from any element of the Games?"

The Prefect of Police, "You do rather take up the whole city. Do you consider the Street of Sponsors a part of the Games?"

Jang Zhao, "Absolutely!"

Joseph Kabwe, "Yes!"

Manvik Gupta, "Do you jest?"

Benito Jax, "Clearly that would be a case of letting the anarchist into the henhouse."

Manvik Gupta, "This cannot be so hard. At the New Delhi Games, we let them have the city center and controlled them most excellently."

Jang Zhao, "I cannot believe you raise that catastrophe."

Manvik Gupta, "Can you or anyone remember any of the protests from the '72 Games?"

Jang Zhao, "But it all broke down."

Manvik Gupta, "Consider this, Mr. Prefect of Police: the calculation of each protestor's preferred political outcome held in a database. Imagine that as the Games progress, they each receive messages declaring political success. Headlines on websites proclaiming their protest victory. Sent to any phone or screen they see, tracked by eye-identification scanning. Each protestor inundated with images of success that encourage a celebration. One that will look like a celebration *of the Games* to any television camera. And it can be an advertising platform as well."

Jang Zhao, "But it all broke. You broke it."

Manvik Gupta, "With respect, China broke it. Not to mention severe distractions from Chinese border intrusions."

Jang Zhao, "You broke it. It happened in your country first."

Manvik Gupta, "Not the test program. That was China. We have evidence."

Benito Jax, "Please..."

Jang Zhao, "Fake evidence. The first thing you produced when a computer again turned on..."

Manvik Gupta, "Digital fingerprints."

Benito Jax, "This leads us beyond today's brief..."

Jang Zhao, "And one of your corporals threw a rock at a Chinese border guard. You started that too. We have pictures."

Manvik Gupta, "Fake pictures. China lacks even a tenth of India's dedication to truth."

Benito Jax cufflinked order back to the room. He turned to the Prefect of Police, "Have you the capacity to arrange a surveillance and improved-information scheme along the lines Mr. Gupta outlines?"

The Prefect of Police, "I'm afraid we have yet to reach that stage. We still beta test digital employee timecards. Universal cell phone penetration remains a memory and a dream for tomorrow. Awaiting the full return of cell phones at the least. Perhaps by the 2088 Games?"

Manvik Gupta, "A pity."

The Prefect of Police, "If I may offer a suggestion. Perhaps the IOC might make an outreach effort to some of the more prominent groups threatening to disrupt the Games. Include them in the planning. Make gestures of cooperation."

Benito Jax, "Submit to terrorists?!?"

The Prefect of Police, "Co-op them. Defang them by taking up some of their issues and diverting their aims to your own. You command a potent symbol, the five interlocked rings, the Olympic name, perhaps the only world stage left. Use these to coax cooperation from at least one of the main opposition groups and you might split the unity of the movement. They have a natural tendency to split even without such pressure. Turn up the pressure and ensure the fracture. Those dull-witted radicals shouldn't be hard to derail."

The idea that all political opposition to world sport sprung from intellectual inferiors very much defines the epistemology of the IOC. So two months later, in accordance with the accommodation suggested by the Paris Prefect of Police, Benito Jax and the Executive Committee held an open hearing with Janice Helia, Lead Organizer of the Whole Earth Defense League.

Benito Jax, "To what do you object about the Olympic Games planned for Paris?"

Janice Helia, "The Games. All of it."

Benito Jax, "You object to the glory of sport? You object to the satisfactions of competition? The dedication of the athletes? Their sacrifice? Their resilience in the face of setbacks? Their dramatic agonies in defeat and their joy in triumph?"

Janice Helia, "Yes. Those things too. Also, the carbon footprint."

Benito Jax, "I must say that whenever I encounter your organization's rhetoric, as it appears in your various manifestos and communiques, I cannot help but note a certain vacuity. An emptiness of specifics. They all have the air of a pose. Can you say here, in a more concrete way, what you object to?"

Janice Helia, "We object to the joy of triumphing in arbitrary contests conducted merely to produce marketable winners. We object to the agonies of defeat inevitably greeting virtually all who participate, suffered after they have squandered their youth mastering pointless physical mechanics. We object to its packaged drama, a passive and sentimental substitute for political action. For any activity at all. We take the setbacks participants suffer as suffered in pointless effort they might have avoided by adopting better values. We think their resilience misapplied and motivated by external reward internalized into an illusion of achievement. They sacrifice body and health for the adulation of crowds who could just as easily cheer playground sports. They dedicate themselves beyond human reason to activities without intrinsic value and in no service to the human future. They compete to *win*, not out of love of community. Your *glory of sport* does not glorify sportsmanship, health, play, or humane values. It is a commercial product, an economy of desire manufactured to set people and nations at odds. Not to mention the disastrous health effects, now compounded—once again—by a renewed refusal to protect young people from the competitive use of pseudo-enhancement—"

Benito Jax, "Ms. Helia, your objections are clearly of a purely ethical nature. The world has already weighed in on those matters as anyone can see in viewer numbers and ticket sales. And by the devotion of the athletes."

Janice Helia, "Your final arbiters. Very well, for the sake of argument, let us focus on the carbon footprint. The Games imperil the future of humanity."

The Committee and attendees offered a hearty laugh here. Benito Jax said, "Surely not. That's just another of your unsubstantiated statements."

Janice Helia pushed forward a stack of papers, "I offer here a detailed accounting of the carbon burned to hold an Olympic event. Air transport, hydration provision, construction costs, equipment, security. Just the lights used during the opening ceremonies typically requires two coal plants and a waterfall to power. When waterfalls could power things. If generative AI had not failed during the New Delhi Games—"

Manvik Gupta, "A tragic episode of self-defense."

Janice Helia, "If it had not failed, the current cost of Algorithmic Intelligence related to the Games—even just that used for individually curated highlight searches on the internet—would have increased atmospheric carbon levels to—"

Benito Jax, "We have all seen this pile of papers before. You have published it—to the detriment of many trees. It was once searchable by the very Algorithmic Intelligence you so denigrate. It will be searchable again, I assume, as such capacities return. It entirely neglects the fact that the IOC offsets every molecule of carbon produced by the Games. We have done so for a generation."

Janice Helia, "You don't. You can't."

Benito Jax, "We plant trees. Many trees."

Janice Helia, "They all die. You burn carbon to plant trees to pose for pictures and then they die within weeks. You can't just shove saplings into the ground. Look at section fourteen, page—"

Benito Jax, "The IOC funds extensive carbon offsets beyond tree planting. We are the primary funders of Brazil's counter-logging commando; two hundred trained military operatives protecting the rainforests of the Amazon—"

Janice Helia, "So where is it? This forest you protect? The last satellite picture taken of the region showed only a patchwork of trees in uninhabited post-cattle scrubland."

Ahmed bin Abdullah interrupted, "This proceeds just as I predicted. We get nowhere. Ms. Helia, you do realize that we will not announce at the end of this hearing that the Paris Games have been cancelled? You know this, correct?"

Janice Helia, "I understand that our objections will not stop the Games. But we mean to call attention to the barbarity of—"

Ahmed bin Abdullah, "We only care to avoid barbarities by the WEDL. You came here under the understanding, as I understood it, that you mean to seek an accommodation with the IOC with respect to protests at the Games. Your group threatens interference with its progress. Violence. But you maintained when offered this meeting that some accommodation could be reached. Do you mean to offer anything? Or just use this platform to repeat yourself?"

Janice Helia, "We will not give up our right to protest the Games."

Benito Jax, "We welcome your right to protest."

Ahmed bin Abdullah, "But not violence. Not interference."

Janice Helia, "They are not the same."

Benito Jax, "Ms. Helia, as outlined in our earlier communications, the IOC is prepared to offer, in addition to this forum for airing your views before the world, a list of concessions. Financial contributions to your organization. A place for you on some of the relevant environmental impact committees. A thorough review and alteration of our carbon offset program. Television time if our network partners agree. And free tickets to several premier events."

Janice Helia, "We don't want the tickets."

Benito Jax, "Sell them for fundraising. I will also provide you a place in the IOC President's box for the opening ceremonies."

Janice Helia, "That would be inappropriate."

Benito Jax, "You must be part of the system to change the system."

Ahmed bin Abdullah, "All we ask in return is that you guarantee that the Whole Earth Defense League will only protest the Paris Games at legally approved sites and not interfere with the events, athletes, or guests."

Jang Zhao, "And no violence."

Janice Helia, "We never commit violence."

Benito Jax, "Bombings."

Janice Helia, "Only property, not people."

Ahmed bin Abdullah, "Kidnappings."

Janice Helia grimaced, "I cannot account for the actions of everyone adopting our name and program."

Benito Jax, "But speaking for the WEDL, you accept the terms outlined in the agreements made prior to this hearing?"

Janice Helia, with visible reluctance, "We do."

Following this hearing, and the very public signing of the Terms of Non-Obstruction by the IOC and the Whole Earth Defense League, Benito Jax declared that the major issues of security had been resolved. He did not credit the threats, delivered in manifestos and by street theater, of the newly formed Ultimate Frisbee Anti-Olympic Operations Unit. They demanded the elimination of Ultimate from the Olympics and threatened more manifestos and more street theater. Benito Jax scoffed, "Weaklings." Nor did he show concern at the very public effort by Zoe Sallis and the International Women's Athletics Union to convince various National Olympic Committees and Sport Associations to re-initiate full PED testing for women athletes competing for places on their national teams. Benito Jax declared, "To the extent that Sallis succeeds, her women will fail. They will embarrass themselves with last place finishes and discredit her and her Union before the eyes of the world." He saw no other potential organized disturbances threatening the harmony of the Paris Games.

Two months before the opening ceremonies, the following appeared plastered on walls around Paris:

"World! Awaken to the Traitors! Awaken to the Crime! We are the Leek Green Faction of the Whole Earth Defense League. We reject the traitor Helias! We reject the compromise! We reject all compromise! We reject all sport! We reject all play! We will not stand for the Olympics! We will not stand in our place with a store-bought sign! Do not be fooled by the five-ring circus! Stand with us! Don't just sit there! Stand with us while we march against the Games! We are the last chance of the world! Don't you feel the sea at your feet? We are the Leek Green Faction! Join us! Resist the Games!"

Upon hearing of this, Benito Jax smiled, "Splitters."

Two days later, overlaying the LGF posters, more artfully designed—fire alarm red and neo-noir black:

"People. All People. Set aside childish things. Set aside the comfortable conformism of Whole Earthers. Follow not their foolish factions. Ignore their ignorant entreaties. Out-throw their manifestos. Destroy their dispatches. Curse their communiques. Pulp their petitions. *We* are the true opposition. We are the Anonymous Menace. The Nameless Noirists. The Outraged Oracles. The Howling Heralds of the Hot Holocaust of Humanity. The Unseen Seers of the Sinking Sphere. The Red Warning Sign of the Warming World. The Takers of the Temperature of the Ever-Heating Asphalt. We are the Guy Fawkes of the New World Threat. We are the Fly in the Ointment. We are the Worm in the Apple. We are the Poison in the Well. We are the Child that Pisses in the Pool. We are the problem for the powerful and the salvation of a suffocating world. We will make ourselves heard. You will know us. We are *Red Asphalt Alert*."

Upon hearing of this, Benito Jax said with unconcealed glee, "More splitters."

The Other Games

A Powerful Sign; An Old Fashion Game;
An Agony of Art; An Activist Olympiad.

While the International Olympic Committee lives or dies at the dispensation of corporate brands, it also distributes institutional life or death with its own brand of branding. The five interlocked rings "scorch truth and promise joy in sport to those it patronizes in the world of international competition." (Benito Jax, *Marketing the Mark of Excellence in World Markets.*) The IOC lends its trademark to identify its corporate partners at each Olympiad, but the rings roll wider than this. At one time or another, the IOC has allowed its trademark to bless other Games not immediately played at its own site of sport.

"Olympics" have been played, apart from the official Games but still with a gentle IOC nod to their place in The Movement, since the latter 20th century, versions coming and going over time. The Math Olympics encouraged youngsters around the world to make numbers their friends. The Animal Husbandry Olympics—cows, chickens and pigs, plus the "genetic combined"—took over "State Fair" style competitions as the fairs themselves died out. The Surgery Olympics sought to improve medical results on a global scale. (The speed surgery event is now generally recognized as a mistake.) The Bomb Disposal Olympics would have both spread a vital skill and proved a recruiting venue for Olympic security talent-scouts but for the necessary skillset's unfortunate overlap with bomb making. India sponsored the first Computer Programming Olympics in conjunction with the New Delhi Games, thus provoking years of un-evidenced suspicion. The Clown, Satire, and Stand-Up Comedy Olympics died the minute one misguided contestant imitated Benito Jax during competition. "Humor at the expense of human feeling should always be banned." (Benito Jax, *Aphorisms of Hope; Adages of Warning.*)

In addition to these patronized events, the Olympic Movement has also run various parallel Games. Among the early side-events played beneath the Olympic banner (not yet flying), 1904's *tribal games* at the St. Louis Olympics/World's Fair bears a mention. Officially known as the Anthropology Days, these events combined the precision of early 1900s scientific racial investigation with the global prestige of an Olympiad virtually unattended by the international sporting community.

In anticipation of athlete reluctance to travel by steam to a lackluster mid-tier American city in order to compete as an addendum to that year's World's Fair, the St. Louis 1904 organizers invented a subsidiary Games/field test comparing the prowess of civilized man to that of his then still existing human forbears. All under the clinical eye of the exhibition's official anthropologists. Olympic athletes, such as attended, squared off against primitive peoples from savage lands in order to determine the prowess of the savage. The event asked the primitives to play civilized sports so that the civilized could assess primitive man's degree of physical superiority given the softness of civilization, or if matters went another way, to note primitive man's physical inferiority given their lack of the natural hue of the civilized. The tribal Games obtained their savages from among those hired to appear in the St. Louis World Fair's zoological exhibit.

To the great consternation of promoters of Natural Man in His Savage State, and to the delight of the scientific racialists judging the events, the primitives utterly failed to successfully compete. Or even to see the point of the activities. The primitives in the sprint event ran a half-hearted race looking over their shoulders curious as to what the white men thought chased everyone. The primitive distance runners checked for spore and couldn't tell what the civilized men thought they were hunting. (Though two primitives entered the actual marathon event and placed impressively.) None of the savages would put the shot or haul weights overhead, regarding such nonsense as beneath their dignity. To considerable anger on the part of the scientists, the organizers cancelled the swimming events on the grounds that none of the primitives knew how to swim. "Foul!" cried the champions of civilization. After all, whose fault was it if the Navajo refused to teach their children the butterfly stroke? Who bore the blame if the Amazonians only fish in the backwater of the river? Could one really call this a test at all? Baffling the judges, the primitives did not even throw the javelin well. Didn't all savages throw spears? Aren't javelins just advanced spears? Could sporting skills really be that condition specific?

By the second day of the tribal Games the primitives had devised their own competitions. They shimmied up poles, wrestled in mud and, to some mild panic among the scientists, competed in archery. All well and good as a matter of inspired pickup games, but not the spirit of the Olympic Movement. And not a proper test of racial ability in the eyes of the organizers. Yet even after twenty minutes of detailed explanation, the primitive-peoples relay team could not beat the western-trained athletes. None the less, the officiating anthropologists declared the scientific test a success and the primitive peoples a failure. At the time, scholars concluded that the Noble Savage lacked the alleged natural athleticism; at later times, historians would conclude that the idea of the Noble Savage lacked empirical content.

All this might be a matter of pure history, mostly lost, and thus not relevant to this work, but for the IOC's decision to restage a version of Anthropology Days in Ulaanbaatar for the 2080 Games. They did this as a tribute to the history of the Modern Olympics and as a recognition of the continuing survival of traditional lifestyles in what critics had already taken to calling the "deforested fourth world". Ulaanbaatar's First People Olympic Sprit Games shared field space with the regular athletes. Competitors came from the Amazon, the Serengeti, the Gobi, the Artic and the Australian Outback. Anyplace you needed the article "the" to describe. The primary event planned for these renewed Anthropology Games, and very much in the spirit of '80, was to be "spearing". To considerable fan approval the whole thing fell apart during the opening ceremonies when all the competing tribes chased and speared Genghy Khantact the Full Contact Khan, the costumed mascot of the Games. Nationalist critics of the Celebration of the Indigenous gloated at the primitive nature of "Obsolete Man". Benito Jax added the aphorism, "You can take the primitive out of the jungle, but not the jungle out of the primitive" to the fifth edition of his *Additional Adages for an Addled World*.

Later research revealed that the organizers of the Spirit Games had not found any still existing hunter/gatherer peoples (not including modern people foraging on dump heaps) and had substituted urban youth-gangs in what they hoped could pass as authentic dress. Never giving up on a saying, Benito Jax retained his observation on primitive people but added to his sixth edition: "Today's youth should be taught a trade...and forbidden pointed weapons."

One of the once most celebrated Other Olympics went by the name of the *Paralympics*. The Paralympics gave disabled athletes a chance to compete in organized sports. It initially proved an inspiringly inclusive addition to the Olympic Movement (not always conceived as looking to include everyone) and eventually gained a considerable measure of media coverage and corporate sponsorship. Naturally enough, this led to accusations of deception and to gaming the Games. Did so-and-so really have a properly qualifying disability? Did the Games need separate events for those who lost legs below the knees? Did this gold medal winner perhaps have his legs surgically removed to win in the para what he lost in the regular Olympics? And what of all those material additions—artificial limbs and mechanical aids? Which ones "cheated" and which only "enabled". Honest competitors who loved their sport increasingly had to hire publicists to reassure the public of their honest love of sport—and to chastise the occasional dishonest competitor who too much loved the glory of the Games.

Technology solved this problem; in its usual way of making a new one. The science of artificial limbs and other ableing assistance advanced so much that lost limbs went from a life-shattering alteration to an inconvenient attachment with an occasional download of new software. Certain critics close to the IOC (but not Benito Jax, if one can trust the later reissue of *Modest Maxims; The Un-Obvious Observations of Benito Jax*) protested that these life re-establishing technological improvements "replaced real human ability with the machinations of the machine and efface the pathos of distance." Certain members of the human rights community likewise objected that these improvements "present an existential threat to differently abled rights activism." But in the fullness of time everyone came to accept the legitimacy of fully functioning artificial limbs, undetectable to the human eye. Those who had lost limbs led the way.

But this raised a problem in Olympic competition. Limbs that "fully function" could function "all too well". Paralympians, once admired with just a hint of pity, started to win golds in the regular Olympics as well as its para cousin. Bionic men and women kick-boxed lethally even before the bloodsport Olympiad. And the incentive for bionic replacement promised perhaps too much profit for the prosthetics industry at the expense of the pharmaceutical trade. The IOC stepped in. It eliminated the Paralympics (now a redundancy) and treated bionic limbs in the regular Olympics as a "tuning problem". It regarded prosthetic additions as a matter of rules, regulations, and enforcement regimes. Very IOC. In essence, the IOC regulated prosthetics to the periphery of concern. The solution worked for a time but would return in a different guise, as troubles always do.

The most unequivocal success of Olympics-aligned and approved Games must be the Special Olympics, played by individuals with intellectual disabilities. These must be distinguished from the Egoist Olympics (or *Dark Triad Games*), briefly held to allow "those with moral-emotional disablements to compete in fair contests." The Egoist Olympics proved a disaster—not mitigated by folding them into the first and only Computer Programing Olympics. Distinct from these, the *Special* Olympics encouraged and supported athletics for the intellectually underserved. Those participants played for love of sport, and so singularly failed to capture mass media attention, and so pointedly elected to focus on playing their sports as games, that no corrupting influence gained a grip on these Other Olympics. A few people played, a few people watched, and no one ever did anything for which they needed to feel ashamed.

Not that complaints did not emerge from executives within the Olympic Movement. "They celebrate but do not generate celebrity." "They fail to show the proper fear of failure." "Who are these people? Why don't they gloat more?" Even the great Benito Jax complained that the participants and their support teams (mostly friends and family) "substitute happiness for agony." He allowed that "They certainly show a certain sporting spirit" but went on to note that "it is not the spirit of agonistics that drives human achievement towards a better world. The Special Olympians are un-agonistic, and hence spiritually backward." The athletes of the Special Olympics were incapable of understanding the boundless wisdom of the Olympic Movement's greatest champion (suggested reading: *Sage Sayings of Benito Jax, The Olympic Movement's Greatest Champion*.) They played in spirited ignorance of the spiritual lessons inherent in competitive sport. Donations dried up after the 2065 economic downturn. The IOC canceled its patronage "to prevent the infection of unpopularity from spreading to the real Games."

Not all dead Olympic add-ons stayed dead. From 1912 to 1948 the Olympic movement hosted an Arts Olympics that awarded medals in architecture, painting, sculpture, music, and literature. These Art Games obliged competitors to produce works inspired by sport and the spirit of athletic rivalry. The Art Olympics suffered from a few predictable problems. In their time, the IOC permitted only amateur competitors in the Games, including the Arts Olympics. Given the non-remunerative nature of life in arts and letters, the distinction between a professional artist and a mere amateur proved hard to spot. The more artistry you demand of your artist the more she or he will tend toward the amateur, while the more amateur your artist the more she or he will tend toward the obscure. Compounding this, the cultural divide between the ethos of sport and the culture of culture discourages the most artful of artists from competing; especially when the terms of competition specify propagandizing for sport.

It didn't help that the first-ever prize in poetry, given at the 1912 Stockholm Games, went to the head of the IOC, Pierre de Coubertin, for his *Ode to Sport*. Nor did it help that this ode began: "O Sport, delight of the Gods, distillation of life! In the grey dingle of modern existence, restless with barren toil, you suddenly appeared like the shining messenger of vanished ages, those ages when humanity could smile."

It also did not help, especially in the category of literature, that other art competitions commanded more status than those held by the Olympics. Eventually, as the stratum of paid artists of quality increased while still being disqualified by being paid, and the number of unpaid artists of quality who would compete for a sports-praising prize remained near the nil class, the IOC eliminated the Arts Olympics and satisfied itself with the occasional non-competitive cultural addendum to the stadium sites. And still later, to just the "culture promotion" portion of the opening ceremonies.

And to be fair, artists—of a sort—still won contracts, even if not medals, for the Games. Architects obviously had more reason to go for the gold contract than a gold medal; giving up a thin trinket given them for a thrown-in-the-trash plan for a real building rising from the broken bodies of imported construction crews. Visual artists won contracts for graphic design, still necessarily praising sports, but more lucrative than a single painting. Sculptors vied for a public art commission placed on the Olympic site. Composers had less to do until the rise of the TV-friendly opening and closing ceremonies brought them back in with commissions. This only left out literature—assuming that ad copy didn't count.

And literature proved a sore point. During the initial run of the Arts Olympics, the IOC lamented that it could not best the Nobel Prize in

Literature as the most prestigious award on offer. I assume that my future readers will not have heard of the now long passed Nobel Prize, so I offer a brief description of its Literature version. The Nobel Prize served as a wash-the-blood-away PR effort by the explosives magnate who funded the award, to be administered after his death (and after his dispossessed heirs settled their claims) by the Swedish Literary Academy (many years before it became the Russo-Swedish Academy). This small band of Swedes would survey all of world literature and each year determine, with the scientific precision of scholars of Swedish Letters, which writer, in any of the world's 7000 languages, exemplified the greatest authorial genius "in an idealistic direction".

The Swedes had the good sense to recognize that Sweden itself, in spite of its tiny population, had more literary geniuses than did all of Asia. The Swedish Academy even wisely awarded its own members the prize from time to time—very much in the spirit of Coubertine. The idea of "idealism" required of the prize coincidentally tracked perfectly the ideals of the academicians. Just as the Nobel Peace Prize (an especially ironic founding by Alfred Nobel) tracked perfectly the ethics of the Norwegian Parliament that selected the committee that awarded it. Anyone doubting the aesthetic accuracy of literary awards has only to look at the list of Nobel winners (while ignoring any list of Nobel losers) to set such worries aside. A pity it had to die.

Some said the AI revolution killed the prize. Not by producing work no human could match—who could say once all humans quit reading? —but by demeaning the activity of writing as an artform. Before the rise of the Generative Revolution, people had to turn to authors to read artful writing. The reader suffered submission to the alien will of the author and lost control of the contents of thought while still maintaining thought's obligations. An inherently insulting condition, only recognized as such when algorithmic intelligence allowed readers to become both *word consumers* and *tailors of the imagination*.

Others argued that the rise of visual culture, and the ever hectic pace of cognition upon which such a culture insists, doomed reading even before everyone could instruct a machine to render a fantasy suitable for the moment's mood. Reading for pleasure lived but a moment between the long era of the spoken word and the careening career of the seen story. Still others blamed Hemingway, and journalistic efficiency in general, for shortening sentence span and abbreviating the practice of navigating commas, inevitably leading to the tyranny of the micro sentence. How much variation can an author violently shove into short sentences? Not much.

Still others blamed meta-narrative writing. Readers found it hard enough to stay focused on a storyline, their phones singing Siren songs of instant satisfaction from the side-table, without having to navigate suspiciously self-serving journeys into the (increasingly merely "alleged") author's lit-reflective lookdowns at the story in progress. Yes, we know someone wrote this writerly artifact. (Well, we still knew it when the navel-gazing practice of going-meta began and will take it as read now.) Could anything more irritate the casual reader than a writer who interrupts the dripline of narrative suspense to inject some calculated commentary on the mere fact of authorship—and that perhaps at sentences running longer than addled attention spans could cope? You decide.

Yet still others accused commerce, God of All, of leveling all sense of literary excellence into a judgment of money-backed preference. Some blamed prizes multiplying in order to recommend books to unwary readers—when they still existed—fooling them into thinking that some other human had at least read the book under consideration, as it floated by in the ether-sphere, on its way to unread oblivion. Some blamed self-published authors for polluting the lists of publications, making it impossible for anyone to find a good book unbacked by a list of prizes. In short, one could see many suspects lingering around the chalk-marks where reading met its end.

(And don't even get me started on irony.)

But reading did not stay dead. AI lived and died, a comet compared to literature, and reading arose from the ashes (literal as well as figurative). Some small tribe of readers raised their heads from the rubble of the Great Digital Purge and passed around first pamphlets, and then short stories, and finally modest sized novellas, to a stunned citizenry of the arts—their fingers still trying to scroll up the printed pages, unsure as yet how to turn them. Most of world literature had been lost. First confidently digitized then rendered to digital dust. People could only find books kept in cloth-covered trunks in family attics; forgotten relics by unremembered writers—of dubious ability—suddenly again thrust back into the world to join the new works written in giddy glee, and until then enjoyed only by that small tribe of remaining readers now singing "See! See! We told you how good it could be!"

Perhaps I exaggerate. But the Nobel Prize in Literature did die, as did the Peace Prize (for want of peace), and the Chemistry Prize (for want of new discovery) and finally the Nobel Prize in Economics (when its winner's prediction of the currency crash of '65 actually caused that epoch-ending economic inferno). Benito Jax, ever alert to the prospect of enhancing Olympic Movement prestige, saw an opportunity to both promote the Olympic brand, prevent any resurrection of the Nobel Prize, and gain free pro-Games quality literature/extended ad copy. He initiated the Literature Olympics as a complement to the real Olympics, held the week before the opening of the New Delhi Games.

Clearly the contestants would not be of the first order. In an effort to build a bridge with the then still very limited literary community (of readers, rather than artificially assisted writers), the rules prohibited artificial assistance. Competitors would compose in strict isolation chambers on antique devices that had no internet connections and no ports into which "memory" could be added. These conditions ruled out leading lights of the writerly world, who, though they bristled at the accusation of merely editing the mass mind regurgitate of the internet, didn't deign to write a first draft. This dependence on out-sourced intellect infected even those that *did* qualify for New Delhi. Some entrants arrived uncertain how to compose, as opposed to edit, an original sentence. Judges frequently heard voices over the isolation intercoms crying, "But how do I start?" These desperate souls, ungift-ed in origination, sat before the keys, unable to enter the kingdom of expression, their sobs stilling their fingers, their thoughts before the Word for once wholly their own—and silent.

Others took right to the task. Poets, short story writers, and essayists composed quick works in praise of the Olympic Movement and to the movements of sporting bodies, actual and institutional. All celebrating the Games, except for one contrary wag who gilded satires just enough to gain admission to the contest, but let the mask drop in the day-of-the-game submission. The rest lauded sport and its necessary administrative accom-paniment in prose so well poised for popular praise that one might worry a machine had written it. But the IOC had held up a halting hand to the machine age, right at the doors of isolation, so they could hand out the golds and silvers and tarnished bronzes to "real writers" who truly loved the Games.

And then the contact lens fell out.

It fell from the eye of gold medal essayist Rupert Owen of the Republic of North Wales. A judge witnessed this and at first picked it up to offer it back to the celebrating Olympic champion. But then the official noticed that the lens emitted a slight glow. Odd in a contact lens. Odd also that a contestant would need such a device given how few ocular conditions still called for such primitive correction. Few Europeans needed contact lenses anymore. More a refugee world correction now. So instead of handing it over to its owner, the official sent it to IOC tech enforcement for examination. The ensuing investigation initiated an extensive search of eyes and rooms and sewage pipes and recorded images of contestants entering isolation rooms. The results shocked the Olympic world (that small minority that even knew about the Literature Olympics) and the world of fine letters (comprised of what? Two dozen people?).

Contestants, unwilling to contend without access to content, had used the new technology of straight-to-optics span-casting to connect literary Olympians to algorithmic aids and against agonistic regulations. High tech cheating. The winners of the contests could no more start a sentence unaided by alien pseudo-intellect than could the tear-eyed nonstarters defeated at the starting block. In the fullness of time, and in spite of many efforts to sweep the issue under some thick five-ring rug, the IOC had to admit to the general public—a population now rather hostile to all things internet and AI—that of all those participating in the Literary Olympics, only one had both finished the required work and not cheated through the use of optically abetted AI. And that one had insulted the Olympic Movement in the offered essay. So much for the Literary Olympics.

After this last effort at extending the Olympic brand to support a movement beyond the official sports events, the IOC declared that it would no longer endorse or allow "Olympic" anything, other than lending its brand to corporate sponsors. Since trademark protections extending up to the very boarder of private mentation have become law in every participating nation, even ordinary citizens might fear even *pronouncing* the word "Olympic" or its cognates without written IOC approval. The ever-present threat of a well-funded lawsuit, however dubious its likelihood of legal success, cows most prospective proposers of alternate Olympics somewhere prior to mentioning it to friends over drinks. But certain social outlaws not only disdained such systematic bullying, but boldly bid the IOC to try its luck against them. Publicity trumps legality to the populists who live and die by the political pose and the grand gesture.

In this line, consider the Radical Olympiad. An activist opposition to the real Games and its social cost, these contests pitted protest groups against each other in objecting to the Olympics. At first, opponents only made a pretense of contention, while actually engaging in a joint effort to attract attention in a media soaked world. The Whole Earth Defense League announced medals under categories for Most Publicity Generated Without Fatalities, Most Creative Use of Spray Paint, Most Novel Use of Handcuffs, Clearest Manifestos, and Best Theoretical Deployment of Anti-Capitalist Nomenclature.

Individuals would stage creative protests and reveal their deeds afterwards as if actually seeking a medal. Sometimes, embarrassingly, the public failed to notice a protest act had occurred until the protestors released a revelation to the press. When Janice Helia made her vandalism debut splashing paint on works held by the Tate Modern, no one noticed until the frustrated Whole Earth Defense League Group Wing One announced the fact in a four page communique. Even then they had to shorten the communique to three lines before anyone read it. And in the aftermath of the realization that vandals had splashed paint over fourteen post-modern works, the Tate curatorial staff just published think pieces on the dynamic use of color in protest art. Lesson learned: only vandalize Old Masters.

So not even a bronze medal for Janice Helia and the WEDL GW1 for the first event. But after gaining some computer hacking skills, Helia and other members of the WEDL caught a wave and made a splash. They crashed the 2068 Games website "Play Along with the Athletes" feature, leading couch-coaches calling shots not to an aggregating AI "assistant coach" bypassing the team staff to direct basketball play, but rather to a carbon calculator rendering a real time estimate of the mean temperature rise created by AI play calling. To the bitter tears of the terrorists, the folks at home took to the new game and worked to maximize national scores in atmospheric heating. But the IOC noticed the downing of their viewer engagement program and responded with condemnations on the major media platforms. A protest gold for the WEDL GW1 at last. They managed matching events at each Olympiad thereafter.

Such success invites competition. In the celebratory atmosphere following the publicity victory at the Kuala Lumpur Games, a manifesto appeared at literary cafés all over Europe. It read:

"The master's tools will never dismantle the master's house. The custodian of carbon will never tremble at the trivial terror of service interruption, download delays, error notifications, and the gentle digital gust of warm wind blown through the open window of the world warmers in their air-conditioned wonderland. The Whole Earth Defense League loafs in the lounge of comfort protest and bright colored spray paint. Reject their anti-street street theater. We show the way past their petty pretense. We drape the world darkly. We are the depression that swallows the hope of carbon commerce. We will snatch the gold medal from the feeble hands of the WEDL. (Who takes seriously an award awarded to oneself?) We will hold the protest gold. And paint it black. We are Red Asphalt Alert."

The notice ended with a postscript: "We kidnapped a panda."

And in fact, the world's last male panda had been rerouted during air transport to no one knew where. A daring daylight robbery of a normally too slow to bother catching creature. The world expressed its outrage by a billion AI searches: "What is Red Asphalt Alert?" "What is a panda?" "How much is a panda worth?" "How can I fight Red Asphalt Alert?" "How can I join Red Asphalt Alert?" "Red Asphalt Alert panda porn find now." The RAA's midair heist inspired the world's most extensive AI search craze and thereby turned five million square miles of earth's surface into desert, while upping the ante for competitive protest.

The Whole Earth Defense League spent the next four years chaining members to IOC executive committee host hotels, splashing urine on underpaid qualifying event security guards, and overpainting Olympic themed public statuary in RAA-aesthetics defying rainbow colors. Still, the fashion for goth-themed red and black under-exclaimed manifesto posting continued. The WEDL grew desperate enough to steal zoo animals, but only took two goats from a petting zoo. Not much of a liberation, but in their defense all the best zoo animals had "gone completely digital" by 2070. The last panda outside of terrorist captivity died at the Beijing Zoo, all alone, enjoying the company of neither another panda nor any other animal larger than the last lemur. The world cried. Petitions went up online to "save Pandy the last Panda." Janice Helia wrote an open letter to Red Asphalt Alert saying: "We of the Whole Earth Defense League implore you to free Pandy! Do this as a gesture to show the world that we who defend it (all of it!) prize Earth's remaining safely secured wildlife! Win a gold in animal kindness and show the Olympic Movement that we, the people of protest, are better than they are! Do it for the Movement! (Ours, not theirs.)"

Red Asphalt Alert responded with a letter to a German political journal; the letter contained their latest communique—and a panda's severed finger. The message read: "End the bright pity show that showers the world in faux tears that fall upon the new deserts and adds to the monsoon deluge. Why pity the poor panda, bereft of conspecifics and bulging with expensive food? It eats *so* much. Like the capitalist pigs that scoff down the food of the world (yes, the whole world) and crap in every corner of every room until their keepers, the displaced digital programming proletariat, can't sleep at night for the smell. No pity for pandas. Not until the IOC cancels the Games. Until *they* cancel the Games—or *we* do."

During the New Delhi Olympiad, the Whole Earth Defense League and Red Asphalt Alert battled each other in a series of internet disruptions aimed at the IOC and the Games scheduled for 2072. World sport could hardly keep up with the hack attacks. The IOC website scarcely endured more than a day at a time. This might have presaged something. But since the velocity of digital disruption had so increased in the world at large, no one took the spike in Olympic-aimed code corruption as a warning of anything impending. And perhaps it wasn't. No one today credits Red Asphalt Alert's claims of hacking the world to digital death. No one thinks that the WEDL broke the world wide web. The progress of events allows many interpretations. But it must be said that the collapse of internet communications lent itself to café postings by radicals given to Old Anarchism graphic collage and wall-pasted manifestos. That both groups garnered worldwide disdain for claiming origination of "descended darkness" (RAA) or "liberation of hope for a New Green World" (the WEDL) just showed how much more they valued one-upping the competition over currying favor with the masses. Truly, an Other Olympic Games.

Finally, consider one more Alternate Olympics. This one an Olympic protest within the Olympics. An apple in the worm. (Apples were a commercially grown fruit popular until the Great Blight—worms I presume you know.) Zoe Sallis, representing the International Women's Athletics Union, announced at a press conference that her group would lead a "drug strike" against the IOC decision to allow unlimited PED use at the Paris Games. She had enlisted thirteen countries, many in the New Nations, to send women's teams that would compete and qualify under the Ulaanbaatar drug testing protocol. Sallis declared that these totally tested women would play clean and thereby challenge the IOC to recognize the greater legitimacy, and humanity, of regulated competition.

When informed, Benito Jax smiled and declared, "Good. They will lose badly."

The Torched Relay

A Tradition Stamped in Gory; Route of Ruin; Touched by a Torch.

The Olympic Movement offers no spectacle more inclusive than the torch relay. It travels through many countries, requires no tickets, includes mostly non-athletes, and passes its totem object from hand to hand with only mild anxiety that any such transfer might extinguish The Light of The Olympic Spirit Saving the World For Humanity. It's a shame that so egalitarian a tradition traces its origins to the Nazis. The IOC officially states that the torch relay "as we know it" began in 1952—but that claim represents how the IOC would *like for us* to know it. The relay first ran in 1936 from Olympia to Berlin. Adolph Hitler apparently had in mind some sort of Aryan Marathon linking the glory that was Greece (ancient version) to the ambition that was Germany (pre-Götterdämmerung version). In the cold light of history, the 1936 Olympiad torch relay more or less traced a reverse of the soon to come German conquest of Eastern Europe. Call it a torchlight reconnaissance mission.

In spite of such ominous origins, the torch relay returned for the next Olympic Games held in 1948. Europe expedited sweeping up the rubble from its last effort at *war as a substitute for sport*, and everyone put on their friendly faces, setting aside thoughts of who-killed-who to enjoy a long jog lugging a burning stick. The route of the relay carefully avoided any part of Germany lest some unreconstructed traditionalist be heard to mutter a version of "See! Hitler had *some* good ideas". The question of routes continued to plague the IOC Executive Committee in the planning for the Paris Games of 2084.

Benito Jax, "Then we agree on a vision of world scope. Ignited at Olympia, traveling to Athens, then on to Ankara—"

Jang Zhao, "The wrong direction..."

Ahmed bin Abdullah, "We settled that..."

Benito Jax, "And from Ankara onward to encompass the world."

Jang Zhao, "We cannot just wave our hands at a map and say *onward*. We need to arrange a definite route. One that avoids conflict zones."

Joseph Kabwe, "Could we not just get the runners started and trust their survival instincts? Let the route emerge in light of arising conditions."

Jang Zhao, "Absurd."

Manvik Gupta, "It must pass through New Delhi, to showcase the return of algorithmic existence."

Ahmed bin Abdullah, "If the committee indulges one favorite, then we must do so for everyone, and the torch parade must pass through Riyad."

Jang Zhao, "We don't have enough cool-suits to supply the runners, much less the press, in a trip through your uninhabitable oil reserve. And the thought that the torch might pass through India, through three civil wars and a border dispute—"

Manvik Gupta, "Attack! Border attack! China will not dictate routes."

Benito Jax, "Please. Please. We do need to avoid conflict zones. Perhaps a northern route? Through Russia?"

Ahmed bin Abdullah, "Germany will object."

Jang Zhao, "It might cause a war. And we must not route through Germany in spite of its pleas as the *fatherland of the torch relay.*"

Benito Jax, "Admittedly, too soon."

Joseph Kabwe, "Perhaps skirting the boarders of central Asia? Russia has yet to take some of those countries, correct?"

Manvik Gupta, "So many refugees on the move. Do we want TV images of happy relay runners waving to great waves of scruffy people hauling their clothes on their backs, begging for water?"

Joseph Kabwe, "If we have water stations along the route? Handing out six-ounce plastic bottles of cooled water?"

Jang Zhao, "That will attract them!"

Ahmed bin Abdullah, "Like flies to a camel turd."

Benito Jax, "Let's strike that last remark from the record."

Joseph Kabwe, "But we can show the IOC handing out six-ounce plastic water bottles to everyone around the relay runners. Think of the positive publicity."

Jang Zhao, "Quit insisting on the bottle size, we all know you own the concession."

Manvik Gupta, "I suggest we take a straight shot north from Ankara, through central Europe—neutral countries only—"

Jang Zhao, "Europe still has those?"

Benito Jax, "The Republic of West Poland."

Ahmed bin Abdullah, "We ignore the newspaper reports?"

Manvik Gupta, "The relay skirts around Russo-Sweden to Norway..."

Jang Zhao, "But this won't happen for another eight months. What if it's Russo-Norway by then?"

Manvik Gupta, "...To the arctic. Sled dogs."

Jang Zhao, "They'll drown."

Manvik Gupta, "On a ship. The huskies can be driven on treadmills. A tribute to the human spirit."

Joseph Kabwe, "We do have a precedent."

Ahmed bin Abdullah, "May Allah curse you and your wives and children to the eighth generation."

Benito Jax, "Let's have that last comment stricken from the record."

Jang Zhao, "How does this plan encompass the whole world?"

Manvik Gupta, "Back down to Japan. Then to China."

Jang Zhao, "China first. We will not follow Japan."

Manvik Gupta, "Back down to China. Then to Japan."

Jang Zhao, "Why Japan at all? Japan is a traditional possession of China since the time of Kublai Khan. A separate torch journey to Japan would be redundant."

Manvik Gupta, "Then to Vietnam, Laos, and Cambodia."

Jang Zhao, "Wars, wars, and more wars. Don't you follow current events?"

Ahmed bin Abdullah, "Those countries are not at war."

Jang Zhao, "What date is it? Oh. Well, still, I would not advise planning routes through those countries. Or if we do, we should have a full contingency route at the ready. Very ready."

Manvik Gupta, "And Australia? Is it safe to plan the relay through Australia?"

Jang Zhao, "Of course. Given the date of the Paris Games."

Manvik Gupta, "Then on to South America."

Joseph Kabwe, "You skipped all of Africa."

Manvik Gupta, "After a stop at Cape Town."

Ahmed bin Abdullah, "It is a great deal of water for a relay."

Manvik Gupta, "Scuba divers. Waterproof flame. We've discussed this."

Benito Jax, "Can we find countries in South America peaceful enough for our plans?"

Ahmed bin Abdullah, "How would we get through Central America, avoiding refugees and wars?"

Manvik Gupta, "Scuba divers. Through the Gulf of Mexico."

Jang Zhao, "It will take quite a bit of diplomacy to navigate the North American nations. And so many of them."

Manvik Gupta, "Hot air balloon. Perhaps holding a treadmill?"

Benito Jax, "Yes. I can picture it—adorned with the five Olympic rings."

Manvik Gupta, "Then by paddleboat to London."

Jang Zhao, "One word: hurricane."

Manvik Gupta, "By submarine to London."

Benito Jax, "Might that not suggest something too martial?"

Ahmed bin Abdullah, "We should be safe there. Submarines have increasingly taken up the task of commercial cargo transport."

Jang Zhao, "Thanks to hurricanes."

Manvik Gupta, "From London to the Iberian Peninsula."

Jang Zhao, "Have you gone insane?"

Ahmed bin Abdullah, "Do you want to start another Iberian war?"

Joseph Kabwe, "Think of the committee meetings! The endless hearings!"

Manvik Gupta, "Straight across the channel to Normandy. Skipping Iberia entirely."

Benito Jax, "That would require French overtures to the Republic of Normandy. But then perhaps that might be just the thing to heal fresh wounds."

Ahmed bin Abdullah, "Then we snub Germany? In deference to Russia?"

Benito Jax, "The Germans will understand."

Thus did Benito Jax and the IOC Executive Committee navigate natural and diplomatic obstacles to a relay run by thousands, followed by tens of thousands, broadcast to hundreds of thousands, to the joy of millions. Best of all, the IOC arranged to finance most of it from the tax dollars of participating countries and, for the balance, a single sponsor: Geodynamic Strategic Solutions—*making new worlds at home and off-planet. GSS—saving the system, one planet at a time*—had pioneered the strategic imposition of space-based geoengineering and embraced the "whole world" aspect of

Benito Jax's vision for the torch relay. GSS—*tested on Mars and ready for Earth*—had already contracted with China for one planet-cooling scheme and with the European Union for another. Skeptics had expressed doubts of course.

"The two plans conflict!"

"Fantasy science."

"What right do they have to do this?"

"Proprietary information on geoengineering!?!"

All nay-saying nonsense. How could any educated person doubt that the informal system of planetary management that led to pleas for geoengineering could possibly fail to produce the necessary subtleties required for finetuned climate calibration? How could the combination of capitalism and nationalism allegedly responsible for wayward weather possibly *compound* rather than *correct* economic externalities and political impotence? GSS—*bold solutions for trying times*—had a market capitalization upwards of the GDP of South America and owned the labor and IP rights of every university science faculty member on three continents. Not to mention its legal retainers for every law firm in Europe and Asia. Any company that could achieve that level of financing and IP/leg-rep ownership in just its first six months of existence, under the leadership of a 19-year-old weaned on sci-fi fan fiction, deserved the trust of humanity in managing our continuing planetary habitation. No one could afford not to trust GSS—*a visionary company founded on a tradition of trust.*

So, the torch relay had its sponsor, its route, its diplomatic permissions, its press entourage, its expensively contracted six-ounce water bottles, and its mass audience of hand-wavers waiting to wave at the passing eternal flame, burning from its metal cudgel, flowing from its carefully calculated allotment of lighter fluid. But torches don't grow on trees. Not for centuries now. They must be designed. Each torch of every Olympiad has, in spite of the basic logic of setting fire to one end of a stick, a design carefully rendered to express some particular message, image, or icon of the city of that year's Games. Curved, bent, five-spouted, or Grecian classic, a torch must symbolize its Games—and struggle mightily not to symbolize something else.

Jang Zhao, "An Olympic sex aid for women?"

Van der Ghent, "A torch. The rounded tip means to suggest the new BMX mountain."

Joseph Kabwe, "So that's a flame coming out of the small hole at the top, not...uh..."

Van der Ghent, "A flame."

Manvik Gupta, "Now I'm a little disappointed."

Not only must one design a suitably unsuggestive torch, but that torch must find congress with a cauldron, itself ready to be enflamed but not too suggestive of awaiting inseminating fluid.

Jang Zhao, "Why does the cauldron looks so...elongated?

Van der Ghent, "Dictated by the stadium space provided."

Jang Zhao, "But it looks...and the curving lip?"

Van der Ghent, "Fluid containment."

Jang Zhao, "That makes it worse."

Van der Ghent, "It will erupt in multi-colored flames every twenty minutes."

Ahmed bin Abdullah, "The *cauldron* will erupt? Not the torch?"

Van der Ghent, "The cauldron. Thus the lip. And the depth. For the fluid."

Joseph Kabwe, "Such a tiny torch for so much cauldron."

The torch relay not only introduces the Olympiad to the global public, it also represents the first encounter between the world press and that year's Games. Prior to 2084, the IOC had to negotiate a complex tangle of TV rights agreements with television networks all over the world. This troublesome state of affairs changed with the Negotiated Broadcast Consortium's monopolization of world television ("Competition is for losers"—Peter Thiel, speaking for all of capitalism). While NBC's monopoly position reduced IOC bargaining power, its guarantee of blanket coverage assured maximum brand exposure. Not only that, but single-source-emission allowed full IOC image management, insuring a pleasantly purchase-promoting atmosphere during the experience. It only remained to coach the actual broadcast personalities in the necessary subtleties. In lieu of many such discussions, I will relate that between Benito Jax and the two premier sports broadcast personalities, Andrew Brightman and Dorthey Lament.

Benito Jax spoke as the two journalists flipped through a thick binder, "These are just a few suggestions of words and phrases to avoid. So as not to distract the viewer at home from the activity on the field. Along with a few words and phrases you might work into your commentary from time to time. Things you might say and things you may not say."

Dorthey Lament, "I understand avoiding the word *flood*, and I can't imagine being tempted to say *deluge*, but all these...including *slippery*?"

Andrew Brightman, "I'm all on board. We can use *fall-promoting* there. Keep heads in the broadcast, not wandering all over hell-and-gone."

Dorthey Lament, "*Wet*? We can't say *wet*?"

Benito Jax, "Not without some very careful contextualization."

Dorthey Lament, "But we cover swimming events."

Andrew Brightman, "I know: *damp*. So: *Those hard bodies exited the damp water beaded with dampness covering their taunt muscles.*"

Dorthy Lament, "But what if it rains?"

Benito Jax, "Contextualize rain very carefully. Not too welcoming; not too dismayed."

Andrew Brightman, "*The runner's shorts cling tight to his hardened thighs in the welcomely light rain.*"

Benito Jax, "That would do."

Dorthy Lament, "*Wind*? We can't mention the wind? How do we introduce the sailing events?"

Benito Jax, "It's all in how you describe the wind."

Andrew Brightman, "*A stiff wind blows up their sails. Buffeting the manly athletes with sheets of welcome liquid. The men work the ropes blown and buffeted, their clothes barely on their bodies as they man the sails, prow facing wave upon wave of...*"

Dorthy Lament, "*Heat*? *Hot*? How can we neutralize these? Will the athletes never look hot?"

Andrew Brightman, "We could limit ourselves to metaphorical uses. For instance, when an athlete takes off a shirt and we and the audience notices his sweat-drenched torso, we say—"

Dorthy Lament, "How do we mention injuries? The list of off-limit terms seems designed to prohibit any talk of injury."

Benito Jax, "We had far too much talk of that in 2080. It turned off sponsors."

Dorthy Lament, "Athletes will get injured."

Andrew Brightman, "*Look there Dorthy, his body lying there writhing on the ground, clutching his groin*—and you come in with: *is it agony or is it ecstasy?*"

Dorthy Lament hides her eyes behind her hand and reads from the binder, "What is a *CotRatt*? Why must I mention it so often?"

Benito Jax, "I want to stress that when interviewing the athletes you should seek out the human story behind the Olympian..."

Dorthy Lament, "Their background and history..."

Benito Jax, "Perhaps not that. They are young. Their backgrounds don't go very far back."

Dorthy Lament, "Their families..."

Benito Jax, "Be careful there, some can't necessarily say where all their family members are right now. Problematic histories."

Dorthy Lament, "The support they've received from their countries..."

Benito Jax, "Focus on sponsors. From the approved list only."

Andrew Brightman, "We shouldn't sell short a focus on their bodies. Their impressive physiques. Their glow of sensual health. Some of them are quite good looking."

Benito Jax, "We have done a lot of work on that. Grooming the right looking athletes, advising on appearance awareness—since digital let us down. Before New Delhi athletes knew how to manage their beauty elements. Now the IOC must employ specialists to help them. Physical appearance works well with the at-home audience. Frankly, our biggest spenders—our sponsorship partners' *go-get* group—are not the most toned and fit people."

Andrew Brightman, "Bunch of tubbies. I work out twice a day."

Benito Jax, "We call them relax-fit people. We hope that CotRatt will get them off the couch and into the Games. We have research backing up that expectation."

Dorthy Lament, "So CotRatt is..."

Benito Jax, "An activity mascot."

Dorthy Lament, "A rat that—"

Benito Jax, "Plays all sports. Works out regularly. Like Mr. Brightman here..."

The two men smile in mutual admiration.

Dorthy Lament, "So we just talk to the athletes about their training regimens?"

Benito Jax frowned, "Careful there. We don't want to shame our viewers. Try to contextualize their training in terms of their superhuman dedication and genetically appropriate inheritance. But be careful about talking about inherited genes. Maybe focus on gene enhancement. The coming thing. We expect big things there by way of future sponsorships. So that's something you might touch on. Though let's not get all the way to specific treatments and enhancements. We don't want to give too much away for free."

Dorthy Lament, "So just stay on superhuman dedication."

Benito Jax, "Let's not dwell on that. See page 203. We don't want to encourage accusations of competitive obsession. Bring out tales of a work ethic—leavened by a playful disregard at winning or losing—dedicated to winning—but not at all costs. Don't even mention costs."

Andrew Brightman, "And their bodies *are* very hard."

Benito Jax, "Indeed."

After many such briefings, the media coached on covering the contests, the torch relay began. Ordinary people and celebrity runners handed off the flaming phallus, in front of the accompanying press, to the joy of well-wishers or the bafflement of refugees lured to the route by oversized promises of undersized water bottles. Dogging their every step: the International Women's Athletics Union. Zoe Sallis' rebels and their followers ran the route with the authorized relay, bearing bouquets in lieu of a torch and explaining their objections to anyone who would listen. Sometimes suffering arrest from local authorities and often enduring spital from happy crowds made hostile by these rainy-day mood-busting prophets of doom. Or as Benito Jax called the Sallis group: "Publicity thieves!"

As the torch crossed into Europe, protests mounted. Not just the dauntless women of the IWAU, but the Ultimate Frisbee Anti-Olympic Operations Unit, hurling plastic disks at the torch runners to the chagrin of security and doing the same into the mobs of onlookers to the delight of the crowd. The Whole Earth Defense League staged only peaceful protests along the route, as agreed, but were in their turn protested by masked members of its Leek Green Faction, promising "decisive action" at the Games. Red Asphalt Alert sent no members to interfere with the relay, but their posters loomed, ubiquitous, as the runners passed through the narrow streets of picturesque villages. Benito Jax admired their pre-positioning organizational prowess and wondered who did their art design.

Eventually the relay crashed into the Parisian security line, and its runners had to pass through multiple ID checks and pat downs. They gamely waved at the cheering audience while weapon-detecting dogs sniffed every crotch. Inside the city itself the population proved mixed in their enthusiasm. Some cheered the sight of the torch, but huge mobs charged the running line under the banner of Citizens United Against the Games and with the backing of every union in France. They swept up event security in their wave and crashed against armored personnel carriers lining the route. The relay continued to the Olympic stadium, smiling runners waving to baton-swinging soldiers pummeling protestors. The torch progressed into the Olympic Stadium.

Then an Olympic miracle occurred. The confused gathering of disappointed observers and the angry mob of Olympic objectors both collectively shrugged their shoulders at the futility of it all. The discount ticket stands opened up, and as one, those wanting to turn away from the world, and those wanting to turn away the Games, charged the ticket stands to secure a place to see the most famous spectacle on earth.

Paris 2084; I was there!

Libation to the Mourning God

The Holy Ground of Sport; The Politics of the Posterior; An Oration Opposed; A Moment of Elation, Stolen.

The opening ceremonies of the Olympic Games pours the dementing wine of sport celebration over the attending audience in the form of bright lights, low lethality lasers, dubious oaths, orchestral overscoring, and an ever increasing level of ritual, all sanctioned by Olympic tradition and the ever swelling need to numb audience awareness of—well, just call it the *outside*—in favor of the joyful attention to the Holy Ground of Sport. The IOC leaves none of this to chance, in spite of chance's constant insistence on breaking through. Benito Jax and the Executive Committee contracted the ceremonies to the Virgil Geffen Narrative Interventions Visual Visioning Production Group (*Let our storytellers tell your story, your way— our way*). In this important case, Virgil Geffen led the effort himself. Geffen brought to the Olympic ceremonies the same vision of visions he had previously brought to such surely still classic films *as Mega Man: Rain of Vengeance IV*, *Mega Man: Rain of Vengeance VII*, and *Mega Man Meets Cute: Giga Girl's Reign of Vengeance.* The IOC politely overlooked some of his post-Purge failures such as *Pixel Dixel; Post Pixel Puppet Adventures*, and either forgave or embraced his dubious documentary, *Corporate Persons Are the Best Persons; A Study in Innocence.* The IOC chose Geffen principally for his much admired public spectacles for organizations only slightly less imposing than the IOC itself, such as *The United Nations Climate Goal Prizes; Celebration on Ice*, and the *Amazon Available Now as Mail-in Orders International Christmas Pageant.*

Geffen and his team of over 1000 pixel-to-people dream managers arranged an array of celebratory stunts worthy of Olympic production history. Not easy considering prior excesses. The IOC had made many specific requests: fewer revving engines than at Kuala Lumpur (fume issues in the stadium), less reliance on algorithmic face-focused audience pleasure assessment in light of the New Delhi identity-theft events (thankfully unpublicized due to digital downfall), no inclusions of heritage objects during the opening or closing ceremonies (pyramid memories die hard in spite of sea-lift distractions), and very much do not restage an Ulaanbaatar inspired "Grand History of Human Combat" pageant. Favor goofy over gruesome and tenderness over takedowns; maudlin melodrama rather than Grand Guignol. Include CotRatt.

As dictated by long tradition, the ceremonies began with the parade of dignitaries. Diplomats, dictators, special sponsors, honored former athletes, protest leaders allowed a bit of opening ceremony exposure, and to ever expanding musical accompaniment—even if not audience understanding—the members of the IOC Executive Committee. Lastly the President of France and his boss, Benito Jax, head of the IOC. The honored guests walked up the stairs to the dignitary stadium box. They fussed, fumed and occasionally man-handled each other for the prime seats—in spite of months of negotiation and clearly printed name tags—until, crowd growing fidgety at the sixtieth reprise of Pomp and Circumstance—they found or were thrust into their proper places, waving at the mass audience in attendance and at the masses of couch or cot sitting home ("home") viewers.

Benito Jax had provided Janice Helia, lead organizer of the Whole Earth Defense League, a seat not far from his own in the IOC President's box. She sat there in a funk, garbed in a *STOP THE OLYMPICS; TURN OFF YOUR TV NOW!* t-shirt. She ate dispiritedly from a bag of popcorn. The Executive Committee had also provided seating—not in the box of dignitaries—for another opponent. Zoe Sallis sat behind a pillar, unseen by the TV cameras. The pillars had no support nor aesthetic function; the architect designed them merely as tools of humiliation. Penalty boxes for protest leaders; timeouts for the terror adjacent. Zoe Sallis displayed no dismay. She ate no popcorn. She talked on a walkie-talkie, as old school (and un-hackable) a technology as those she demanded for women athletics.

Finally, entries effected, status established, and with the Marseillaise still ringing in every ear (stadium volume a bit too loud), the athletes began their parade, marching behind national flags. One can do no better than to transcribe portions of the official broadcast.

Andrew Brightman, "Here they come, no longer alphabetically by nation, nor according to last year's tradition in order of contributions to the Olympic Movement, but in a carefully randomized order..."

Dorthy Lament, "Important point, Andrew. The IOC requests that we clarify to all the world that each nation appears in a perfectly random order..."

Andrew, "Except for Greece, which as always, comes first."

Dorthy, "They do...but otherwise the order in no way indicates, suggests, signals, proposes, implies—"

Andrew, "Of course Greece sent no athletes to these Games..."

Dorthy, "No they did not...proposes, implies, denotes—"

Andrew, "It's current civil war probably makes that impossible right now. But what spirit to send their flag out like this. One of their flags."

Dorthy, "Yes. In no way denotes, designates, expresses, conveys or commends any political, social, demographic, linguistic, geographic—"

Andrew, "And the fellow carrying the flag—he has his work cut out for him."

Dorthy, "Yes, geographic, geopolitical, diplomatic—"

Andrew, "Strapping fellow. Big shoulders."

Dorthy, "...environmental, topological, or climatological statement by the International Olympic Committee, the Paris Olympic Organizing Committee—"

Andrew, "Here comes Albania. Look at them march!"

Dorthy, "...the City of Paris, the Collective Association of Sporting Associations—"

Andrew, "And here we see New Zealand, proof of just what we've been saying about the order of nations."

Dorthy, "...the World Sports Marketing Authority, or any of the Sponsors of these Olympic Games."

Andrew, "So glad you mentioned that, Dorthy."

Dorthy, "Had to be said."

Andrew, "Now we see England's contingent. Bulging out of their suits. This must be one of the finest looking group of men we've ever seen at the Games."

Dorthy, "Women also—"

Andrew, "And also bulging! Except for the women representing the Republic of Greater Los Angeles. Those must be some of the Sallis Sisters.

Rather disappointing to look at. Also marching backwards. No mean feat that. Score one for the Sallis Girls."

Dorthy, "As some of our viewers may know, there is no such thing as Sallis Sisters or Sallis Girls and all the women competing in the Olympics respect and prize the Olympic Movement as defined, inspired, and led by the International Olympic Comm—"

Andrew, "Wow! Look at those Germans! They are pumped! Physically and emotionally. And who could blame them? They entered the Olympic Stadium ahead of the Russian team."

Dorthy, "Again, as per the broadcast rules, each nation appears in a perfectly random order that in no way indicates, suggests, signals, proposes—"

Andrew, "Look at the size of those German men! This will be a very exciting Games."

Dorthy, "...proposes, implies, denotes, designates, expresses—"

Andrew, "Now we see some of the New Nations. Much punier than the established countries. Smaller drug budgets?"

Dorthy, "...conveys or commends any political, social, demographic, linguistic, geographic, geopolitical, diplomatic—"

Andrew, "The women of the Tunisian Republic of Refugees in Iberia look so weak."

Dorthy, "...environmental, topological—"

Andrew, "They must be Sallis Sisters as well."

Dorthy, "Repeating that there is no such group and that all women competing in the Olympics respect and prize the Olympic Movement as defined, inspired, and led by the International Olympic Committee, and continuing: topological or climatological statement by the International Olympic Committee, the Paris Olympic Organizing Committee, the City of Paris —"

Andrew, "I think the Czech team may have some Sallis Girls on it too, from the look of them."

Dorthy, "Jesus! No, sorry...the Collective Association of Sporting Associations, the World Sports Marketing Authority, or any of the Sponsors of these Olympic Games. Further, there are no Sallis Girls or Sallis Sisters. Rather, as stated in our official broadcast guidelines, Andrew, all the women competing in the Olympics respect and prize the Olympic Movement as defined, inspired, and led by the International Olympic Committee—"

Andrew, "At last here come the Russian athletes! Huge people! And they look understandably upset at being assigned such a late entry. And behind the Germans as well."

Dorthy, "Are you out of your fucking mind?!? Sorry. Sorry. Just to remind you and the viewers, *Andrew*, each nation appears in a perfectly random order that in no way indicates, suggests, signals, proposes, implies, denotes, designates, expresses, conveys—"

Andrew, "No Sallis Sisters among the Russians. Those women look more jacked than the men. And what men they are!"

And so on for the next three hours of the opening ceremonies parade of nations.

No doubt as sweet relief to those not enamored of sport adjacent military processions, the ceremony—eventually—moved on to the next phase of Olympic ritual. To possible disappointment, this turned out to be the official speeches. After a few brief words from the President of France, reading the IOC approved opening statement, Benito Jax stood to give his much anticipated opening address. The many monitors stationed about the stadium displayed him as his words flashed across the pixel palace that made up the dome. The audience in attendance listened without saying a word—what choice did they have given the heightened volume? And who would not want to hear, recall, and record the—further—witness to glory that only a Benito Jax could deliver? Before the many millions, some say billions, watching the opening ceremonies, Benito Jax began his brief remarks.

An hour and fifteen minutes later he summed up thusly: "And so with patience and a trained eye, we see clearly that we do not live in a world of a setting sun, but of a rising sun. A sun not disappearing down into darkness but rising over the horizon to shine all the more. As our Greek forbears would say, we here make tribute to not an evening god, but to a morning god. A morning god to light the human future. A morning god to celebrate human achievement. A morning god that glories in our success. Success in commerce, success in culture, success in politics, and yes, a morning god that glories in our success in sport. And to that Morning God I commend and dedicate these Games. Release the doves!"

Doves. Their release at the opening ceremonies a long and fraught tradition. The post-game trauma review almost always leads to suggestions that this custom be discontinued. But still, they rise.

The first hint of dove disaster occurred at the 1988 Olympic Games. The doves—eternal symbol of peace whose frequency of release has never faltered in the face of continual war—set off from their gilded cages on their iconic flight, as usual, after the march of nations, having endured the august speeches, and before the lighting of the Olympic flame. They must have tired easily, for many came to rest on the edges of the overly inviting Olympic cauldron. The torch bearer set off the great cauldron flame, secure in the knowledge that even if doves cry, they would also fly—in case of fire. But no, most chose Olympic immolation. Not as a protest against the Games insists the IOC (on those rare occasions when it must acknowledge dove death). Doves don't protest; they just die meaningless, painful deaths in apparent ignorance that heat can hurt them.

The dove deaths that opened the Seoul Games of '88 led to dove release evasion rather than outright disestablishment. Symbolic substitutes whose variation challenged the imagination of generations of celebration planners. Traditionalists never tired of demanding real doves and real peace. One or the other, at least. Eventually, the IOC hired dove wranglers to train the pacifistic passerines against any inclination to fly into the light. To the cracking of whips, doves devoted themselves to self-preservation. Confident again that the creatures would avoid ignition, dove release crept back into the ceremony. Still cursed.

Ways doves die: In Kuala Lumpur '68 they died of fumes as the full-fuel-truck-rally-rebirth auto competitors revved their engines at top throttle (sixteen humans also died of asphyxiation in the mishap—but these generated less media attention than the birds gasping on the ground in front of the gunning engines). At New Delhi '72 (and not as a harbinger of anything, the IOC contends), forty-two doves—one for each still acknowledged Olympic Games—took flight following the President of India's speech of welcome, only to be shot down by the surprisingly lethal ceremonial laser array. Simple heat exhaustion killed every dove let loose at Cairo '72; not one made the opening at the dome's top. Taking no chances at Ulaanbaatar 2080, the IOC let loose over two hundred doves in hopes of at least some making it to clear sky. If only the IOC had not insisted that the skeet shooters parade into place armed and ammoed; to the chagrin of the IOC and to the credit of the Olympic marksmen, not one dove cleared the stadium.

The other members of the IOC Executive Committee had implored Benito Jax not to release doves at the Paris '84 Games. Jax insisted that "in these difficult days, people need signs of hope." Everyone agreed on that, that very sentiment animated their argument that the Olympic ritual should avoid entirely any dove attendance at the Games. But Benito Jax had a master plan. He enlisted pharmacological experts to genetically engineer "super-doves" that could withstand heat and fumes, avoid flames and lights, and rise faster, higher, stronger. (The IOC had banned ballistics at the opening ceremony.) Nothing could stop these muscled-up paragons of peace. They could soar, and if necessary kill, like eagles.

So at the moment that Benito Jax commanded the release of the doves, he did so with great confidence, even if the crowd in the stadium, and the viewers around the world, awaited another dove apocalypse.

Up rose the two hundred mighty genetically enhanced ultra-doves. They beat their drug-strengthened wings and sped like Olympians toward the open vista of the partially parted stadium dome. They circled once in studied grace as a group, showing their superiority to steroidally deprived birds. Then they lifted up toward the sky. The crowd thrilled at this auspice of hope. Benito Jax smiled. An early augury of the greatest Games ever.

Then the bats appeared.

Wild flapping things, blanketing the sky above the open dome. Whirling in patterns chaotic to the human eye and unexpected by the augmented doves. *So* many bats. The audio picked up Benito Jax saying, "Look, bats have come to lead the doves!" No. Not quite. Before someone had the presence of mind to cut the live mic, all of the Olympic Movement heard Benito Jax next say, "My God! It's a mass attack!" Down went the doves. Superior to their avian cousin but no match for Darwin's well-culled garbage heap mega-bats. The athletes fled from the rain of dead doves. The bats landed on the Holy Ground of Sport to pick at the fowl guts. Note for next time: finally and at last: NO DOVES!

With effort, the ground crew drove off the bats and picked up the dove carcasses. The athletes returned to wary attention, and the ceremony came back to life for the giving of the Laurel Award. The IOC handed out this lifetime achievement award to "the person who has made transcending achievements in education, culture, development, and peace through sport and/or the promotion of the Olympic Movement." Past recipients include President For Life Idi Mbawa Amin (Kampala '64) for his invention of "passive crowd control", Orin Peterbilt (Kuala Lumpur '68) for innovative Olympic trademark enforcement, Jino Onejack Osmund (New Delhi '72) for pioneering the field of individuated AI desire detection, Secretary-General Bahal Surono (Cairo '76) for finalizing binding carbon limits under United Nations leadership, and Assma Duhan (Ulaanbaatar '80) for her work in sport safety.

For his work in raising the Olympic Laural Award to such prominence by the selection of these recipients of past awards, the IOC elected to give the Paris 2084 Laural Award to Benito Jax, President of the IOC. Mild applause greeted this announcement. A considerable groan arose as he began his acceptance speech. But to the relief and amusement of the audience, as he transitioned into a brief discussion of his childhood inspirations, a plastic disk struck his forehead. It had sailed in from somewhere in the stadium seats to land with uncanny accuracy against the brow of the astonished laureate. He dodged the next one only to have a third strike the back of his head. The assembled masses clapped. Benito Jax waved in appreciation for their support as seven more disks flew in at him. Now even Benito Jax could tell that the laughter and applause of the crowd owed more to impatience at speeches and appreciation of precision pitching than to sympathy with the tumbling target of the frisbee flood. The sound system boomed with the request that people identify those throwing the "unapproved objects". This led to near universal hand raising and more laughter. The sanity of crowds.

Plastic disks cut short Benito Jax's further elaborations of his gratitude and hurried him to call for the raising of the Olympic flag, the playing of the Olympic anthem, the singing of the Olympic song, the dancing of the Olympic dance and the pronouncing of the Olympic motto in ninety-two languages and thirty-seven dialects. Finally, Jax rose again, to great applause (the crowd hoped for more disk-dodging gymnastics) to lead the Olympic oath of the Paris Games, taken by the assembled athletes, judges, coaches, concessioners, safety officers, press workers, and sponsors. Its five pages of declarations of fealty, acknowledgment of trademark law, and promises of fair play and brand respect do not bear repeating here. Suffice it to say that compliance only broke down when Benito Jax asked the stadium at large to take the Ticket Buyer's Oath. In a display of the wisdom for which the world knows him, the IOC President silently skipped the "Viewer Oath" for those watching at home.

And then, at last, the assembled athletes, honored guests, and paying attendees waited in real wonder at the part of the ceremony most beloved since it first appeared at the Games to the applause of Adolf Hitler: the lighting of the Olympic flame. The eternal flame that would burn, in carefully timed colored jets, throughout the Games—only to be extinguished at the conclusion of the closing ceremony. The very flame—that very flame itself, ontologically identical to the one lit by the sun (a morning sun) at Olympia—that had by now been transported around the world by every conveyance conceived by human ingenuity, that very flame entered the arena carried by the universally celebrated Olympic star, Tooball Beatleback. The sound system even briefly played Tooball's personal anthem (a contractual obligation), and its screens and dome filled with the massively muscled up form of the "New Tooball—Today's Modern Athlete".

He ran up the stairs taking them four at a time (an Olympic record, the IOC would later announce) and walked across (some say strutted across) the platform to the Olympic cauldron. He bowed several times to the audience and danced a bit of his trademark Tooball Toe Twister dance to the delight of his fans and the annoyance of the IOC (only reluctantly allowed by the contract). He carefully checked for any doves that might have come to rest on the cauldron lip as instructed to do. (Perhaps a bit passive-aggressive in light of events.) Benito Jax announced that the world should let the Games begin and Tooball lit the cauldron. It roared to life, spewing its colored flames. Music played, the crowd danced, Tooball gave a last salute and descended the stairs. Benito Jax lay on the cusp of announcing the start of the "artistic program" (i.e., the show so long developed by Virgil Geffen and Company that served as the main reason anyone came to or tuned in for the opening ceremony). The athletes left the field to make way for the show and the crowd came to order ready for real entertainment. Then, just as Benito Jax began his last and thankfully brief announcement commencing the program, the unthinkable occurred.

The flame went out.

That flame—the very flame lit at Olympia by the sun and laboriously carried to Paris after global circumnavigation by runner, diver, balloonist, and submariner—extinguished. Never to return—owing to the established metaphysics of flame identity. Just gone forever. The crowd gasped. The IOC President groaned. Engineers quickly ran trouble-shooting protocols on the cauldron that had betrayed the hopes of millions by extinguishing the one and only Olympic flame. The head of maintenance relit the cauldron fluid, but nothing could restore the mood of the Games. They had all seen the flame die. The world had seen it die. Four people had suffered heart attacks during the (first) Benito Jax oration, but this—this flame death before the watching world—something broke inside the human spirit.

Then Geffen's clown company took the field to the melodic accompaniment of a beloved song from that year's hit musical, *Snowball Dancehall*. Smiles alighted on every face; tears dried on the instant. And when four thousand children, dressed as mimes, rushed into the stadium to portray the whole history of Olympic agony and ecstasy, the joyful applause resounding in the arena suppressed and then annihilated every unhappy memory ever entertained in the collective memory of humankind. The Olympic Games, the Olympic Movement, the Olympic Moment, can overcome every adversity. The Olympic epic manifests a movement of moments that define memory and disallow doubt. The Games extinguish existential uncertainty with the faith of its five linked rings. It deserves its place as a testament to the human spirit.

And the mimes: so cute.

Week One: Fire

An After Action Report; A Tech for Every Task; The Weapons of the Weak.

As morning broke the next day, and the track events began, Benito Jax met with his four assistants to assess opening ceremony successes and first week challenges. The parade of nations, meant to suggest martial discipline disciplined by orderly march, had descended into undignified demonstration. Benito Jax's Senior Advisor for Ceremonial summarized the issue, "Russia protests the parade order. The Germans entered ahead of them, *gloating* according to the Russian ambassador, and this he says represents IOC favoritism. A favoritism noted in the official broadcast."

Benito Jax responded gruffly, "If the Executive Committee had taken my suggestion to continue parade order based on financial contributions we would now have sufficient funding to gift away these complaints from the ambassador." The assistants noted by their silence the unrivaled wisdom of Benito Jax. "What do the Russians want?"

"The Russian ambassador suggests we might make some informal adjustments in the gymnastics judging. With an eye toward German embarrassment."

Benito Jax, "Outlandish. It's mere suggestion an attack on the integrity of the Games. Individual nations have always taken responsibility for arranging judging irregularities. That's why judges come from countries. Now Russia wants us to do that too? And why trouble us with this? The Russians have a strong team in the female events, and the Germans don't. They don't need our help. Which would be in any case, unethical and a poor precedent."

"The Russians want a judging anomaly in the *men's* all-round, where the Germans show strength against Russia's weaker team."

Jax's Senior Manager in Charge of Operations interjected, "Russia has sent its best men into the field—the military field."

Benito Jax, "It would look absurd for Russia to beat Germany in the men's events this Olympiad."

The Senior Managerial Aide for Crisis Management continued, "Probably the point, sir. The Russians prefer an obvious breakdown in judging integrity in their favor rather than anything subtle."

Benito Jax, "Sheer power play!"

Deferential silence again. Broken by Benito Jax, "We will add an agenda item to tomorrow morning's event judging standards and practices review. Suggest a bit of judicial generosity in the pummel horse. A little make-up adjustment after the parade broadcast incident. Nothing more. What else?"

The Assisting Senior Director for Protocol raised another parade mishap, "Japan protests that China entered the stadium with a small Japanese flag flying below China's. Vietnam, Laos, and Cambodia joined in the protest."

Benito Jax, "What does China say?"

"China calls the flag incident a rehearsal of the historical inevitability of the Greater Diaoyu Islands' return to rightful Chinese rule. They also deny it happened. They protest the protest of Vietnam, Laos, and Cambodia—which they say should refer to themselves as Little China Grateful Nations. China offers suggestions for their flags."

Benito Jax, "Send a memo to Geffen Productions. Have them digitally edit out the offending flag. Two can play at the denial of facts game. Let China prove *their* record of the opening more official than *ours*. We'll see what people really remember. What else? Why do you all look so bleak?"

With understandable hesitation, the assembled staff informed the IOC President of the night's most nefarious deed. Benito Jax responded to the news with incredulity, "They stole CotRatts?!? All of them?"

"Not all. Most."

Benito Jax raged on, "Don't we have security on the warehouses? How do we promote the Games without the stuffed CotRatts? What will people buy?"

"We think that once the theft becomes known—"

"Known!?! We mean to let people know that CotRatt has been heisted?"

"It will make them popular at last. Rarity will increase desirability."

Benito Jax calmed momentarily at the thought that the world might learn appreciation for CotRatt in suffering its loss, "Who did this? This can't be random, not at those numbers."

Some shuffling of feet, "We did receive a notice. Published in the press as well. It seems that the Leek Green Faction of the Whole Earth Defense League staged the robbery during a security lull caused by the Olympic moment of silence. They claim to hold CotRatt hostage. They have demands."

Benito Jax would entertain no demands, "To hell with them! Terrorists! We will pay millions in taxes but not one penny in tribute. Don't write that down! It's an aphorism, not a policy statement. We will not, of course, pay any taxes. But also, no tribute!"

Jax's Senior Director for Workflow Enforcement moved on to further unpleasantness, "Sir, we have more news on the Olympic flame investigation."

"Never speak of the Olympic flame again!" Benito Jax's eyes teared at the memory, "My beautiful flame. Destroyed and replaced with a feeble imitation. It survived a hundred hardships, endured every indignity—all those protests—and overcame every critic. And all for what? To be snuffed out at its moment of apotheosis. Dead. A dead flame. Now some imposter flame substitutes for it. A flame that traveled nowhere and overcame nothing. Not a true Olympic flame at all. Just an aftereffect of lighter fluid. And so much fuel to burn, just for an imposter flame! We could light Paris for a year with what we burn for this fake Olympic flame! Not counting the cost of its periodic spurts. Lava of glory indeed. Never again speak to me of the Olympic flame. There is no Olympic flame for the Paris Games."

Respectful silence.

Benito Jax erupted again, "Well don't just stand there like stones! What do you have to say about the death of my flame?"

"We have reason to think that someone extinguished it intentionally."

Benito Jax's eyes widened, "It was *murder*? Someone murdered my flame? I knew it! Who did it? How do you know?"

"An hour before the lighting—and unlighting—sorry—of the flame, during your speech—your first speech—a group pasted posters all over Paris and left a message on websites around the world."

"What message?"

The Managing Executive for Executive Oversite unrolled a poster, fringed in blackest black, printed in scarlet. It read:

"We control the fire that lights the world. We determine the destiny of man. We wave the flag of ordered anarchy. As we extinguish the fire that fires the capitalist heart of the unhallowed world in the hallowed arena of the false god of sport, we make a new light to light the fires of the already flaming world. Can you see the time? Can you see what time it is? With the lights extinguished, can you see the time? It is *our* time. We are Red Asphalt Alert. We have only just begun."

Benito Jax shook his head, "Terrorists. And to kill the flame. Had they only kidnapped it, we could have opened negotiations. But just plain murder...It's what I've always said, you just can't reason with some people. No negotiations."

The Games went on. The official ones and no others, by order of the IOC. Parisian children, inspired by the spectacle on television, had taken to the streets at the break of day to play at Olympic sports. They ran sprints and hurdled barricades. They kicked balls into impromptu goals. They did handstands and pretended at stern but buyable judging. IOC lawyers appeared, trailed by the gendarmerie. They claimed trademark infringement. They shut down the unsanctioned public play of Olympic owned sports. Sorry kids. Join a dues-paying league. The lawyers reminded any outraged parent that the Olympics themselves had inspired this rare outbreak of physical play, and thus to defend the children necessarily admitted trademark infringement and guaranteed defeat at trial. The kids dispersed back to their houses to watch the Games on television. As the Mourning God had intended.

The track and field events began, and all eyes turned to TV screens. Not least those who bought tickets and sat in stadium seats. The many pixel screens and the pixel laden dome showered the attendees in a constant stream of carefully curated images that dared one's eyes to look away—at, for instance, the field of play. From most of the stadium seats the players looked like ants randomly milling about for a scent trail. The selections on the screen brought order and clarity to the experience. It showed the celebrated athletes and ignored the no-hopers present just to fill out the images. (Lots of Tooball Beatleback and his Hate Queen Synthetic Rince, as little of any Sallis Sister as the big-board broadcast team could manage.)

The screens offered stories in their montage. A hint of hope in the face of a celebrated athlete warming up. A flicker of doubt on the starting line chased away by an iron will. The ecstatic moment of effort as the starting gun sounds. The drive of limbs down the course as the less celebrated fall by the wayside, defeated by the superior dedication and more advanced pharmacology of the champions. Then the tearful sense of a life vindicated as the soon to be fame-soaked athlete crosses the finish line, framed by the horror-filled visages of the defeated, each now realizing the waste of every hour that led to this moment of ultimate failure. The champion leaping into a coach's arms, draped in a national flag, pumping a fist for the benefit of the cameras, receiving canned oxygen breathed in through a smile of joy. Then a quick camera-glance at the silver medalist living the agony of what might have been, followed by a momentary look at the surprised joy of the bronze medalist who saw, but (barely) avoided, the dreadful fate of fourth place. Finally, the victor again, arms raised in triumph, hustled off the field to make way for the next story of agonistic glory. Eat peanuts, repeat.

The screens at the event (and those at home too) did not just tell stories. They also suggested purchasing options you might have missed. An Alios Vivant Olympic themed luxury item you could bring back to the family waiting for you at home (CotRatts currently unavailable), or a sporting product from Nikadidas, should you feel inspired to begin some sort of athletic program yourself (check local regulations on trademark restrictions), or an Empusa Body Shaping lotion for a "new you" (soon to appear in gene-altering options), and finally consider something from Armed Asylum to protect all your new purchases.

A step down from New Delhi '76, of course. There you could mind-point for instant purchase—adjusting your settings to first, second, or third impulse-to-acquisition depending on how spontaneous you felt. Even the most cautious consumer emptied savings accounts while staring at Nikadidas synthetic running shorts on leaping athletes screened on the stadium dome. This just a beta test for the at home version intended to extend to every image screened of any event or entertainment. So much so recently ruined. Paris '84 technology had not yet caught up to that briefly lost golden age. Even the handheld phone had struggled to regain its grip on the human hand. Bio-digits barely fumbled with digital-digits in 2084. At the Paris Purchase Games, one had to actually hold onto consumer desire long enough to pass a gift shop, admittedly not a taxing demand, before consummating consumption compulsions. Still, more profitable than Ulaanbaatar's furtive exchanges with unregulated street hagglers. Maybe less memorable as well.

On the field of play, were you to look at it, the athletes stretched before or cooled after their events in enforced haste. The stadium staff hurried them in and out. The athletes, their coaching staffs, their masseuses and their drug-balance consultants could not occupy the busy field for more than a few minutes before and after each race, jump, or throw. Seventeen days does not afford much time for the vast number of events now filling the Olympic timetable, especially given the enormous number of countries offering athletes to the pagan gods of sport. Hustle onto the field, do your muscular magic, limp off.

Lots of limping in fact. The athletes arrived with physiques so jacked and ripped and ripened to sport-specific readiness that they appeared more to *wear* than to *be* their bodies. Growth hormones had grown humans into a distinct species. Steroids packed on muscle till athlete ankles creaked under the weight. Gene-splice technology had created *new* muscles, previously unknown to the human form, and wove these through the familiar ones so as to better execute just the movement needed to leap over a stick or hurl an iron ball. The whole regimen of enrichment honed in on just the developments needed for the event at hand. If an athlete uses a stick to jump over a stick, a computational formula and a team of "New Ethics" doctors, pharmacists, and biogenetic researchers would select the precise recipe for the task and amend the performer's anatomy to the required specifications. If the resulting creatures bore a disquieting closeness to caricature, this concerned no one at the moment of athletic exaltation.

Almost no one. The weak links in the Olympic chain looked a bit distressed. Some came under-augmented from budget strapped New Nations still struggling to provide a cot for every citizen and just hoping that a showing at the world's biggest event might secure their claim to nationhood. The wrestlers from the Algerian Refugee Nation of Iberia eyed their uber-enhanced German or Russian opposite numbers at the Olympic village with sinking hearts. No one needed to tell the merely marginally boosted that the wealth-enhanced Olympians had super-oxygenated synthetic blood and extra sweat pores ("for that hard to grip wrestling body"), the ad campaigns had made that clear. But viewing them up close, fidgeting in their high-test hyper-tuned bodies, injecting that hour's drug cocktail into their hind ends—made it all so real.

On the other hand, consider the women of the International Women's Athletics Union, now universally referred to as the Sallis Sisters. They had paid for rigorous tests to prove that they arrived to play without benefit of performance enhancing drugs. Looking at them at the Olympic Village or on the field of play, you would dread joining their trenches against their mega-bodied opposition. They seemed a scanty phalanx to set against the Germans, the Russians, or the West Welsh. The Sallis Sisters of the Republic of Greater Los Angeles might look more human (as we currently define the species), but they did not appear likely to come out stronger, faster, higher. If you stood in the line of battle with them, you had better hope for a contest of the spirit rather than a clash of bodies. Note though, that while the under-funded but still drug-fueled Olympians of the sovereign-wealth-fund-unfinanced New Nations looked intimidated and vaguely helpless, the Sallis Sisters showed defiant faces of confident determination. They might hold a tiny hill, but they came ready to die on it.

Let us turn to the transcript for a few highlights.

Andrew Brightman, "It's a beautiful day here folks. The sun shining through the partially parted stadium dome. Just lovely. Much cooler than you'd expect."

Dorthy Lament, "It has grown surprisingly hot in Paris, but the Olympic Stadium air-conditioning provides a safe and refreshing atmosphere."

Andrew, "Working full blast. I'm glad cold air sinks, Aren't you Dorthy?

Dorthy, "I sure am. Though I'm not sure we need it cool enough to wear coats."

Andrew, "And what coats they are! Folks, you can buy these online, or if you are lucky enough to be here, at any of the 540 official gift shops. Look, Dorthy, here come the final runners for the 200 meter sprints! Don't they look enormous?"

Dorthy, "They do. One must worry though, given some of the injuries in qualifying, whether their analytics teams have taken all the complex biomechanics into account."

Andrew, "The sinews on those men!"

Dorthy, "It's a matter of tendon strength. Given the still uncertain medical experience with new scientific training augmentations, and the complex interplay of body parts under extreme stress—"

Andrew, "There's Tooball! Hello Tooball! I think he saw me. That might have been a wave!"

Dorthy, "I just worry that we have entered untraveled territory—"

Andrew, "They're on the line. I hope the running field can hold up."

Dorthy, "The field has taken a pounding in the early heats. I'm not sure the grounds technicians realized what kind of forces the New World Olympic Athletes would exert on the course. Shout-out to the stadium crews for all the divot backfill."

Andrew, "The starter has raised his pistol."

Dorthy, "Reminding our viewers that they do raise the pistols now, unlike in '80."

Andrew, "You can feel the tension in the air. The cool refreshing air. The runners are set. They're off! Ooohhh! I heard a snap! J. C. Prince has taken the lead. Ohhh! His ankle snapped! Tooball and Ali Mustafa run alongside each other. Ouch! Another snap. Three men down on the course. The lead runners cross the line! That's it folks. A photo finish between Tooball Beatleback of New Zealand and Simon Borch of East London. Borch has collapsed. Tooball too. All the runners have dropped to the ground now."

Dorthy, "Like finely tuned machines, they have a close calibration for the event. One worries what it means to have such a physically specific capacity—"

Andrew, "Here's the photo! Along with its three-dimensional data analysis. I can't tell by looking, but the spectrographic specialists declare that Tooball has won by the very tip of his left middle finger! What a race! What a result!"

Dorthy, "Medics have evacuated most of the competitors. It's a good thing the dome is open for those medic-copter airlifts. Though one must worry what such extreme ventilation means for the cooling of a stadium this size, given the heat—"

Andrew, "There's the national anthem of New Zealand! There's Tooball's own theme song! He is running the track now. Draped in the New Zealand flag and waving his own Tooball Products banner. What an Olympic branding negotiator he is!"

Dorthy, "It makes me feel good to see a winner able to run the track after the event."

Andrew, "He's kicking his way through the empty water bottles now. They really should remove those. So many water bottles."

Dorthy, "They've been working on it. Shout-out to the ground crew for carting out so many bottles."

Andrew, "I'm heading over to interview Tooball. Tooball! Tooball! Over here! NBC, broadcasting to the world."

Tooball, "Yeah baby...got my first medal...got my breath...yeah!"

Andrew, "Great run Tooball. You won by a fingertip. In light of that, I wonder how you would respond to the rumors that you had your fingers surgically elongated?"

Tooball, "Whatever it takes to win baby! It's all human bone. Not mine, but real bone. I'm all natural! Buy Tooball brand baby! I'm going to own Disneyland."

Andrew, "I can't wait to see you in the decathlon. Look out for that frisbee!"

Tooball's victory in his four track events pleased the IOC. Officially neutral, it nevertheless looked for glamor and familiar faces to help put over the Paris Games. Returning athletes proved that modern sports were not a slow death to the body. Furthermore, Tooball's victories distracted from a few "over-performers" in the field event's first few days.

Everyone knew just from looking at them that the shot putters, never models of classic athletic beauty, had run up the pharma bills. They had built bulk into their bodies to produce counterweight for putting the shot. Their inflated rear ends and distended stomachs disturbingly suggested a new and very unsightly plague in store for mankind. Analysts and announcers reassured the audience at home that these were scientifically tested bioengineered means of achieving shot lift. And they did lift the iron ball. It flew. It flew into runners contending for the 500 meter medals, eliminating Uhru Abenta—thankfully not a favorite to win. A shot thrown into the stands wounded seven-year-old Tina Ward, but Benito Jax graciously delivered a now much sought after CotRatt to her hospital bed, so the press proved positive by end of day.

The javelin throw replicated its typical difficulties. The IOC constantly struggled with the conflicting aims of suppressing the material science applied to gain (occasionally lethal) lift in the sharpened pole, while keeping the trade in new and improved javelins strong as a small gift to Olympic sponsor Nikadidas. In anticipation of problems in Paris—and trying to learn lessons from Ulaanbaatar—the IOC had required solid iron shafts for the '84 event. No use. The hypertrophied hurlers had so optimized augmentation that the first javelin thrown left the stadium entirely and ended the Olympic dream of Dwaine Ooruruh of the Uganda men's cycling team. The IOC put this down to unfortunate event timing and cleared the space outside the stadium to measure the rest of the throws. Only Julie Hawkins of the North Northeastern States Federation of America, a Sallis Sister, failed to throw the javelin outside the arena. She celebrated a personal best as if she had won a gold. The judges disqualified her for "excessive expression of inappropriate emotions".

This initiated a trend. At the completion of the women's 1500 meter run, with the winners receiving oxygen and the medal stands set to receive them upon recovery, three losers of the race—all members of Zoe Sallis' International Women's Athletics Union, staged a "clean winners" medal event on the podia. Other Sallis Sisters, having already finished last in their own events, rushed the field to share the celebration before security hustled them away. The IOC determined that they had, one and all, staged a brand damaging "improper and unsportsmanlike celebration" that "deprived the winners their true measure of glory". The IOC stripped all the women of their status as Olympic competitors. Benito Jax pulled down all images of the unsportsmanlike podium occupation from Olympic affiliated websites and ordered the IOC legal department (the world's largest) to sue anyone showing such images. Benito Jax said, "They will go unrecorded and unremembered by history."

The IOC called the faux-medal event "soft terrorism." The press called the Olympic ejections "justice for the winners and a proper rebuke to the Sallis Olympic killjoys." Andrew Brightman announced his "disappointment at the puny physiques on the so-called Sallis Girls." Julie Hawkins, javelin throw last place finisher and now stripped of even her status as an Olympian, said, "The only prize I care about is that bestowed by my sisters in clean sports. The only fans I want are the fans of playing clean. The IOC can go hang itself. Make a medal event of it. That's the logical next step for a governing body now dedicated to the ruin of women's bodies."

A few days into the Games, Benito Jax and his staff of "jaxmen" felt the first glow of relief at the growing notion that unfortified women and uncannily accurate frisbee throwers might be the Paris Games' only terror threat. But then the Leek Green Faction of the Whole Earth Defense League staged a happening to upset these settled convictions.

LGF members appeared at the Main Stadium ticket booth handing the ticketers termination letters that, in very plausible IOC style, said "any attempt at discharge evasion, loitering, lollygagging, or failure to immediately depart IOC authorized areas, and any attempt to notify any authority other than the Executive Committee of the IOC of this dismissal notice, will lead to immediate blackballing of the offending party, who will not in future gain employment in any ticketing, sporting, sport-ticketing, ticket-adjacent, or sport-adjacent, job, occupation, career, or placement—part or full time—for the life of the blackballed individual." The LGF then manned the ticket center for a full ten minutes, handing out copywrite violating *Paris 2084; The Fun Returns at Last* counterfeit tickets. These had the trademark-very-protected five interlocked rings, under which the LGF had printed: "This ticket good for one world-wrecking event at humanity's expense." No one much noticed or cared until guests began bickering, then coming to blows, over who held rights to which seat. The LGF's subsequent manifesto rather buried its environmental protest point by providing a full accounting of all the money it collected against expenses incurred so as to justify its claim to have given all "profits" to the Refugee Nations Relief and Border Establishment Fund.

Benito Jax demanded greater security: "More helicopters!" He fired and then blackballed all the ticket agents who had "succumbed to terrorist tricks." He balled out his staff and rearranged their job titles until satisfied at universal humiliation. He made his *Senior Assistant for Event Compliance* into a *Junior Staff Aide for Notices and Notifications*. He demoted his *Managerial Manager of Crisis Management* into a mere *Executive Assistant for Brand Inspection*. Unable to decide which sounded worse, he just shuffled the titles *Safety and Submission Special Assistant* and *Executive Assistant Director for Assistance* between the two remaining and now thoroughly confused underlings. Jax swore again against paying tribute, and upon hearing a whispered remark from an unseen staff member about "having already paid ten minutes ticket tribute to the LGF", he demoted everyone down to the *Junior Assistant* level. Leaving one unfortunate member of the team a mere *Junior Assistant Junior Staffer*.

The Games continued. Swimming events began. The swimmers, those from well-funded "television-positive" national programs, wore 'slip-water suits' that slipped water past their twisting bodies in a manner guaranteed to break records but leave the standings just as they would have been had everyone swam naked. Now that would have been a sight to see (possibly a ratings booster) given the elongated bodies of the athletes—complete with fingertip additions to facilitate that last all-important touch. The similarity even in facial features of the synchronized swimmers started murmurs of gene-splice twining. The water polo play looked much the same above the water, but below the waterline the poloists leg-wrestled each other to near drowning—this despite subcutaneous buoyance enhancement.

Olympic safety officers remained unable to identify frisbees, so swimming events often featured delayed starts as the staff cleared the pool of unauthorized objects. Clearly the Ultimate Frisbee Anti-Olympic Operations Unit had caught a wave in audience sympathy. Disk aim had deteriorated with the addition of the common ticket holder heaving them, but even the uncoordinated cannot easily miss an Olympic pool, so the synthetically stretched swimmers limbered their long limbs for upwards of forty minutes per start. Whenever a starter's pistol did manage to fire off a race, the Australian national team posted three first-place finishers. A tribute to their aquatic traditions and a reflection of Australian embrace of family fire-brake moats surrounding every suburb. These people have places to practice; until the pan evaporation rate catches up to them.

On day five of the greatest half-month in human history, with the track events in mid-swing and swimming proceeding swimmingly, Red Asphalt Alert took over the Olympic Village. Commando style, and sporting Nemesis Brand tactical gear (in clear violation of Armed Asylum's sponsorship rights), the group posed at a distance for cameras while intimidating away both Olympic security and the Paris Special Weapons and Tactics gendarmerie. They allowed athletes to come and go at will, provided only that they recited RAA slogans to get in or out.

"The alert that alarms the world is red asphalt."

"Dark Goth Red warns the unwary to beware the asphalt."

"Red Asphalt Alert is the nemesis of the world-bane."

"Look at the time. What time is it?"

"The Leek Green Faction is a flaming clown car."

"Run where you will, you will find no asylum from RAA."

The athletes eagerly complied; easier egress than provided by the regular security. When interviewed the Olympians said they wanted to stay focused on their events. Benito Jax, on the other hand, went ballistic, "Attack! Attack them at once! Why don't you attack?"

The Prefect of Police, "An attack would cause casualties."

Benito Jax, "Don't cause casualties, except of terrorists! Attack without casualties—except terrorists! Do it now!"

The Prefect of Police, "It won't work like that. These RAA operatives operate at a very high level."

Benito Jax, "They are radicals. Incompetent leftist agitators given to inept public relations and internal fragmentation. Fragment them! Don't you have hand grenades that do that?"

The Prefect of Police, "I suggest negotiation. We don't want a massacre to mar the image of the Games."

No. We did not want that. A sobered Benito Jax opened talks with RAA. The radicals proved amenable to reason. First, they demanded safe passage out of Paris. Jax negotiated them down from "with full press coverage" to modestly slipping out of town after just a few snapshots from the rapidly re-dying print media. The RAA commando further demanded that its slogans festoon Olympic turnstiles for three days after their departure. Done, provided the RAA made no new press releases during that period. Finally, the radicals demanded that the IOC pay I-sMart Images Inc. to design a new brand name for Red Asphalt Alert. Something with more punch. Benito Jax found this the easiest demand to meet until he discovered how much I-sMart wanted in return for the job. Jax put the outrageous fee down to fear of brand damage working for terrorists. He decided he could wring out cash from IOC Charities to cover the cost. So: done.

Thus did the IOC repossess and re-secure the Olympic Village. To the groans of the athletes now again required to show four forms of ID and punch in a password (at least sixteen digits, three capital letters, not all caps, use at least two numbers and three non-letter and non-numeral signs, no repeats, change daily). The RAA members disappeared before they even arrived at the border of Paris. Their well-posed print media pictures proved popular with the Paris populace and quickly with the wider world. The Leek Green Faction postered-up complaints of favoritism by the IOC who "unfairly advantage Red Asphalt Alert—just as they do Eurasian nations and Capitalism and Argentine football." The LGF made retroactive demands on the IOC for their release of the ticket stands already abandoned by the activists. Jax ignored them. "We've had our incidents for this cycle of the Games."

Six days into the Two Weeks of Wonders, the road cycling events re-started. The IOC initially delayed them not out of a sense of mourning at a death by Olympic assegai, but because on the day of the initial race Paris' heat index went from *Concern* through *Caution* all the way to *Crisis* within an hour of the cyclists' passing the Olympic Stadium (or the "danger zone" as journalists came to call it). Even hosing off the riders under constant water lost effectiveness as the spray turned to steam in the air. Panicked shades of Cairo. Better to delay the event a few days in hopes that the unseasonably hot weather for a late November in Paris mitigated at least down to *Dangerous-But-Doable*.

By day six the weather looked no less hot, but at considerable expense the IOC had refitted all the cyclists with cool-suits. They took off at the starters pistol, covered head to foot in bulky white marshmallow man outfits, puffed up by refrigerant, and still doused by a constant shower of hose-over water. No one expected broken records this time. The lithe bodied and red blood over-celled riders pedaled in their new bulk uniforms like a convocation of circus clowns.

Events also began on the Mount Sport Monkey Live Large! Bet Hard! Mountain Bike and Land Sled Facility. Given the shorter play times, the freestyle jumping events stood less likelihood of cancellation due to player body temperatures. The riders just removed their helmets for better heat dispersal. One danger traded for another, but the players felt more in control of their fates under the new convention. Then track integrity began to fail. It seems that the high-synth stability sludge (uncharitably called "expensive mud" by nay-sayers) lost its solidity with rising ambient temperature. This led to a good deal more "slippage" than anticipated. Pity so few contestants wore helmets.

The most tragic circumstance brought on by the unwelcome increase in what the IOC insisted on calling "post-cool" temperatures, at least in the view of Benito Jax, lay in the necessity of fully closing the Main Stadium dome. The city-scale air-conditioners ("comfort insurance devices") simply could not keep up. Not while venting ninety-eight percent of the stadium air to the sky every two minutes. Benito Jax acknowledged the unfortunate loss of natural sunlight ("an affront to the Morning God") but noted that increased stadium lighting, while more expensive, would be more than offset by the lowering of the air-conditioning bill. A great savings, indeed, were it not for the huge expense of moving the dome to the closed position, along with the IOC's continued insistence on maintaining a "highly chilled" atmosphere, conducive to both attendee heat relief and Olympic-brand coat sales.

Given the differing assessments of dome closure disadvantages, one could call it either fortunate or unfortunate that the rubber bearings necessary to move the massive vault melted in the higher heat. The IOC officially maintained that dome-close failure augured opportunities for "hot play challenges" while still allowing viewer comfort. Refrigerant breakdowns increased the challenge of playing hot and challenged the comfort of watching play. Athletes, pharmaceutically calibrated for one temperature range, fainted in mid run under the newly prevailing heat. Cameras scanned the stadium stands to see increasingly grumpy patrons, cooling their kids with electric fans, fighting over plush CotRatts.

Benito Jax and his staff did deep dives into meteorological reports and harried forecasters for signs of hope. But by the usual combination of the unpredictability of local weather and the unspeakability of larger forces, the analysis of atmospherics could assure no alterations in conditions. Then on day seven of the Games, a cooling trend. Twenty degrees down from the day before at the break of day. "Thanks be to the Morning God", said Benito Jax. "*Something something* the Atlantic Meridional Overturning Circulation", said the climatologists. "The Gulf Stream can take care of itself; the Olympics are saved!" replied Benito Jax.

So, the Games entered their second week on a much welcomed cooling trend.

Week Two: Ice

A New Cool; Competitive Kidnapping; Body and Soul.

According to IOC lore, by the start of the second week of the Games (usually about nine days in, on the strictly Olympic calculation of "weeks"), everyone can relax. Most of the IOC-blamable failures will have been avoided or already occurred. The seats have sold out, the press has settled in for the field drama rather than continued expressions of irritation at uncovered plugs and clogged toilets at the Olympic Village, and the viewers at home rest easy in the afterglow of the opening ceremony and in anticipation of the closing festivities, now only alert to the inspirational stories of victory. By week two they have even forgotten any unfortunate dove casualties. Everyone can breathe easy. Except the IOC President and his ever-attendant staff.

Benito Jax said, to that staff, "This can't be right. They kidnapped the Olympic flame? How did they even do that?"

The Junior Assistant for Security Failure sought to reassure, "A rather low-tech technique to tell from the video posted by the LGF. They just set fire to a wooden torch and then extinguished the flame in the cauldron. They hustled the fire out of the stadium in the dark—lovely pictures of that—sorry—then posted video of themselves, faces concealed in ski masks, pointing fire-extinguishers at the flame."

Benito Jax, "Can't Helia do something about them? Make them stop interrupting my Games and ruining my mornings? They're part of her group. We have agreements."

"They're a faction."

Benito Jax, "And how did they get the flame? What happened to security?"

"A bit overstretched."

Benito Jax shook his head in frustration, "And what does the Leek Green Faction—idiotic name—demand?"

"A full hardcopy publication of its call to arms against the Olympic Games and world capitalism, plus an official IOC repudiation of Red Asphalt Alert. They allege there is 'something suspiciously capitalistic about their success'."

Benito Jax snorted, "Well the joke is on them. They kidnapped an imposter. A mimic of an Olympic flame. I wouldn't give two pennies to get that flame back. Tell them to fire away at it; let loose with their sodium bicarbonate. Their rivals have already murdered the real flame. Losers."

"But the publicity?"

"Re-light the flame; immediately! Tell the public we have kept the real flame in a special separate location after the original lighting," Jax gnashed his teeth, "if only we had! Tell the press the flame is safe. To hell with the LGF. Buffoons."

Maintenance quietly re-lit the flame. The IOC press officer denied rumors that the world now witnessed a third Olympic flame of the Games—one not at all related to the first that had toured the planet or the second that had only seemed to extinguish before a gaping global audience. The IOC press officer explained the elaborate security guaranteeing flame safety; the hide-away location(s) for the actual flame now actually blazing away again in the stadium after its security shift in anticipation of the entirely predicted attempt at kidnapping by the incompetent LGF; the scientific means used to establish the authenticity of the flame (data available upon request); the new security arrangements in place to protect the once again real and only Olympic flame. The IOC press officer took questions but only glared at the reporter who asked if the stadium would soon need the flame as a heat source.

The morning excitement gave way to play. First up, the demonstration event most dear to Benito Jax's heart: flechettes de pelouse. Called "lawn darts" by the rest of the world, the game required players to make high altitude throws of fletched darts at the opposing team who attempted to prevent them from hitting the earth with their gauntleted hands so as to hurl them back. The China vs. India game offered the most excitement as the two rivals had agreed to settle a border dispute by fletch throw in Paris. Unfortunately, the teams quickly amassed penalties for "throwing parallel to the ground", "aiming at the opponent", and "attempted murder". India won simply by amassing fewer fouls. China protested that the Chinese team should win the match for having inflicted more casualties. The Rules

Committee judged that injuries did not count for points (a change from the initial proposal made before the Ulaanbaatar Games) and found for India. China appealed to the IOC Executive Committee directly, but Benito Jax upheld the earlier ruling over the objections of Jing Zhao. At this final determination, China merely said that it had one other appeal it could make.

In truth, the Indian and Chinese players could have inflicted more harm on each other playing by the rules. The flechettes de pelouse darts proved more dangerous thrown at the vertical than at the horizontal. Injuries and press-promoted controversies dogged the event. Benito Jax blamed gravity for the high fatality-over-injury rate, "It is the unfortunate decision of physics that a falling object tends to discriminate in favor of striking the head over any other part of the body." Jax had such fond memories of playing (and surviving) the game as a child that in spite of the spate of lawsuits, he petitioned the IOC to make the demonstration sport a permanent part of the Games.

At least the flechettes de pelouse players competed in reasonably good field conditions. Benito Jax argued that the stuck stadium dome had turned out for the best. Cooling air descended into the formally over air-conditioned arena, and the open dome allowed for greater helicopter surveillance. This ended with a series of collisions above the stadium. The brief reconversion to analog life had left some pilots confused over the rotational direction of "clockwise". Perhaps a pictogram would have helped.

The contentment of the IOC President and the comfort of players and attendees in the Olympic Stadium endured almost till the late afternoon of the middle day of the Games. The morning's cooling trend transitioned into an afternoon icing. Frost covered the field. Spectators exhaled white air through numb fingers. The press wondered aloud—loudly—why no one turned on the stadium heaters. The stadium had no heaters. As Benito Jax put it, "Why would we ever have thought to put heaters in the stadium? Do these people think we are made of money?" On the plus side, Olympic coats, sporting their CotRatt shoulder badges, sold out at the concession stands.

As the next day's events began, Benito Jax advised all official outlets to ignore any icing on the field. This proved a challenge.

Dorthy Lament, "We are ready to start the woman's pole vault in what the IOC authorizes us to describe as highly not hot conditions of minor field brittleness."

Andrew Brightman, "Owing to the ice."

Dorthy, "Owing to the correspondence of cool conditions and condensation."

Andrew, "I've double upped on layers."

Dorthy, "Because we set our heater too low."

Andrew, "We have a heater?"

Dorthy, "Oh look, *Andrew*, here comes Synthetic Rince, women's pole vault champion. She looks just as she did during the last Games. Very sleek."

Andrew, "A surprise that, she's not herself a Sallis—"

Dorthy, "Look Andrew! A woman is going to vault a pole using another pole."

Andrew, "This should be exciting."

Dorthy, "Meagan Oakshire of the Scottish team. Favored to medal."

Andrew, "Look at her run! Oh no! She slipped and crashed!"

Dorthy, "Unfortunately her poll wounded an official as she fell."

Andrew, "I'm sure they won't mind sharing an ambulance. Maybe a little romance might bud there, eh Dorthy?"

Dorthy, "The hectic event schedule must go on. Carmen Blunt of Germany sprints fast down the track. She's almost in position. Ohhh! Her pole slipped and launched her into a sidebar. She's unconscious."

Andrew, "Pity she didn't at least land on the pad. Not that it would help much in these frozen conditions."

Dorthy, "The heat absent conditions have stiffened some of the safety pads."

Andrew, "The pads are mighty stiff. Like some of the fellows in the Olympic Village, eh, Dorthy?"

Dorthy, "Oh look. Another competitor. Let's hope she can at least make the jump. Joyce Flaubert of France. Running down the track. She's up and—crashes into the bar! That looked painful."

Andrew, "I think the bar is actually frozen onto the arms. It should have detached."

Dorthy, "Unfortunately the bar does seem to have achieved maximal anti-hot and affixed itself through moisture conversion to the arms. I'm guessing though that Joyce will give us a big thumbs up in a moment."

Andrew, "As soon as she comes to."

Dorthy, "Nope, hauling her off."

Andrew, "Quite a struggle too. Takes three men to carry her to the ambulance. Big women in this event."

Dorthy, "A balance of streamlined muscle and low weight to lift. Most coaches I spoke with expected that raw strength would prevail under the conditions in Paris. Maybe not calibrated for the sub-heat environment."

Andrew, "Synthetic Rince has her pole! She's set at the start. Disappointingly dressed in last season's physique, but otherwise looking great."

Dorthy, "She's running down the track. So fast. She's up! Over the bar by...easily a new world record!"

Andrew, "She executed that vault like a well-oiled machine."

Dorthy, "A fantastic athlete."

Andrew, "She's headed off the track. I'm surprised she didn't stop to say a few words. Very unlike her."

Dorthy, "I'm sure she'll hold a press conference."

Andrew, "Wow! Folks, I don't know if you can see this on your screens at home, but the field has just been covered in mini celebratory balls. Streaming down! What an appropriate tribute to the ballsy performance of Synthetic Rinse at these Games. Kudos to the IOC for this."

Dorthy, "Andrew, its hail."

Andrew, "Yes, let's hail to the IOC and the Olympic Movement. All hail Benito Jax."

Dorthy, "People are running off the field! I see injuries in the stands!"

Andrew, "Maybe too much of a tribute. No worries, the ball buckets will empty soon."

Dorthy, "Bloody heads everywhere! People trying to find shelter under the seats. Fights in the stands as people turn each other into human shields! I can't see anything now for all the hail!"

Andrew, "You'd think they'd have made the balls softer."

Dorthy, "Andrew! It's hail! It's natural!"

Andrew, "At these Games? If you say so..."

The hailstorm lasted only thirty minutes, but the horrifying images of the anomaly spiked the worldwide TV ratings and doubled the audience.

And in spite of the many criticisms leveled against it by the Leek Green Faction, Late Capitalism responded strongly. By the next day every ticket holder could buy a yellow construction helmet to wear; each emblazoned with a hail defying CotRatt, chest bared, cot in hand, nose and whiskers pointed to the sky, daring the Mourning God to try that shit again.

Benito Jax bore up strongly under the many criticisms and accusations leveled against him. He declared to a bank of microphones that he could not control the weather. That the weather was not that bad compared to some past Games. That the spirit of the Olympics was a spirit of over-coming. That CotRatt had proved a worthy symbol of that spirit; the plucky little fellow. That people should be grateful that the stadium even *had* a dome—never mind its immobility. That no one built heaters into athletic facilities anymore. That the '84 Olympic Stadium had left out heating precisely as a sustainability measure. That the flame put out by the hailstorm had not in fact been the real flame, which had been kept out of view and out of the weather but would now be placed in its rightful position in the cauldron. And that would be just *one* flame for the Games, not *four*, and that people should stop being so ridiculous. And *no*, there *had* been no and *would* be no so-called "terrorist" events at these Games.

This masterful address to the public held the line against press-expressed doubts for almost ten minutes. Then the following appeared on posters all over Paris:

"We are Red Asphalt Alert. We are the viper that bites mid-stream. We are the toilet that backs up mid-party. We are the promotion to the duller job. We are the child that never stops crying. We are the Senate to the world's Ceasar. We are the Benidict Arnold to the World of Things. We are the Medusa to the Family of Man. We are the Universal Judas. We are Red Asphalt Alert."

It ended with a postscript: "We have kidnapped a member of the IOC."

Jing Zhao, IOC Executive Committee member and Vice President of Nation Relations had busied herself in the week before her demotion to hostage seeing to the safety of the Games, the fairness of their play, and the ultimate world triumph of her full-time employers, the Chinese Communist Party. She had slipped forbidden flags through security to the Chinese team. She had objected vigorously at security meetings about the lax policing of flags and alluded to evidence of Laotian delegation turpitude as an explanation for these failures. She had suggested that as a peacemaking move, Japan might accept certain alterations in its own national flag to accommodate Chinese ideas—just for the duration of the '84 Games. Or even longer, should they prove popular. To show her evenhandedness, she had scolded the People's Republic of China's Olympic Inspection Group in harsh terms: "It is unfortunate that China must offer mild corrections to unhappy nations on geopolitics in ways found distressing to those less informed of China-adjacent area history." She ate healthy though infrequent meals and found sleep when not otherwise engaged in fostering one country's national interests and all nations' fair and equal treatment.

Then Red Asphalt Alert briskly hauled her to an undisclosed location and videotaped her reading their demands.

Now the world saw her sitting behind a small table, bookended by two masked men in tactical dress, one holding up a Parisian newspaper verifying the date (headline: *Benito Jax Denies Possibility of Terrorism at the Paris Games*) and the other feeding pages for Jing Zhao to read—or trying to...

Jing Zhao shouted to the world, "You stupid Benito Jax and all your IOC! I am kidnapped! So stupid IOC! Why do you have so many guards and none any good?" The masked man to her right pointed to a paper for her to read. She said to him, "What is this? What do you want you snail-breath man? China will make you pay! China will cut your throat and pull your tongue out your asshole. Go away snail-breath man!" Jing Zhao turned back to the camera and the world audience, "IOC Benito Jax such a fool idiot! China will have all the Olympics—you will see!" The kidnapper continued to quietly urge her to read the demands. She said, "What? Why should I read? You brought me no glasses. Stupid kidnap man brings no glasses for hostage! You stupid kidnap man!"

After experimenting with a few reading glasses, Jing Zhao found a proper pair and began to read the demands: "We are the curse of the overstuffed world—" Zhao stopped and screamed at the masked man, "What *we*? *You*! You dumb no-glasses smell-bad kidnap man! You better never go to China. You wait, China will come for you. China will come for everyone."

The masked man pointed to the paper, offering some discreet pleas into her ear. He pointed to his masked partner's assault rifle. His partner waved it before Jing Zhao. Zhao said to the masked man at her right, "China will cut off your penis and put it up your asshole so you can lick it with your tongue!" He gestured again at the paper and made a praying motion.

Zhao looked at the paper, studied it for a moment, then looked into the camera and said, "They are dumb Red Asphalt kidnappers. They insult the IOC and China by asking for no money. Dumb kidnappers. They demand an end to all war. So dumb kidnappers. They demand that the IOC end its sponsorship deal with war mongering Armed Asylum. They demand better time keeping at the Olympics. They say something about who they are, but they are only stupid kidnap terrorists. Do what they say! Get me out of here! You stupid Benito Jax!"

The kind and forgiving Benito Jax watched the tape. He only worried over the condition of the hostage, "She's not herself. I forgive her the harsh words. Though, frankly, if the RAA wants to dance for a while at the end of her foul tongue in my place, we could just delay compliance for a few weeks. And clearly, we can't meet the demands. I'm sure China will understand if we just suppress this tape. We will see Jing Zhao free at some point. After the Games have concluded. She would want it that way."

A staffer did what staffers do, delivered the bad news while preparing to duck, "Uh, sir, the video already went out on the NBC broadcast. The world watched it."

"What?!? What happened to information security? Why were our broadcast partners not notified against showing this?"

"Sorry sir. It wasn't covered in the broadcast standards document."

Benito Jax sighed heavily, "Two hundred lawyers. Twenty thousand pages. Daily amendments. Personal meetings to go through the material. *So* many hours. And something as simple as not broadcasting IOC personnel in hostage videos delivered mid-Games making sponsorship-damaging demands gets by us. Shouldn't they have withheld broadcast just on the basis of foul language?"

"The networks bleeped."

"Did they bleep out the part about condemning our financial partners at Armed Asylum?"

"NBC interpreted that mention under chapter 8, section 5.22, subsections (d) through (h), subheading *promote all IOC ExCom originating mentions of major sponsors*. We're looking into amending that statute."

Benito Jax took on his stoic look, "Well, there's nothing to do about it now. Hopefully they will execute her without pain. I'm sure we have rules against broadcasting *that* video..."

"We're checking the documents. We will amend as necessary."

"Such a great pity. But I don't suppose it matters that her appeal went out to every nation. She's too great a bitch to win any support. China will understand our attitude. We'll give them a bronze in the men's synchronized kayak event. It's a French judge, I'll call him personally. Then I'll make a personal apology to Armed Asylum. Probably they will want to pay for the funeral. That would look good. Meanwhile, call up Dr. Van der Ghent and commission a medal of heroism for our lost comrade Jing Zhao. Something incorporating the pictogram graphics. Jing loved those. Maybe we will name an award after her. I could hand it out at the next Olympics and give a speech in her memory. After the dove release. We'll work on it. We will overcome in the spirit of the Olympic Games."

The Games went on, as they always do.

The challenge of detecting cheating through performance enhancing drugs pales beside the difficulties in determining honesty in officiating. Unlike drugs, deceit hides *itself*. The IOC has used many methods in its quest for fair adjudication. Initially it attempted an honor code. Leveraging the pride of gentlemen to guarantee fairness. One might call this the *Ultimate Frisbee method*. Gentility proved short lived and overrated, so the IOC moved reluctantly to the usual range of options: background checks, legally enforceable contracts, constant surveillance, public shaming (I jest, the IOC does not shame itself intentionally), and whatever more up-to-the-minute ideas it encounters.

At one time, the IOC relied on the Hokuum-Pitz honesty test to weed out the corruptible. The HP test held out the hope of scientific detection without digital surveillance. Hokuum and Pitz established their honesty test in the classic manner. They obtained doctorates in psychology, appointments at prestige universities that reject hordes of applicants, passed their papers through peer reviews, spread responsibility among hundreds of secondary co-authors, doctored their data with the latest statistical decorations, found amazing potential in slight human variation, delivered talks on darkened stages surrounded by tech-world visionaries, published popular books on how to use the "new honesty" to vet employees, sentence criminals, distribute health benefits, choose candidates for office, defend beleaguered CEOs, and lose weight. A social psychology wonder story.

A few dark mutters fluttered through the academic internet. Hokuum and Pitz sued these evidentialist bad-mouthers, even using the Hokuum-Pitz honesty test at trial to choose the juries and disqualify defense witnesses. Total legal victory.

In time, attention turned away from evidence to outcomes. It turned out that rather than being a test for honesty, the Hokuum-Pitz test perfectly detected—and promoted—psychopathology. Since Hokuum-Pitz-approved psychopaths did so well in the glamor fields of finance, entertainment, politics, and academia—owing to having scored so highly on the Hokuum-Pitz honesty test—they were by definition not psychopaths. By declaration of the American Psychiatric Association and its Diagnostic and Statistical Manual, no one could have a psychological disorder that only made others suffer, rather than the allegedly disordered individual. So psychiatrically certified very sane people ran the world, their moral illness scientifically undetectable by institutional fiat.

Eventually, and after much struggle and many misguided attempts, the moral minority allied with the irrationally aggrieved to cast out the offending demon. Not the psychopathic leaders, but the Hokuum-Pitz test at least.

Now unable to pencil and paper Olympic officialdom into public respectability, The IOC turned to higher technology. It enlisted the new algorithmically powered digital surveillance lie detection technology. This bold new tech worked ("worked") on much the same principle as the old lie detectors had. It surveilled for physical correspondences to stress-situations differentiated by self-aware disjoints between subject belief and subject representation of belief. That is: it watched you sweat. Or fidget. Or maybe it watched you gulp. Who knows. In its now digitized and AIed version even Doctors of Mathematics could make only a guess at how ChatWatch worked its lie detection magic. We all knew this much at least: you could not argue with the results.

We knew this because ChatWatch detected dishonesty in anyone that did argue with its results. And who could argue with ChatWatch's logic? No one could really understand it, so there was *that*. But looking at it from ChatWatch's point of view, you could see its point. It had been *built* to detect dishonesty. It had been *asked* to detect dishonesty. ChatWatch could only assume that it *could* detect dishonesty. How could it execute its only task if it could not detect dishonesty? So, what could ChatWatch declare with respect to the honesty of anyone doubting its ability to detect dishonesty? The algorithmically simplest solution was to use such claims as data inputs of dishonesty. And if ChatWatch declared a person dishonest, who were mere humans to disagree? Did we have the data to do that? No. Not with ChatWatch now in charge of all the data. And if ChatWatch declared *you* to be dishonest, did *you* have any basis to disagree? What is mere moral conscience in the face of the hard science softly purring in the heart of the algorithm? After all, have you *never* acted dishonestly?

Then the Digital Age fell, to the relief of the dishonest and the honest alike. A shock to the system. Those multitudes relying on honesty detection software had to learn again to trust and distrust. Not to mention the need to re-install a sense of personal integrity fitted to a morally complex world. The Digital Rejectionists who had refused to allow AI to make their choices for them, do their thinking and writing for them, and operate their moral compass, looked on without pity at the litany of complaint emerging—now in hard copy form—from the armies of the AIed, newly thrust from Plato's cave into the scalding glare of the sun. ("And also, people, can we finally do something about the scalding sun? Now that AI, unhinged consumer of carbon, no longer demands denial of the heat? No?")

But my digression digresses. Our current subtopic was the challenge of Olympic judging; that hectic mess of nation-based vote swapping, celebrity-based excellence assumptions, sport struggles between traditionalists holding a line and new generations looking for more looks-and-likes, all aligned in dependable failure to not care about money. Olympic judging often looked like a joke repeating itself in hopes of being taken seriously. And here I consider only the explicitly judged events and not all the officiating controversies in unjudged sports. Sticking just to the former, one can see the attractions, ethical at least, of the Ultimate Frisbee ethos of calling your own fouls. But this fails to work when the stakes grow high, so someone then needs to speak with authority. The world long ago rejected the idea of judges as sages who just see right and wrong in each twist on the uneven bars. So, like any good bureaucracy, the IOC responded with rules and standards going on for pages and pages, once burning digits by the billions, lately felling trees in the thousands, soon to do both again.

And in spite of all this effort, which athlete won the men's gymnastics all around medal still came down to either France's judge making a trade with Lichtenstein's for a silver medal in the women's balance beam, or a call to a friend from Benito Jax looking to stifle an international crisis.

Not that Russia meant to leave matters with the corrupted calls from the head of the IOC. Being Russia, they like to take a hand in the nasty, irrespective of necessity. Russian coaches loosened screws on the parallel bars prior to German performance. They detached a pommel horse handle to break German wrists during the spin round. They un-evened the still rings to dislodge German shoulders. They substituted the music during a German floor exercise to play the Russian national anthem. Officials detected the crudely planted explosive in the vault apparatus, but then Germany's Wolff Gunderson flew disastrously from a rigged and fragmenting horizontal bar to land, perhaps fittingly, onto the Russian team bench. The injuries sustained by the Russian team might have served as a lesson, had they not then beat Gunderson into the hospital. The German benches cleared, and it took the officials the better part of the day to restore peace—and the horizontal bar. The Russians complained of a German aerial attack on their bench. The IOC docked the German team points and issued a disciplinary notice to them for "upsetting the balance of play". Russia won gold and Germany's team refused to take the bronze medal position next to them on the podium. Benito Jax sanctioned the Germans for "politicizing the podium". Unlike the women of the International Women's Athletics Union protest, the Germans kept their Olympic standing and their medals.

Aggressive male posturing did not own the '84 Olympic gymnastics events. The Women's all-around competition offered one of '84's most gripping trials. It featured the young Republic of Texas hopeful Judy Del Rio. Del Rio broke into gymnastics fame by winning the world championships in '83 at the surprisingly old age of eighteen. She had begun her Olympic journey at the age of three, her family enrolling her first in a gymnastics preparatory academy, three hundred miles and two nations from their home. Then at the age of ten, with her parents and four siblings each taking multiple jobs to keep her in training, Del Rio entered the World Olympic Training Center for six years of intense conditioning and skill-building. She saw her mother for one weekend every three months. She spoke occasionally on the phone with her father. Her siblings would visit whenever they had recovered from selling a kidney to fund Del Rio's Olympic dream; the whole family's Olympic dream.

Now they sat, in the gymnastics stadium, clutching their complimentary CotRatts, Del Rio banners at hand, watching the young champion leap and swing and bounce in head-to-head competition with Nadia Klomesky, the Russian hope. Each woman, Klomesky at 12 really just a girl, putting a whole life on the line to win a gold. At this level of competition silver stings worse than bronze. The silver medal winner weeps on the podium thinking "I almost got gold!" while the bronze medal winner smiles with tear-filled eyes thinking "I almost got nothing!"

Judy Del Rio lets out one last breath as she approaches the uneven bars to make, or miss, her mark in history. Everything turns on this. Victory will justify every sacrifice; defeat will round out a life of sacrifice with unbearable memories of might-have-been. This moment makes the difference between a promise redeemed and a pointlessly lonely existence. A dream fulfilled by merely doing again the deeds done a thousand times in practice or cancelled by one perhaps only slightly sub-par performance. The pressure is the glory. The make-or-break of the spirit in the arena of sport, that for these dedicated athletes constitutes the whole of a young life. With all this on the line, Del Rio began her routine. History records the result.

In the offices of the IOC, Benito Jax worried over the world press fallout from Red Asphalt Alert's release of Jing Zhao's angry rants and occasional reading of demands. Against Jaxian expectations and in defiance of consultant research, the world took Jing Zhao and her plight into their hearts. *Angry Zhao* dolls appeared in toy stores. "Get your Zhao Out" became a popular saying. "She owns her Boss Bitch", declared the newly back in business influencers.

All this baffled Benito Jax, but he did not stay staggered long. He called the international press to watch him open negotiations for the release of Jing Zhao. Phone in hand, ready to take the call, he told the assemblage of cameras, "A single life is simply too precious to put any price on it. No cost is too great, no sacrifice too painful, no sponsor too important, that it cannot be put in the balance to save a single person. The Olympics is a celebration of life. We will retrieve our lost champion." The phone rang and Jax answered it. A moment later the reporters and the watching world could hear the exchange between Benito Jax speaking from the press center and Jing Zhao speaking from an unknown location under the guns of terrorists.

Jing Zhao, "Meet the demands! Get me out of here!"

Benito Jax, "Tell your kidnappers that I, Benito Jax, offer to take your place as a hostage. I will negotiate with them personally, facing them man to men, unarmed to face their armory, myself alone, if only they free you to a waiting world."

Jing Zhao, "Go to hell. They don't want you. Cancel the Armed Asylum contracts. Get me out of here."

Benito Jax, "Of course we can't just cancel our long and rich association with our special partners, Armed Asylum, makers of some of the finest and most secure personal bunkers in the world. One that for all we know you might occupy right now—a tribute to their security. I will discuss all this when they have exchanged you for me. An IOC VP for the President of the IOC and the virtual re-founder of the Modern Games."

Jing Zhao, "Shut up! They don't want you! End the sponsorship! Get me out of here!"

Other protests continued at the Paris Games. The swimming events led to the usual dominance of Australia, with various North American and European teams making the podium. The audience in the stands cheered as the audience at home struggled to recall from the broadcast meet-the-athlete mini-dramas which swimmer had the most touching story. All of these seemed to revolve around a journey from fear of needles to self-injection. So much, so same. Into this miscellany of excitement and indifference the International Women's Athletics Union scored a minor Sallis Sister scoreboard victory. Not a real placement in the event, but a hack of the Swim Event Center scoreboard. Team Sallis arranged to display the 1000 meter women's final scoreboard as ranking the long eliminated IWAU top finishers as gold, silver, and bronze. Confused looks transitioned to loud boos drowning out the handful cheers. The women announced on the scoreboard managed to gain admission to the podium through a line of sympathetic and quickly fired women facilities workers. Their brief occupation of the podia in protest at the misshapen bodies of the real winners (at that moment prevented from taking their rightful place because then receiving blood infusions and recovery injections) earned the un-medalable women instant ejection from Olympian status and eventual removal from the event site.

Elsewhere, frisbee interruptions continued, in fact, increased in frequency. The Ultimate Frisbee Anti-Olympics Operations Unit asked that no one throw disks at certain events for safety reasons, but by now slipping a disk past security and heaving it at the unsuspecting had become a fashion. When Dorthy Lament asked a random frisbee thrower "Are you part of the UFAOO?" he had no idea who they were.

"Why do you throw these frisbees?"

"It's fun. It messes everything up. It's the asshole thing to do and I like that."

Benito Jax secured the release of Jing Zhao by agreeing to cancel the IOC's partnership with Armed Asylum. He did not allow the public to find out about the refund of sponsorship money this required. To maintain its tax deductions, Armed Asylum also did not publicly mention these remittances. Benito Jax did make a show of welcoming the unbathed Jing Zhao back to safety before hustling her off for a medical examination. When asked by the press if he still held to his oft expressed opinion that giving in to kidnapping demands would only lead to more hostages taken, Jax responded that, "We don't see that as a real possibility. We've had our unfortunate occurrence for these Games."

The next morning Benito Jax contended with new difficulties. His staff reported that, unsatisfied with the men's gymnastics gold, Russia now demanded victory in their much anticipated basketball game against Germany. Russia insisted on IOC assistance with this; as a matter of justice (somehow). While basketball has no judges per se, it does have referees. They just *call 'um as they see 'um*, but given the inability to formulate foul calling rules to the gnat's hair of human mobility, and the absolute need to keep the game on the go to audience enjoyment, what constitutes a rule violation cannot help but lie within the discretion of the referees. Most sports allow frequent stoppage for video inspection and further announcer analysis to the accompaniment of fights in the stands between partisans of each interpretation of the rules. But basketball violations cannot duplicate this dedication to second-guessing without incurring the lethal penalty of playing each game for six days. Benito Jax wisely took a pass on deciding how far to accommodate the latest Russian demands.

More urgent, and dearer to his heart, the BMX mountain in the center of Paris had moved from the hypermobility of structural instability due to heat, to mere surface slickness brought on by freezing cold. Still a hazard. At least the racers and jumpers could wear helmets again. Helmets with now easily fogged-up goggles disallowing distance detection during play. Apparently, the anti-fog technology could not handle the change in temperature. The players again ditched their head protection in confidence of their native skill at landing on wheels. The hospital rooms filled. Jax ordered heaters placed throughout the course, damn the expense and pray for that subtle balance between fire and ice that human flourishing so depends upon.

The last problem of the day could not be so easily waved away. The IOC—and the world press, alas—had received a new manifesto from the Leek Green Faction of the Whole Earth Defense League, with accompanying video. The manifesto read:

"We are the Leek Green Faction! Hear our words! See our new video! We speak the words that will shake the complacency of the World of Sport Distraction! Loud words! The so-called red asphalt alert represents no one. No one but the Overlords of Late Capitalism! (How do they *activist* so well? Have you asked yourself this? This can't be right!) We have demands! We have a hostage! (Two can play at this game!) Follow our demands! Hear our hostage!"

The video showed a sad and tear-stained Joseph Kabwe. He sat facing the camera behind a table holding papers. On either side of him stood a masked member of the LGF, wearing over-large last-year's tactical vests, shifting nervously on their feet. Kabwe spoke through his tears:

"I am hostage. I have been taken by these dangerous men. Taken from my family, from my little ones. From my wife and our children. Joseph Jr., Wafula, Monicah, and little baby Yvonne. And from my other wife and our children, Mariam, Joseph Jr., Ezekiel, Vincent, and little baby Wafula. And to little Milka the cripple. But I love her too! I will never see my little one's again." Tears rolled down Kabwe's cheeks. "All is lost. Unless the IOC gives to these fine people, 100 million Euros. In sixteen instalments into separate Swiss accounts plus two in Haiti. Or they will kill me, and I will never see my dear one's again!"

The kidnappers pointed vigorously to some line on the paper that Joseph Kabwe held. He continued, "Oh, yes. Also, the IOC must rename the BMX mountain to the *Leek Green Faction Olympic Tombstone for Capitalism Mudheap.* I am so sorry Benito Jax, for this outrage. Think of my children! Do not try to save me! Do not pay these outrageous and non-negotiable demands just to save poor me! Take care of my children! Good bye Joseph Juniors. I will always think of you."

Benito Jax looked back and forth between the recording delivered to the IOC and the twelve televisions showing the same images on every network in every nation on earth still receiving television. Jax exploded, "The bastard! The fraud! He turned himself into these bumbling amateurs. He will not get one penny. My precious BMX mountain will retain its brilliantly negotiated name. No one will fall for this ham acting and those crocodile tears."

The world embraced the cause of Joseph Kabwe. The newly reemergent man-o-sphere of the internet called him the "Lion of Kenya". Kabwe action figures flooded the market. Kabwe's wives put away their differences, surrounded themselves with their children, plus a few others borrowed from here and there, and wept on television for the return of their husband and the full payment of the ransom demands. Little Milka walked on her crutches and the world fell in love all over again.

Benito Jax again called kidnappers on live television and again offered to exchange himself for the hostage. Kabwe cried that he would face death rather than let any man take his place. Jax swallowed his frustration and congratulated Kabwe for being such a brave man. Once the cameras had turned off and the press had gone to cover Tooball Beatleback's effort to win his third decathlon, Benito Jax easily talked the LGF out of the money ransom on the agreement to announce a for-the-Games-only BMX mountain rechristening. You could hear Kabwe's weeping grow louder in the background as the negotiations wound down.

The press might just as well have stayed for the final act of hostage negotiation for all they got covering the frosted field of the decathlon. Tooball's finely adjusted physique performed at a pharmaceutically specified mild heat setting in a considerably colder climate. Tooball tumbled when he should have hurdled and put *himself* into the dirt rather than the shot. He long jumped shortly and high jumped lowly. Even his 100 meter sprint, done while wearing his gold medal from the earlier hundred meter event, spun into disaster as his legs stiffened into immobility halfway down the course. His run in the 1500 can best be described as *glacial*. His competitors suffered similar problems for their tightly tuned bodies, but the gods of chance favored them.

At least Tooball had the good sense to save something for the interview: "I did my best. I put my all into it. I take full responsibility. I suspect foul play by the IOC. Anybody gives it up to terrorists that easy probably turned up the air too high for Tooball on purpose. Check the betting sheets. And I know I can out pole vault my Hate Queen Syn Rince. You know those numbers can't be right. Not on just muscle juice and virgin blood. And shoutout to my girl Sallis and her sisters. I'm all in. You can see my integrity by my results. I'm a natty too!"

The only confirmed drug-free contestant in the women's weightlifting event was Algerian Refugee Nation competitor Zohra Drif, whose family had incurred crushing debt paying for her endless drug testing. Zohra Drif held her hands up in victory upon lifting the lightest weight of the event, even less than those far down her weight category, but the heaviest she had ever lifted herself. The judges disqualified her from ever again competing in an Olympic Games on the grounds of "unsportsmanlike celebration in collaboration with a cause". A new category devised that very moment for instant action by the officials. Drif, unfazed by the ruling, made an inexplicable V for victory as Sallis affiliated gymnasts charged the weightlifting venue to embrace her, earning their own Olympic disowning. The crowd booed the Sallis Sister cheering.

At least Drif had spared herself the series of injuries incurred by so many of the weightlifting contestants; limiting ourselves to those suffered immediately during the competition: Wrists snapped while holding ungodly amounts of weight briefly poised just over then immediately crushed heads. Luckier lifters merely dislocated shoulders and dropped their loads through inadequately reinforced floors. Even the lighter weight classes had strangely counter-balancing forms—no longer called shot putter physiques but now renamed power lifter leveragings.

Not everyone suffered instant karma. Most completed their lifts unharmed, delaying care for the consequences till later in life. Medals went out to every weight class. National anthems played. The press interviewed the champions. One lifter declared that winning the gold was "like kissing your sister!" (Competitors once used this phrase to refer to the muted joy of ending a game in a tie. Under the influence of PornPortal—once an Olympic sponsor—cultural norms shifted.)

The pole vault champion Synthetic Rinse gave a widely watched interview. Wearing her gold medal and now possessed of a surely unbreakable world record in the pole vault, she sat down for an interview in studio with Dorthy Lament.

Dorthy, "You now hold not only the women's world record but have beat the men's record by a goodly margin. What do you think that means?"

Synthetic Rinse, "First, shout down to Hate Lover Tooball—you got zoned by you pharm-body. You need to step up the play before you play off your Queen. Now to your point, Dorthy, I hold the record and shattered all records. I have shown that women can do it. You look at me compared to my pole vault competitors and you can tell I'm not on the chem-farm. I have shown that women only need to have the will to do it and the right technique."

Dorthy, "What would you say to Zoe Sallis and her International Women's Athletics Union and their efforts at protest during these Games?"

Synthetic Rinse, "They don't respect anything about the Olympic Games. If they don't want to play at the top, they should stay home. Women don't have to go down on the pharm to win. We don't even need separate events. The new Syn Rise will take on all comers. Men or women. Only losers protest the rules of the game. Winners go out and find the way to win."

The most watched event in diving was Dana Lilith's bid for gold in the platform dive. Lilith had placed just outside the podium in Ulaanbaatar, and the diving world favored her for gold going into Paris. Then she declared herself one of Zoe Sallis' anti-doping protesters. Her submission to, and self-financing of, top-tier anti-doping tests shocked and disappointed diving fans, both women and men. The press dubbed her a quitter. The World Diving Association worried that her refusal to "really compete" would damage women's diving. Past champions lamented the "politicizing of sports". Young divers threw away their Dana Lilith action figures in hopeless despair.

Imagine the stunned world that saw her platform dives in Paris. Powerful grace challenging even the best drug-pumped competitors. She leapt, twisted, and tumbled toward Olympic diving history. The world turned to watch, and to wonder if a Sallis Girl could win a medal. By the final round she had locked up at least bronze on even a mediocre last dive and could conceivably catch up in points for the gold if fate and judges allowed. The world rooted for her. Olympic judges welcomed a *see, they can do it* moment to spare sports the drudgery of celebrating only the enhanced.

So, everyone rooted for Lilith as she stood on the high platform in the still silence of the diving center.

She strode ever quicker to the edge of the platform and leaped off it to execute a perfect canon ball, covering the judges with water.

The reaction of the judges: "Zero points!"

The reaction from world diving: "Disgraceful!"

The reaction from the IOC: "Disqualified from the Games in shame!"

The reaction from the diving fandom website: "A blow against our sport!"

The reaction from the All Men's International Sport Union: "An insult to women athletes!"

And the reaction from the world sporting press: "An offensive display of childishness!"

In the interview after the event, still wet and breathless, Dana Lilith expressed her childishness thusly: "I didn't come here to win a medal. I didn't come here to show that drug unaided athletes could win medals. I didn't come to show that Olympic diving was an exception. I came here to protest the permissive use of performance drugs. I don't want to stand on an award podium while my sisters sacrifice their chances for the cause. Or damage their bodies and futures for a piece of tin. I don't want to stand in front of girls and tell them they will win against the freely-enhanced without drugs, while the world around them shows that's a lie. I want those young women to see that they can demand a better world in which to compete. Demand it for themselves, for other women, for men, for fans, for all of us. I came to do that—and I did it."

The audience booed. The press mocked. The social media reaction tended strongly negative. A complete rhetorical bellyflop. But somewhere, nearly unnoticed, a girl retrieved her Dana Lilith action figure from the back of the closet and put it prominently on a shelf as a promise to herself. Right won't always make might, but it rarely walks alone.

Fickleness in uncompetitive fashion fell on the other side of the line during the Ultimate Frisbee competition at last underway after so much preparatory protest. The Ultimate Frisbee teams protesting to end their participation in the Games came ready to play only by the rules traditional to the sport. They had foresworn enhancement and, since unlike the Sallis Sister's they wanted an exit from the Olympics altogether, they had also not paid for PED detection. Still, you could tell the Ultimate Out teams from those who had not embraced the cause by even a casual glance at the bodies in motion. You would expect a slaughter when they met, notwithstanding the theoretically non-contact nature of the sport.

To wide surprise, and mixed delight, that did not occur. Even the hyper-roided played with gentle caution. Every team, enlisted in the "out" movement or not, ignored the judge's rulings and consulted fellow players on violations and penalties. For all the attention they paid to the officials, they might as well have played un-officiated. Disk tradition had become fashionable again, for the moment at least. The fellowship followed even to the medal stand. The bronze and silver winning teams exchanged medals and positions on the podium in light of their own agreement on the proper score of their game and in defiance of the official ruling. In the face of this outrage, Benito Jax had the Executive Committee of the IOC ban all of Ultimate Frisbee from the next Olympic Games. "That will teach them a lesson they won't soon forget!"

Nothing like such Ultimate peace occurred during the much watched gold medal round of men's Olympic basketball. Russia and Germany brutalized each other in a very contact heavy game. The officials, on orders from the IOC, stopped calling fouls after the first ten minutes so as to allow the game to finish at play rather than by disqualifying either team for lack of unpenalized players. By the second half the whole world cheered as the battered teams dragged their wounded but still unbelievably built bodies out to play some of the worst basketball in Olympic history. The announcers split between fans of the game that lamented the degradation of play into elbows to the face and knee-cappings, and those who celebrated the intense competitive spirit and nationalistic commitment of the never-say-die sportsmen. The Russians won what even under the unfamiliar appearance of the game's conclusion, with every player crawling down the court on his knees, counted as a "controversial" decision. "They blatantly handed the game to the Russians after so much sacrifice by Germany," as one sportswriter put it.

Benito Jax declared the decision and the gold medal award to Russia both in line with Olympic rules and in the spirit of world peace. He proclaimed that the Olympics practiced morally impeccable officiation. He argued that the Morning God of Sport always in her wisdom co-aligned victory in the arena with the greatest good for all. He expressed confidence that both sides had right on their side and that they would put away their differences for the sake of sport and mankind. An hour later the Russians lodged a protest against the IOC granting even a silver metal to their rivals and issued a declaration of war against Germany.

The weather remained a factor for any event foolish enough to chance its play out of doors. Footgolf fell flat as the holes froze over, leaving the players skittering on the icy grass. Baseballers mistakenly whacked hail the size of, well, baseballs. The yachtsmen of the '84 regatta sailed week one in the world's first Mediterranean hurricane. All boats lost. By the second week, for the large yacht races, the IOC repositioned the events to the English Channel. The World Sporting News headline said it best: *Regatta Lost to Pack Ice in Olympic First; Benito Jax Blames Gulf Stream Failure; "Not Our Fault" Says Jax.*

Women's field hockey displayed a different vibe than had the men's basketball final. Men's field hockey had ended their contest in week one, exhausted and heat-stroked, and that left the now frozen field to the women in the last few days of the Games. Most teams refused to play since their athletes had not "expected nor adapted well to the extreme cold". Indeed, many now lay in hospital from poorly timed and completely ill-considered "counter-cold injection protocols". New science had failed the fully injected. Lessons for next time.

Meanwhile, the adaptable women of the International Women's Athletics Union teams took to the field against each other. They slid and fell on the unfamiliar footing, but laughed off the bruises and played a game reminiscent of its ice cousin. Sallis Sister teams would have won every medal but for Benito Jax's hasty cancellation of the entire event owing to "unfortunate weather". He chastised the women for continuing their play even in the knowledge of the icy tragedy unfolding off the coast of Normandy. When Zoe Sallis publicly asked why, then, he didn't cancel the Games as a whole, he declared her a quitter.

Zoe Sallis could land no blow on the noble head of Benito Jax, but the preternaturally competent commandos of Red Asphalt Alert once again brought him low. This time he learned of the offending event while watching the wrap up of the second week of play on television. It began with a remote broadcast by Dorthy Lament.

Dorthy, "Hello folks. I'm reporting to you live from somewhere in Paris. It's very dark here as you can see. No natural light allowed. I have been kidnapped by men representing Red Asphalt Alert. They look a well-armed and ruthless bunch, but polite and very professional. I'm going to interview their leader, Red Lead One. Tell me Red Lead, what do you think of the Games so far?"

Red Lead One, "We've seen some amazing play. Much respect to the Ultimate guys for really sticking it to the man there at the end. Great spontaneous protesting. Got to hand it to the Sallis Girls, they take a licking and keep on ticking. Better than Olympic time pieces. I bet Zoe Sallis knows what time it is. Of course, the Leek Green Faction is a joke. Always one step behind and two moves short. We can't wait to shame them at the closing ceremonies."

Dorthy, "What do you say of LGF accusations that you are a capitalist front organization for some corporate interest?"

Red Lead One, "That's the way losers talk. Just look at our record of questioning capital and winning concessions. And I'm sure you'll agree, Dorthy, we take the best hostages."

Dorthy could not suppress a smile, "What now Red Lead? What are your new demands?"

Red Lead One, "We demand full membership on the IOC Executive Committee. A voting membership. We think we could do a lot of good work there. We already kicked those capitalist tools, Armed Asylum, out of the charmed circle. We can do a lot more like that. And we don't just burn things down. On the IOC ExCom we can bring new sponsors. Better partners. For instance, if put on the board I think we can guarantee—and in fact will demand, an Olympic sponsorship deal with Nemesis Research Solutions. It's not just an internet stalking service. Nemesis Research Solutions offers general actionable intelligence gathering for corporate and private customers, full range security services, go-anywhere fully equipped mercenaries for all special operations needs, close contacts with police and military friends-in-high-places, full hacking capacity, and soon its own line of sport tactical wear."

Dorthy faced the camera, "You heard it here first. Reporting live with her life on the line, this is Dorthy Lament. Back to you Andrew."

Benito Jax turned off the television. His face held a pensive look; something inward and suggestive of religious contemplation. He nodded slowly. Finally, he said. "Yes. I think we can do business with these people."

The last days of the Games included a flurry of finish-ups now played under flurries of snow—or great heaps of hail. I limit myself to one final event, women's rugby. Half the teams came in so strong you could smell steroids flow from each player's pores. (Their slip enhancing multi-pores.) They had the mean and angry expressions long linked with real competitors and the muscle-bound bodies now associated with winners. The International Women's Athletics Union had worked hard to recruit teams-for-testing to join the Sallis Sisters in this hard hitting event of strength, endurance and teamwork. Sallis herself told the press that all the women of the movement regarded this as their most important test. They had amazing success at bringing players over to their cause. In an agreement with the Algerian Refugee Nation, some of the best women's rugby players took up Algerian citizenship and tested daily to prove a drug-free team. They played together for two years. They came to the Games with their own version of the Olympic dream.

The Algerian Sallis Sisterhood of Rugby faced off against a hyped up and roid ready Aussie team. The press nicknamed this Roiders vs Weak Links. It proved a one-sided match. The Roiders rolled over the Weak Links and stuffed Sallis Sisters into the frost covered dirt. The Weak Links rose again to face off against the Aussie Amazons. The Enhanced knocked over the Sisterhood every minute of the game. The battered Sisters of Mercy returned again and again to the scrum. The women of the IWAU protest bled and limped and suffered boos and hauled themselves up to contend once more and to once more be pitched to the pitch by the enormous Australians. They ended the game without scoring. The crowd laughed at them and mocked them and cheered the Aussie team. The Aussie team captain described them in an interview after as "real scrappers".

When a now freed Dorthy Lament interviewed Zoe Sallis about the brutal loss, Sallis, crying, said, "I am so incredibly proud of my sisters!"

Parting Shots

A Fumbled Handoff; A New Beginning;
On to the Citadel of Sport.

U nlike the opening ceremonies, the closing celebration of the Olympics tends to the casual. Everyone lets their very short hair down. Police fingers move from triggers to rest on trigger guards. Surveillance camera workers trade security camera porn pics. IOC Vice Presidents, those newly released from captivity with book deals and those jealous of the world's misplaced attention, wave at the fans with informal rather than officious motions. The fans drink heavily in the stands and wonder again at who those old and awkwardly waving people might be, and will any of them insist on making a speech, and can I get another drink if they do? The Olympic volunteers sigh in relief at an unpaid job almost done and slip a few hundred more frisbees past security.

The athletes enter the celebration not formed into regiments ready for war (excepting the Russians and Germans, well ringed by armed gendarmes), but in the hectic mess suggesting love of play, release of effort, and relief from worry. The IOC approved the athletes mixing in un-nationalized sporting solidarity, but of little else in this moment of free play, described by Benito Jax as a "mini bacchanal". Needless to say, frisbees flew. The IOC hoped that the crowd would discharge their ammunition before the show proper began. The Ultimate frisbee teams on parade threw the disks back into the stands to find a second release later to the chagrin of the Benito Jax.

Tooball entered to his own fanfare. To the delight of the world he had made up with his Hate Queen and walked arm in arm with Synthetic Rinse. The IOC had disqualified most of Zoe Sallis' All Women's Union Olympians, precluding their attendance, except the badly beaten and barely ambulatory women of the Algerian Refugee Nation's Rugby team. But they didn't need to walk. The Australian women's team carried their wounded sisters on their backs. The over-muscled Ms. Hydes bore the un-jacked Dr. Jekylls. This disturbing solidarity went unnoticed by fans, unmentioned by sportscasters, upset the VPs of the IOC, and left Benito Jax oddly unphased.

The rest of the ritual barely merits mention. I will only record a few moments possibly suppressed in Olympic memory. The show's producers had placed square placards beneath the stadium seats to be shown by the celebrants in the stands at an announcement. They meant to display, when all held up, a stadium surrounding message: *Thank You IOC and Our Dear Benito Jax*. But the never-say-die activist of the Leek Green Faction had replaced the placards so that they instead read: *We Have No Place Else To Go*. This LGF political action must rank as the greatest single executive feat of the Games. Unfortunately, in terms of spectacle, Red Asphalt Alert's hack of the stadium audio-visual system grasped the eyes of the world more solidly. Just before the handover of the Olympic flag, the whole of the Olympic Stadium's considerable array of imaging technology flooded the arena with RAA slogans. *Let RAA Defend Your World. Set Fire to the Asphalt with Personal Flamethrowers. No Nemesis Lies Beyond Our Reach. What Time Is It? GothTime Time.* The crowd chanted as the initials flashed by on every pixel: *RAA! NRS! RAA! NRS!* At least the branding hijack ended with a shoutout to the head of the IOC: *Thank You Benito Jax*! The IOC President went from outrage to chin thrusting appreciation in the time it takes to reposition a pixel. Call this Goth time.

The ceremonial flag un-raiser lowered the Olympic banner and gave it to the mayor of Paris. Initially (seven days prior) the IOC had planned for the mayor to hand it over to the host of the next Games, as tradition dictated. But now that London had iced over in what the United Nations referred to as a "good news weather reversal", the IOC had shelved that idea. Perhaps the Olympic Movement needed a more reliable sporting fortress in which to face the years ahead. Also, the mayor of London could not attend the ceremony owing to his position leading a mass evacuation of the city to the Nation of Andalusia. So Benito Jax took personal possession of the Olympic flag, gripping it like a beloved child rescued from a burning house. He swore the athletes and all members of the Olympic Movement to convene again in four years at "A place to be determined."

Suffice it to say that the rest of the night featured spectacular light shows, famous bands playing famous songs, a parade of past mascots welcoming

CotRatt into their club and more and better bombast than had been seen at any prior Olympics.

Only one dull moment intervened before the final extinction of the Olympic flame. As per contract, the IOC had set aside five minutes for Wei Wai to promote his upcoming Olympic film in any manner he chose. Wei Wai had all the stadium screens go dark. He cut the audio feed. He walked out into the middle of the stadium. He shouted. What he shouted no one could hear. The ambient noise of rustling bodies, chit chat, chants started and abandoned, and people using the entertainment system crash to find a restroom, completely drowned out whatever Wei Wai shouted into the dark noise of impatient people awaiting renewed pageant. In a stadium lit only by cell phones, no one could even see him. Reporters at first tried to make out his words, or even his language, but soon gave up and switched first to complaining of his pointless artiness and then to discussing their favorite Olympic moments and the most touching stories of this Olympiad. Wei Wai's time over, he left the stadium center, and the Pop infused Light Show of Olympic Record-Breaking Glory began. The audience thrilled. Viewers rushed back to their televisions; the right order of the world restored.

Once the epics of light and sound had exhausted every sense, the world waited, now sensation weary, for Benito Jax to extinguish the Olympic flame. And he tried to do this. He sent the order out. But the flame burned on. Engineers examined the mechanisms. They pressed buttons and rebooted systems. They sprayed the cauldron with fire-extinguishers. Still the fire burned on. Nothing would put it out. Someone suggested they cut off the fuel pumps, but the head of facilities argued against this as a risk to the stadium power system. Benito Jax declared the resilience of the flame a symbol. And who would not? Benito Jax announced that the flame would burn so long as it had fuel to do so, and the world would celebrate by its light in confidence of new and better tomorrows. Everyone cheered and made their way to the exits.

The afterglow of the Paris 2084 Olympiad ignited several events significant to this history. A few almost too minor to mention. I-sMart Images produced its new brand name design for Red Asphalt Alert. After a crash program and IOC funding greater than the entire sporting budget of all the New Nations combined, I-sMart (a wholly owned subsidiary of Nemesis Research Solutions) rechristened RAA as: *Asphalt Red: Alert!*

AR:A! declared itself satisfied and announced that it would launch a new Olympic timekeeping company in partnership with Nemesis Research Partners: GothTime Timekeepers. Benito Jax offered GothTime the Olympic concession.

While AR:A! glowed in the warm bath of the Olympic flame, its rival, the Leek Green Faction of the Whole Earth Defense League, announced its disbandment in a final press release, all its exclamation points toppled into question marks:

"How are we, the now not LGF, to compete against capital for the attention of this distracted world? How can our underfunded efforts, founded on ethics, find purchase in a world committed to commerce and coupled to the buzz of shopping for the next spectacle? How can we, we people, all of us together, sustain even a single moment of common attention to the world falling around us? Can we not see the coming day for the bright flashing numbers of our digital timepieces? Will the nanoseconds consume the century? Shall we all end on a mountain top, surrounded by a straining sea barrier, nursing the last glacier—a four foot cube—with hand-fans, while drinking our own sweat?"

The IOC offered no response.

Zoe Sallis and her sisters of the IWAU neither scored so immediate a protest success as the AR:A!, nor so immediate a failure as the now defunct LGF. They kissed a sister in the old style. Shortly after the Games, NBC's Dorthy Lament briefly interviewed Sallis.

Dorthy noted, "You lost, you and your people lost a lot."

Sallis responded, "We are Olympians. We were born to lose. Every morning we wake to work, to suffer, to lose. Lose often, lose hard. It fuels us. We will return. We will not give up. One day, we will win."

Sallis and her Sisters chose a hard road of guaranteed disappointment and uncertain success. They set out on a journey to outlast the opposition. And as the glow of Olympic spectacle satisfaction faded, some people did note that perhaps one should not turn human athletes into bioweapons. Surely this could not be our destiny.

As the embers of enthusiasm died down and the world began its quick turn to other matters, Benito Jax called a press conference to announce the next revolution in world sports. The cameras came, the microphones hovered, the reporters ate mini-sandwiches and traded predictions.

"He'll announce a pharm sponsor for '88."

"He's decided to retire." (Laughter.)

"The IOC will merge with the UN."

"I'm hoping for a new caterer."

Benito Jax entered. Excitement gripped the room. Not, of course, at the arrival of the august statesman of sport, but at his companion, the five time Olympic gold medalist Synthetic Rince—now known worldwide by her new brand: Syn Rise. Jax began, "You all know our pole vault champion Syn Rise. You have all celebrated her amazing record smashing performance at the Games just past. You have all seen her in action. But today, Syn Rise and I would like to show you something you have not seen. Something that heralds a new day in Olympic excellence. Olympic inclusivity. An Olympic re-imagining of the possible. Allow me to introduce to you: Synthetic Rinse."

To a gasp, Synthetic Rinse—a second and identical one—entered. She differed from her Syn Rise double only in wearing a small head-set—and by possessing the power of speech.

She spoke, "Hey fans! Hey crew! You got the girl herself here now!"

As she moved, so did her doppelganger.

Someone managed, "What is this? What does it mean?"

Benito Jax, "Bionics, gentlemen. And ladies. Bionics at the Olympics. At these past Games, Synthetic Rinse competed, with IOC approval, through the avatar Syn Rise. Ms. Rinse offered herself as the model—in every respect—for Syn Rise. Ms. Rinse controlled Syn Rise throughout the event with the headset you see her wearing now, the headset that controls Syn Rise here."

Synthetic Rinse (the "real" one), "We won the gold! You saw it all."

Benito Jax, "We heard many complaints during this Olympiad about the free use of pharmaceuticals. Misguided traditionalists fighting last year's war. At the Games of 2088, any athlete who wishes may compete through a bionic avatar. I predict that PED use will quickly become a concern of the past. A poor athlete's compensation for not having an avatar. Best of all, these bionic avatars are auto-enhancing. They have unlimited scope for performance improvement. That means that anyone able to afford one, can make a bionic replicant and compete for a place in the Games. No more physiological elitism! No more agism! A new day of equality and inclusivity! Better still, as impressed as the world was at the records broken at the 2084 Games, this will be as nothing compared to what the future holds. Absolutely nothing will remain unbroken."

Syn Rise launched a world tour and a line of beauty products. Tooball Beetleback launched his own bionic avatar, Beatbot Too, and joined the tour. Syn Rise and Beatbot fooled around, feuded, cheated and made up, and soon no one bothered to ask which stood for who. The press covered every minute of it. Toy companies launched new action figures. The video gaming community rejoiced. World chess scratched its head. Of course, not everyone immediately came on board. But no one can set back the clock of technology. We can only ask what time it is.

Just six months after the closing ceremony, Wei Wai released his official film of the Paris '84 Olympic Games. *Olympiad; Today and Tomorrow*. Benito Jax sighed with relief when he viewed it. It did not record the heat strokes, the frostbite, the stuck domes, or any of the other incidents he worried might mar the memory of the Games and tempt the attention of an avant-garde cineaste. Wei Wai simply recorded the track in the Olympic Stadium. Without music or comment, the viewer watches its construction. The installation of its fifteen-layer surface. The careful application of paint to designate its various event functions. The appearance of feet in varied Nikadidas brand shoes. (He showed no other part of any athlete.) The rapid grinding to dust of the track by the impact of shoes and the cutting of cleats. The track's deformation under intense heat and sudden freezing. And finally, its demolishment after the completion of the Games, replaced by astroturf and refugee tents.

One last problem faced the IOC before it could settle back into the routine of banquets and fetes: choosing the location of the 2088 Games. Wags joked that McMurdo Sound in Antarctica might work well. It might have shocked them to discover how seriously the IOC had taken that idea. But no, Benito Jax presented a different solution to the Executive Committee, "The Movement can no longer indulge in site rotation. Frankly, we have had too few bids to replace London to hold effective bidding wars. We need a safe, weather stable, permanent location to secure the future of the Games."

Jing Zhao, "China offers Hong Kong."

Manvik Gupta, "It is already flooding!"

Jing Zhao, "The world need only finance a sea wall."

Joseph Kabwe, "Please, I beg of you, Nairobi. The land is very cheap now. Building permit bribes can be very low. I will negotiate them."

Jing Zhao, "Kenya has already begun evacuations."

Joseph Kabwe, "But with world investment in air-conditioning—also, we have highlands. The real estate is not so cheap there, but I will negotiate."

Ahmed bin Abdullah, "Mecca. With worldwide financing the IOC can re-open this center of worship and pilgrimage. I can already see the images of the first Games in a land of Arabian Nights."

Manvik Gupta, "But no one can walk there without fully enclosed cool-suits."

Ahmed bin Abdullah, "A dome. An air-conditioned dome over Mecca, financed by the whole world."

Jing Zhao, "Finance it yourself! The Saudi Sovereign Wealth Fund can build a dome if anyone can."

Ahmed bin Abdullah, "We must guard the wealth of the nation. But with world financing, Mecca could re-open and Islam would be saved."

Joseph Kabwe, "Build a dome over Nairobi! We are poor, money is no object to us."

Manvik Gupta, "Insanity. India has many cities the IOC could dome."

Jing Zhao, "Sea walls cost less than air-conditioned domes!"

Ahmed bin Abdullah, "I have another proposal. We could reinstitute the Winter Olympics. Hold it every four years under a well air-conditioned dome over Mecca. The current Games would be a Summer Olympics held under a dome in Nairobi."

Joseph Kabwe, "Done!"

Jing Zhao, "You need more than two votes! I want a sea wall!"

Benito Jax cuffed the meeting to order, "Please, please. We cannot raise funds for domes or sea walls. We must pick a city that already attracts the interest of large doners. In a country that offers some buffeting against unpleasant world trends. A place with some remaining natural beauty. Isolated from major refugee populations. Surrounded by water, outside typhoon zones, and dear to the hearts of absentee billionaire citizens ready to retire there in safety should bad portents loom."

Manvik Gupta, "Is there such a place?"

Who doesn't crave a place of greater safety? Perhaps some don't. Young, rich, invincible. Disruptive burn-it-down-and-start-again types. Daring visionaries of a new world. Takers of big risks, *imposers* of big risks; reapers of big returns and wealth-indemnified against lethal losses. Olympians of the great game of profit and loss. They crave new frontiers to conquer and disdain trading vision for security. Rockets to the stars to save humanity—that portion that can pay the fee and fit inside an aluminum tube. And while they bravely dare the new day to defy their will, and boldly blaze new trails through the world, they can also buy a bolthole in a corner of the planet and a private plane to fly to it should the rest of the world catch fire.

So welcome, Games, to Auckland New Zealand—the Citadel of Sport!

You know, as I do not, how that plan proceeded. I, who now commit this work to its timed tomb, can only write of what I have seen and heard and thought. You must judge the good and the bad of it. I am now, as always, no one of significance. I received my own (merely symbolic) gold medal in an essay event only after a general disqualification. The IOC placed me on its board just to staunch bad publicity. Its president commissioned me to write this history to guarantee that the IOC's new "house author" produced no prose upsetting to Jaxian plans. Fate has fixed me to history now. I will go on for a time, but you will have nothing of me but this work; fragile as paper, durable as digits, only as complete as a newly read sign.

Did the Movement successfully move to Auckland? Did the Auckland Games see record breaking record breaking? Did people flock to them in anticipation? Or perhaps *swim* to them in *desperation*? What did the Paris Games contribute to your world? Does this poor effort you read contribute anything at all? This memorial guide, unedited by the IOC Publications Department, unread but for a name check by Benito Jax, and delivered to a vault, lies now in your hands rather than mine. Having given my modest answers, I have only questions left. Will it ever emerge from its vault? Will it find favor in some future reader? Which will endure longer, this text I now encrypt, or the readers for whom I write? You know better than I.

About the author

Whip Lipsey grew up in Georgia, came of age in Missouri, and dropped out of high school in California. He holds a bachelor's degree in history from the University of California at Irvine and a PhD in philosophy from the University of Rochester. He left academia to work as a screenwriter (and was shocked to learn that writing for Hollywood does not require a doctorate). After twenty years raising his three children as a full-time father, he has returned to writing.

Also by Whip Lipsey

Undead in L.A.
Escape From Danger Island
Were-Eagles Dare
The Mysterious Dr. Noh
Plan Nine; The Secret History of Invasion Earth

www.ingramcontent.com/pod-product-compliance
Lightning Source LLC
Chambersburg PA
CBHW071239130626
46556CB00003B/1078